ASSASSINS' RAGE

Recent Titles by Charles O'Brien in this Series

MUTE WITNESS
BLACK GOLD
NOBLE BLOOD *
LETHAL BEAUTY *
FATAL CARNIVAL *
CRUEL CHOICES *
ASSASSINS' RAGE *

* available from Severn House

ASSASSINS' RAGE

An Anne Cartier Mystery

Charles O'Brien

This first world edition published 2008
in Great Britain and the USA by
SEVERN HOUSE PUBLISHERS LTD of
9–15 High Street, Sutton, Surrey SM1 1DF.

British Library Cataloguing in Publication Data

O'Brien, Charles, 1927-
  Assassins' rage
  1. Cartier, Anne (Fictitious character) - Fiction 2. Women
  teachers - France - Fiction 3. France - History - Louis
  XVI, 1774-1793 - Fiction 4. Detective and mystery stories
  I. Title
  813.6[F]

ISBN-13: 978-0-7278-6607-3   (cased)

All Severn House titles are printed on acid-free paper.

Typeset by Palimpsest Book Production Ltd.,
Grangemouth, Stirlingshire, Scotland.
Printed and bound in Great Britain by
MPG Books Ltd., Bodmin, Cornwall.

Acknowledgements

I wish to thank Jennifer Nelson of Gallaudet University for helpful advice on issues of deafness. I am grateful to Andy Sheldon and Haven Fagley for skilful electronic assistance, to Gudveig Baarli for assisting with the maps, and to Jack Leavey for advice on a painter's studio practice. Fronia Simpson, Chris Bachelder of the University of Massachusetts at Amherst, and my agent Evan Marshall read drafts of the novel and contributed to its improvement. Finally, my wife Elvy, art historian, earns special mention for many hours of careful editing and for incalculable moral support.

List of Main Characters
In Order of First Appearance

Anne Cartier: *teacher of deaf children, former music hall enter-tainer, wife of Colonel Paul de Saint-Martin*

Sylvie de Chanteclerc: *goddaughter of Baron Breteuil, distant cousin and childhood acquaintance of Saint-Martin*

Hercule Gaillard: *hack journalist and scandal-monger; radical activist; Duc d'Orléans' agent*

André Dutoit: *Sylvie's friend; curator/clerk of paintings in the Palais-Royal*

Colonel Paul de Saint-Martin: *Provost of the Royal Highway Patrol for the area surrounding Paris, husband of Anne Cartier*

Choderlos de Laclos (1741–1803): *military officer, notorious author of* Les Liaisons Dangereuses, *and secretary to the Duc D'Orléans*

Simon and Nicolas: *two rogues, army veterans, who work for Gaillard*

Lieutenant General Thiroux DeCrosne (1734–1794): *last chief of French police in the old regime*

Micheline [Michou] du Saint-Esprit: *friend of Anne and Sylvie; deaf artist with studio on Rue Traversine*

Marc Latour: *painter at the Louvre, Michou's fiancé*

Lieutenant Maury: *officer of the National Guard, 'Hero' of the Bastille*

Georges Charpentier: *Saint-Martin's adjutant*

Jacques-Louis David (1748–1825): *famous French neo-classical painter of* Brutus

Jean-Sylvain Bailly (1736–1793): *distinguished astronomer, mayor of Paris, 1789–1791*

Louis-Bénigne-François de Bertier de Sauvigny (1737–1789): *last intendant of Paris*

Comtesse Marie de Beaumont: *Paul de Saint-Martin's aunt, Michou's patron, and Anne's friend. She has an estate south of Paris and a Paris townhouse on Rue Traversine near the Palais-Royal*

Joseph Mouton: *young National Guardsman; Harival du Rocher's natural son*

Abbé Charles-Michel de l'Épée (1712–1789): *priest; enlightened, influential founder of the Institute for the Deaf in Paris*

Lafayette, Marie-Joseph etc., Marquis de (1757–1834): *popular, ambitious commander of the National Guard, hero of the American Revolution*

Jacques Harivel du Rocher (d. 1789): *Lieutenant of cavalry; commandant of the Royal Highway Patrol at Passy*

Louis Gagne: *master baker on Rue Sainte-Anne*

Beatrice Gagne: *deaf wife of Monsieur Gagne; former student of the Abbé de l'Épée*

Robert Gagne: *their thirteen-year-old deaf son*

Jacques Duby: *Gagne's journeyman baker*

Inspector Étienne-François Quidor: *Paris police crime investigator*

Pierre Roland: *young magistrate at the Louvre district police bureau*

Thérèse Gille: *widow, works part-time in the duke's palace*

Brigadier Julien Pioche: *officer of the Royal Highway Patrol at Passy; friend of Harivel*

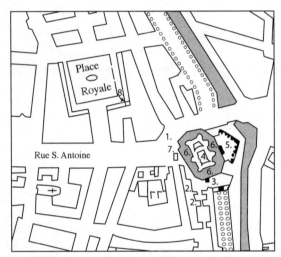

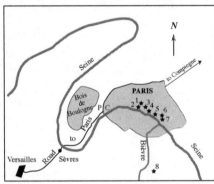

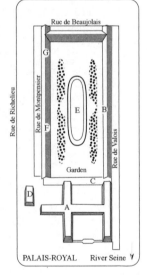

BASTILLE

1. Place de Bastille
2. Barracks
3. Drawbridge
4. Great Courtyard
5. Bastion
6. Moat
7. Guard House
8. Madame de
   Villers apartment

PALAIS-ROYAL 1789

A. The duke's palace
B. Valois Arcade
C. Camp of the Tatars
D. Comédie Française
   (under construction)
E. Circus
F. Café Odéon
G. Café de Foy

PARIS REGION

P - Passy
C - Chaillot
1 - Place Vendôme
2 - Tuilleries
3 - Palais-Royal
4 - Louvre
5 - Place de Grève
6 - Place Royale [des Vosges]
7 - Bastille
8 - Château Beaumont

PALAIS-ROYAL   River Seine

One

The Bastille

'Citizens of Paris, beware,' the man shouted. 'Traitors lurk among you. Ferret them out. Slit their throats. Hang them from the nearest street lamp.'

Anne shivered. He meant exactly what he said. His eyes burned with utter conviction – and hatred. He looked familiar.

On this dismal, rainy morning, Anne Cartier and her friend Sylvie de Chanteclerc were walking in the garden of the Palais-Royal and had come upon a rapt crowd of men and women. Mouths agape, dripping wet, they fixed their eyes on this middle-aged man standing on a table. His body was bent and frail, his face haggard, yet he spoke with a powerful orator's voice.

The two women edged into the crowd for a closer view. Anne whispered in Sylvie's ear. 'I know that man. Hercule Gaillard. A hack writer, extortionist, and a violent critic of the royal family, their servants and defenders. He's changed, looks much older.'

Sylvie nodded. 'He used to work for the Duc d'Orléans, was accused of theft, and fled to London two years ago. He must have somehow regained the duke's favour.'

Anne pulled her bonnet down to cover more of her face. Gaillard would remember her. She had foiled his plot to seize incriminating letters between the Queen and the Swedish nobleman, Comte Axel von Fersen.

'Let's keep a safe distance, Sylvie.' They moved back a few steps and hid behind a pair of stinking butchers in blood-stained aprons, each man holding a meat cleaver.

In lurid detail Gaillard warned the crowd of impending

catastrophe – the King's regiments of German and Swiss mercenaries were poised to attack the city, massacre its inhabitants, and
restore despotic rule. His harangue reached a thunderous call to
arms: '*Aux armes, citoyens.* Defend your hard-won liberty.'

'Yes, with our lives,' came the crowd's swift response. They
flourished knives, axes, and pikes and pledged loudly to destroy
all domestic traitors and foreign hired killers. The two butchers
raised their cleavers and added, 'Blood will flow in the streets.'

Fortunately, Gaillard did not appear to notice the two
'traitors' who had just joined the crowd. For safety's sake, Anne
and Sylvie were wearing the tattered grey woollen gowns and
simple white bonnets of unemployed domestic servants. They
had even smeared streaks of grime on their hands and faces.
In the present feverish climate it could be life-threatening for
Anne to be recognized as a police official's wife. Palais-Royal,
the Duc d'Orléans' vast privileged complex of garden and
commercial property, together with his palace, had become the
centre of violent opposition to the royal government and to its
agents in the city.

The two women moved on to the little puppet theatre in
the Camp of the Tatars, an arcade of wooden shops and stalls
at the south end of the garden. Anne had put money into the
theatre and occasionally produced a show on its stage.

Anne asked Sylvie, 'Do you think André will dare to meet
us this morning?'

'He was reluctant when I asked him last night,' she replied.
'He would come if he could. He's careful to conceal his spying
on the duke and his agents.'

Sylvie's friend André Dutoit lived in the palace. When Anne
first met him two years ago, he was a clerk in the duke's art
gallery. He secretly helped her investigate the gallery director's
attempt to blackmail Queen Marie Antoinette. When the
director left for prison, the duke put André in charge of his
rich collection of paintings but without the title or income of
a director. That post went to the husband of the duke's latest
mistress, an elderly, ignorant gentleman who never set foot
in the gallery. André was outraged but dared not show it. His
family depended on his income.

'How does André manage to get information?' Anne asked
Sylvie.

'He's a personable, clever man and is called upon to work

throughout the palace, serving food and drink, organizing entertainments. The duke's servants gladly share palace gossip with him. He overhears conversations, even searches through the duke's trash.'

Anne felt a twinge of guilt for using Sylvie to gain André's cooperation and for exposing both of them to danger. Anne's husband, Colonel Paul de Saint-Martin, provost of the Royal Highway Patrol, had asked her and Sylvie to help detect troublemakers creating turmoil in the city. They aimed to overthrow the present King and put his cousin the duke in his place.

The colonel's usual sources of information had become unreliable. As the bankrupt royal government's money dried up, some informants faded away or received better pay from the duke. Others were too frightened to work. The duke's agents had threatened to hunt them down. Several disappeared under suspicious circumstances. One of their bodies had been found floating in the river.

Midway through the morning, André finally appeared. 'I can only stay a few minutes. The duke will have at least a hundred guests at his table. The palace staff is overwhelmed. The steward has ordered me to help serve meals. I must hurry back.'

He took a seat on a bench facing the two women, gave Sylvie a fond glance, and nervously surveyed the room. The puppet theatre was empty at this time of day. He relaxed when he saw puppet master Benoit, Anne's friend and business partner, guarding the entrance. They could speak without fear of being interrupted or overheard.

André had news. 'Some seventy soldiers have deserted from the French Guards regiment stationed in Paris. The duke is sheltering them in the palace. They have seized muskets from royal arsenals and are plotting to march on the Bastille today.'

'What do they hope to gain?' asked Sylvie.

'Gunpowder. A large supply is stored there. They say they need it in order to defend the city from the King's foreign regiments, the Germans and the Swiss.'

Anne was sceptical. 'These rebels have no legal authority. The governor won't hand the powder over to them. They aren't strong enough to seize it. The Bastille is a fortress built of thick rock. The garrison could hold out forever if it wished.'

André shook his head. 'With the duke's money, the rebels

plan to recruit a thousand desperate men from among the unemployed artisans in the Saint-Antoine district and assault the fortress. They'll capture it, even if a hundred men must die.'

'Why does the duke support such bloody business?' Anne asked. She had met the Duc d'Orléans two years ago and found him handsome and charming, but also lecherous and untrustworthy. She instantly disliked him.

'In the palace the servants say that the fall of the Bastille would expose the King's weakness and the need for a change. Now I must hurry back.'

'Before you go,' Anne asked, 'tell me what *you* think of the duke.'

'Frankly, I detest him. Granted, I'm biased – he pays me poorly and shows scant appreciation for the work I do. But he's also a bad character, and he chooses agents who are no better than he. Some are ambitious, ruthless military men like Choderlos de Laclos, his secretary. Others are dissolute, venal aristocrats like Mirabeau. And a few are bitter, violent scribblers like the former medical doctor, Marat. If the duke became King, surrounded by such self-serving men, he would ruin the country.'

As André rose to leave, Anne asked him, 'Do you have any advice for us?'

'Yes, indeed,' he replied. 'Beware of two of the duke's men in particular, known only as Simon and Nicolas, both of them former soldiers, ruthless cutthroats. Simon is short, stout and clever; Nicolas is tall, lean and simple – and his right ear is cropped. They're always together. The duke's secretary, Laclos, sends for them whenever there's nasty business to do.'

Later in the morning, while Anne and Sylvie were watching the servants' entrance to the palace, Simon and Nicolas came out with baskets of broadsides. As Simon hurried past the women, he gave a broadside to Anne. She stepped back to read it.

> Patriots! Arm yourselves. Gather at the Bastille. We must force its governor to surrender his gunpowder. We need it to defend our liberties against the foreign mercenaries who would enslave us.

At noon, the garden's little cannon fired off twelve shots. Word came from the Bastille that the patriots had presented their demands to the governor. He had refused to surrender the gunpowder. Baskets in hand, Simon and Nicolas hurried from the Palais-Royal towards the fortress. At the same time, a small group of gentlemen left the palace, led by a tall, thin, sallow-faced man, aged about fifty.

Sylvie whispered, 'The tall man is Laclos. André says he's cold as a fish, but witty. Doesn't care about fashion, or social graces, and always wears the same black coat.'

Anne had heard of his novel, *Les Liaisons Dangereuses*, which portrayed French aristocrats as lecherous parasites. A scandalous tale but everyone appeared to have read it.

Sylvie drew close to the group, then reported back to Anne. 'They're going to join the others at the Bastille. Should we follow them?'

To Anne's eye they seemed harmless – except for the acid in their words. She glanced at the sky. The rain had stopped but dark clouds remained. 'Yes,' she replied. 'Our only danger is getting wet. Besides, I want to visit an elderly acquaintance, Madame Agnès de Villers. She lives near the Bastille. I last saw her several months ago. She might need help.'

At the Place de Bastille the men from the duke's palace melted into a large, excited crowd. Armed with knives, axes, swords, pikes, and a few muskets, they encircled the old royal fortress. Amidst the babble of voices, Anne heard cries of 'death to tyrants, down with despotism, free the prisoners, give us the gunpowder.'

'I think this is as far as we should go,' Anne cautioned. 'If the garrison refuses to surrender, the crowd will surely attack. Many will be killed.'

Sylvie seemed intrigued, eager to draw closer. 'I see women in the crowd. We're in common dress and won't stand out.' With a little encouragement, she would have joined the crowd.

'No, it's not worth the risk,' Anne insisted. 'We'll visit Madame de Villers, a short walk from here. Her apartment offers a partial view of the scene. We can imagine the rest.'

Anne and Sylvie made their way through a rising tide of 'patriots' to the Place Royale. Once an elegant square, it now housed poor but genteel men and women like Madame de Villers. Its tall, uniform brick and stone buildings with steeply pitched slate roofs were dilapidated. Madame de Villers lived on the south-east side of the square in a garret apartment. Its dormer windows looked out towards the Bastille.

A young maid met Anne and Sylvie at the door and led them into a small study, its walls lined with shelves of books. Madame de Villers sat at a writing table by a window, a book open before her. A thin, bent woman, over sixty years old, she was unmarried and in poor health, but her mind was keen. She was remarkably learned in the arts and sciences and enjoyed good conversation. At another window, a telescope mounted on a tripod was aimed at the heavens. A sleek black cat slept on a Turkish rug in front of the fireplace.

Anne introduced Sylvie, then added, 'Excuse our distressed appearance, madame. We feel safer in disguise. The streets are quite unsettled.'

'Yes, I never leave the apartment – I feel like a prisoner here. Thank you for coming. May I offer you refreshments?' Madame de Villers rang for the maid.

'That would be kind of you,' Anne replied. 'And how is Denise?'

Anne knew Madame de Villers' niece from a criminal investigation two years ago. The provost at Versailles had falsely accused her of murder and sentenced her to death. While the young woman languished in prison awaiting her fate, her aunt led Anne to information that exonerated her. Now married and expecting a child, she lived at Versailles and couldn't conveniently look after her aunt.

The maid returned with glasses, a pitcher of cool, sweetened cherry juice, and sweet biscuits. After serving everyone, she withdrew.

Madame de Villers sipped her drink thoughtfully for a moment, then replied, 'Denise has mostly recovered from her ordeal. But she still thinks of the young married woman who shared her cell in the Conciergerie. In her nightmares Denise imagines herself as that woman burning at the stake for killing her cruel husband.'

'Unfortunately, some horrors never leave us,' Anne remarked, speaking from personal experience. She couldn't forget how a corrupt English magistrate had falsely convicted her of beating a man who had in fact attacked her.

The conversation had turned to the weather and other

pleasant matters, when sharp sounds came through the open window. The cat scurried from the room.

'What's that?' Anne glanced towards the window.

'Gunfire,' Sylvie replied. Both women rushed to the window and looked down at the street below. People had stopped whatever they were doing and gathered in agitated clusters.

'The sound is coming from a short distance east of us,' said Anne. She glanced back at her hostess, Madame de Villers, whose dark, deep-set eyes had opened wide with concern.

Anne and Sylvie stared at each other and exclaimed together, 'They've attacked the Bastille.'

Staccato bursts of musket fire came at more frequent intervals, followed by the boom of a cannon.

'May I look through your telescope?' Anne asked.

'Let me show you how.' Madame de Villers removed a cloth cover from the instrument, lowered and focused it.

Anne peered at the fortress. The upper half was visible above the intervening tiled roofs. 'The Swiss are at the battlements, firing down. I can see the buttons on their red coats. The crowd is out of sight, but it's returning fire. A cloud of dark smoke is rising above the roofs. One of the fortress's outer buildings – probably the governor's house – is burning.' Anne yielded her place to Sylvie.

The young woman looked into the instrument and groaned, 'Imagine the carnage in the crowd. At least a thousand men and women are packed together. The Swiss can't miss hitting them.'

Anne shuddered. 'That's like taunting a bear. When blood flows, the crowd will turn into a raging beast.'

'Close the window,' said their hostess, greatly distressed. 'The thought of this death and destruction is giving me a headache. Call in my maid. You should leave now for home while you can. The worst is yet to come. *Homo homini lupus est.*'

On the way down the stairs, Anne asked Sylvie what Madame de Villers had said in Latin as they left.

Sylvie gave Anne a solemn look. '"Man is a wolf to man."'

Late that afternoon back at the provost's residence, Anne learned that Lieutenant General DeCrosne, the head of the Paris police and chief magistrate for criminal cases, had called

Paul to his office in the Hôtel de Police. She bathed and changed into a white silk gown. While waiting for him in the garden, she reflected on the attack on the Bastille. Compared to earlier riots, this one seemed more momentous, a direct challenge to the King's authority, perhaps the opening battle in a larger conflict.

A few hours later, Paul joined her for a light evening meal of cold fruit soup, cheese, salad and wine. When the servant had withdrawn, Paul asked Anne to recall the day's events.

'I'll begin with Monsieur Hercule Gaillard. Sylvie and I heard him holding forth in the garden of the Palais-Royal.' She summarized his message and described its strong impact on his audience.

'He hasn't mellowed with time,' Paul remarked. 'In the present dangerous circumstances he could cause us a great deal of trouble. He hasn't forgotten that two years ago we defeated his scheme to defame the Queen. He will retaliate against us.'

Anne then spoke about André Dutoit's spying in the duke's palace. The duke's men were deeply involved in the attack on the Bastille. She went on to describe what she and Sylvie could see from Madame de Villers' apartment.

Paul listened intently, encouraging her with questions.

At the end of her story, Anne asked, 'And what did you learn from the lieutenant general?' She sipped her wine.

Paul reflected briefly, then said, 'About the time that you and Sylvie left Madame de Villers, a group of mutinous French Guards joined the mob in front of the fortress and forced the garrison to surrender. Several guards dragged Delaunay, the Bastille's governor, to City Hall where an assassin stabbed him to death and cut off his head. The mob approved, called it 'the people's justice,' and paraded on the Place de Grève with the head on a pike like a trophy.'

'How barbaric!' Anne exclaimed. 'In defending the fortress, the governor was merely doing his duty.'

'I agree. He deserved at least a fair trial.'

Anne was growing depressed. 'That's enough. I've lost my appetite. Let's walk in the garden among the roses.'

Throughout the day a light, intermittent rain had fallen, forcing the blossoms to yield abundant fragrance. For several minutes, Anne and Paul strolled on paths among bushes heavy with moisture. Refreshed, they sat down, and resumed their conversation.

'What happens next?' Anne asked.

Paul shrugged. 'The government has withdrawn the foreign troops from the city. They were fanning the insurrection rather than suppressing it.'

'Where are the police and the French Guards, the royal regiment stationed in the city?'

'I asked DeCrosne. After all, he's responsible for law and order in the city. He was almost in tears. He told me there's nothing he can do. The city's police are outnumbered and utterly outmatched. The regiment of French Guards is useless or worse – either disorganized or sympathetic to the insurrection.'

'Did he ask your Royal Highway Patrol for help?'

'Yes, but I declined. My troopers are loyal and dependable, but most of them are fully engaged in the countryside, clearing the area around Paris of bandits and protecting the movement of food into the markets. The few left in Paris are guarding their barracks and its weapons. I've assigned two of them to guard the provost's residence.' Paul met Anne's eye. 'DeCrosne will resign tomorrow.'

'Then the King has lost Paris,' Anne murmured ruefully. 'It remains to be seen, who shall now govern the city.'

Two

Destruction of a Symbol

Paris, Sunday, 19 July

A shout rose from the crowd as a giant stone fell from the fortress. Early on this grey, cloudy morning Anne Cartier and her friend Michou were gazing at the mighty Bastille. High up on its battlements, workmen pried stones loose and cast them down into the moat below.

This was Sunday, the day of holy rest. That didn't matter to the workmen, nor to the large crowd that gathered below to applaud them. The task was urgent. This monument to despotism was to be destroyed without delay. Michou's lips parted, her eyes widened with awe and wonder at the sight.

Anne shared that feeling, but also felt a stirring of dread. Five days ago the mob that forced its garrison to surrender had decapitated its governor and his assistant and paraded their heads through the city streets. The police forces of the city either joined in the atrocities or stood aside. The hapless chief of police, Lieutenant General DeCrosne, resigned.

Paris seemed to teeter on the brink of chaos. Its hungry and fearful people could explode at any moment. The price of bread was rising as the supply dwindled in the markets. Artisans lacked work. Mobs roamed the streets, shook their fists in front of the City Hall.

But Anne also knew of reasons for hope. An elected mayor, the first in the city's history, had peacefully assumed DeCrosne's authority. The new National Guard, a people's militia, promised to restore order in the city. The bankrupt, rudderless royal government in Versailles recognized the city's newly elected council. At the City Hall the King donned the Revolution's red, white and blue cockade, a gesture of sharing power with the people: white, the monarchy's colour, was flanked – and limited – by the blue and red of Paris.

Despite the lingering danger of violence, Michou insisted on this visit, convinced that she would find much to sketch in such a fascinating place. Anne also wanted to satisfy her own curiosity. In hindsight the fall of the fortress was a remarkable event, its demolition no less fascinating. And it seemed prudent to accompany Michou – safety in numbers. The petite deaf artist might accidentally cross the path of a mindless mob and be injured or killed.

As they gazed at the building, a bemused expression came over Michou's face. 'What's the use of a fortress in the middle of the city?' she asked.

'Originally,' Anne explained, 'the Bastille guarded the eastern entrance to Paris. Over centuries the city expanded eastward, and the fortress lost its military purpose. In modern times it became a prison for many prominent people, including the great philosopher Voltaire. The King could send a person there with a stroke of his pen. A prisoner might be tortured and held without trial for decades in its dungeons.'

'How dreadful!' Michou grimaced with disgust. 'Marc tells me that the Bastille is still a bad place and should be torn down.' A painter with a studio in the Louvre, the vast royal palace on the right bank of the River Seine, Marc Latour was Michou's fiancé and mentor and was sympathetic to the cause of reform in France.

'True, it was bad in the past,' granted Anne. 'But in recent years the dungeons have been empty. Very few prisoners remained and they weren't mistreated. Up to two weeks ago, the Marquis de Sade lived comfortably in one of the towers, ate well, received visitors.'

Michou gave Anne a sceptical glance. 'Prisons are always dreadful places, some worse than others. The Bastille *looks* like a bad one.'

She took a sketchbook from her bag, sat down on a low rock wall, and set to work. Anne watched over her shoulder. The Bastille gradually emerged on the page. First, she drew the huge rectangular citadel, its eight towers connected by massive walls. Then, on a smaller scale, she added the surrounding moat, low outer buildings, and perimeter walls.

Finally, Michou held up her sketch for Anne to compare

with the real building before them. Michou's version had an ugly, fantastic, forbidding aspect, its towers taller, its walls more massive than those of the fortress itself.

'To judge from your sketch, I believe that the Bastille's fall pleased you.'

'Yes.' She signed pensively, paused, and then her hands moved again. 'But it caught me, and most people I know, by surprise.'

Anne understood. During the past few years, discontent with the royal government, together with severe shortages of food, had provoked riots similar to this one. The King's troops stepped in and restored order. Things usually calmed down.

'On the fourteenth of July,' Michou continued, 'I was hard at work in Marc's studio, helping him paint for the great exhibition at the end of August. Late that evening, as we were closing the studio, a passing watchman mentioned the attack. But neither Marc nor I gave the Bastille a second thought. All we could think about was the exhibition. Only a few days afterwards did we begin to realize that Paris was different. And despite the bloodshed, the change was probably for the better.'

Michou knew little of the Revolution that had begun in May and culminated with the storming of this royal fortress. As they faced the building, Anne briefly explained the meeting of the Estates-General, the formation of the National Assembly, the King's resistance to sharing his unchecked power, and the present collapse of royal authority in Paris.

'I see; the old monarchy is like this fortress.' Michou waved a dismissive hand at the building. 'The people are tearing it apart, bit by bit. I can't blame them. Misery drives them to lash out at something. But they should know that it's much easier to tear down a bad building than to build a better one.'

'At least today,' Anne observed, 'they are in a good mood.' Despite the grey skies and the threat of rain, the atmosphere around the fortress was festive. The men up on the battlements waved to the onlookers. They clapped and cheered as large pieces of masonry fell to the ground.

The new city council had granted an entrepreneur, 'Patriot Palloy', the license to tear down the Bastille. He planned to sell the rock as construction material. Today, he was selling smaller items as souvenirs in the former guardroom on the Place de la Bastille.

Anne and Michou joined an eager crowd of curious visitors. Men and women, many of them fashionably dressed, were buying door hinges, latches, chains, keys, and other pieces of ironware. Also for sale were beds, tables and chairs, bricks, tiles and small stone fragments, books and textiles.

Michou edged through the crowd to a large bin of books, clothes, and other soft items, bundled in small packages. A genial young woman stood by the bin to set prices. While Anne watched, Michou rummaged through the bundles until one caught her eye. She pulled it out and showed it to Anne. Four dusty books were tied together. The finest was a leather-bound, gold-embossed edition of Pascal's *Pensées*. The other less expensive books were a two-volume edition of Pascal's *Provincial Letters* and a French translation of Thomas à Kempis's *Imitation of Christ*.

'Why have you chosen this bundle?' asked Anne. Lacking any formal education, Michou could barely read and write. Blaise Pascal was a deep and difficult religious author from the previous century. His writing was far beyond Michou's reach. Anne herself could barely understand him.

Michou caressed the *Pensées'* gold lettering. 'This is a beautiful book. I'll enjoy looking at it, even if I can't read it . . . yet.' She showed the bundle to the woman. Anne asked how much.

'A couple of coppers.' The woman held up two fingers, smiling benevolently at Michou.

Michou read her lips, noted the gesture. She took the coins from her purse and handed them to the woman. 'That's a bargain,' she signed to Anne.

'The bundle's yours,' said the woman. 'I thought I'd never get rid of it. Several gentlemen and ladies turned up their noses. Too religious for their taste.'

At a café on the opposite side of the Place de la Bastille, Anne and Michou sat at an outside table with a view of the fortress. The sun struggled between the clouds. Still it gave off summer heat. While waiting for a pitcher of cool cider, Michou untied the bundle and began flipping pages in her books. The *Imitation of Christ* was clasped shut. She opened it, but as she turned the pages, she grew frustrated and disappointed with her purchase. The central block of pages seemed stuck together. She pried them apart and discovered that they were crudely hollowed out to hide an engraved gold case. Inside was the miniature portrait of a young woman.

Surprised, Michou studied it closely. Puzzlement creased her brow. She handed the case to Anne. 'A master did this painting. It must be precious to someone. Certainly, if it were mine and I'd lost it, I'd be devastated. But it's really not mine.' She looked towards Anne, pleading for understanding. 'In my whole life I've never stolen anything. If I were to keep this locket, I'd feel guilty. I have to return it. But to whom?'

Anne examined the design on the front cover, a cross crowned by a wreath of thorns. The engraving was the work of a master goldsmith. On the back side Anne pointed to the goldsmith's mark. 'This might answer your question. Someone should recognize the mark. In the meantime, keep the books and the case out of sight, lest they tempt a thief. The gold case alone is worth far more than the couple of coins that you paid for it.'

The young woman's portrait, Anne thought, might also offer a clue to the locket's origin. She was depicted almost frontally in a bust-length view. Her features were delicate, pretty rather than beautiful. She wore a violet corselet and a rose corsage over her chemise. Rose and green ribbons were woven into her lightly powdered hair. Her head was slightly inclined in a childlike expression of yearning. There was a fragile air about her, like very fine porcelain.

Staring at the locket, recalling where it had been found, Anne wondered if she and Michou had stumbled upon a dark mystery. Why was it hidden away in a prison? That must be investigated and the locket's owner discovered.

They returned to the guardhouse and learned that the woman at the bin was Palloy's daughter. 'Where did you find these things?' asked Anne, pointing to the bin. She didn't mention the gold case.

'Mostly in the officers' quarters. My father, Monsieur Palloy, found your books yesterday in a secret cabinet in the ruins of the governor's house. They had survived the fire. None of them seemed valuable. To judge from the dust and the spiders' webs, the cabinet hadn't been opened in years. Delaunay might not have known about them.'

Anne signed to Michou, 'So it seems that the origin of our mystery may lie deep in the past. That's at least a start.'

A detachment of National Guardsmen stood at the entrance to the fortress. Their officer was speaking to a circle of wealthy, fashionable men and women. Anne and Michou drew close enough for Anne to hear him. He spoke loudly and with forceful gestures. Anne asked one of the women for his name.

'Lieutenant Maury. He's a hero, one of the French Guards who led the storming of the fortress. The next day, they made him a lieutenant in the National Guard.'

Michou set to sketching him. A short, muscular, swarthy man with a wide black moustache and wavy black hair, he had the intense, unflinching look of a daredevil. He was still in the blue coat of the French Guards, but he wore a red, white and blue cockade or rosette on his hat – a symbol of the National Guard, as well as the Revolution. At his side was a sabre, its hilt richly engraved. He touched it often as he spoke, as if depending on it for authority.

Anne translated Maury's remarks for Michou, but she had already caught the gist of them from his lips and his gestures. When he claimed to be the first to enter the fortress during the battle, she signed to Anne, 'He boasts. He might in fact have been second or third. That doesn't matter. He's foolish and daring – that's the point. He would gladly risk his life for a moment of glory.'

He patted a large iron key hanging from his belt. 'The governor's key to the cells. I released dozens of prisoners.'

'Were they badly treated and tortured?' asked an onlooker.

The lieutenant nodded vigorously. 'Their cells were dank, filthy, rat-infested. They were mere skin and bones, dressed in rags. Victims of royal despotism.'

Anne suppressed a strong temptation to object. Maury's account was a mile wide of the mark. A week ago at dinner, the Baron de Breteuil, Paul's patron, had said that most of the prisoners were removed during the previous several months – the Marquis de Sade just fifteen days ago. The remaining six or seven were living well in decent tower rooms, rather than in the dungeons. With no better place to go to, they were content to stay in the Bastille. When money became available, the government intended to tear down the building. It no longer served a useful purpose.

Encouraged by his audience, Maury went on to describe the battle's aftermath and the arrest of the fortress's governor Delaunay. 'We French Guards were going to bring him to the City Hall for trial. Why shouldn't we? He caused the death of at least a hundred patriots.'

Provoked by the lieutenant's slippery explanation, Anne spoke up. 'Was he ever fairly tried?' She knew that a so-called patriot stabbed him to death on the way to the City Hall. The guards should have protected him.

The onlookers shook their heads and murmured at her. Maury frowned. 'Madame, where have you been? Every honest man or woman knows Delaunay's fate. The people were impatient for justice and tried him in the street. They didn't need a courtroom, or magistrates in fancy robes.'

His audience nodded, apparently satisfied with his version of events. Anne could see no point in challenging him further.

As Maury's audience began to disperse, his eyes fastened upon Michou staring at him, a small sketchbook in one hand, a pencil in the other. He bristled. 'What do you think you're doing, little woman?' Suspicion and menace filled his eyes. 'Do you dare to mock me?'

Anne quickly stepped forward. 'My friend means no offence, sir. She's deaf and looks that way at you merely to read your lips and expressions better. Your story greatly intrigued her.'

While Anne spoke, Michou appeared to grasp Maury's problem. With a respectful smile, she held up the sketchbook for him to see.

He glanced at her sketch, then studied it closely and seemed intrigued, flattered. His expression grew almost benevolent. 'An amazing likeness. Well done, little woman,' he said. 'Give me a copy when you've finished.' He bowed to her and swaggered back to his post.

Anne and Michou retreated to the café on the Place de la Bastille and sat again at the outside table facing the fortress. Michou resumed sketching it, while Anne ordered cold cherry soup for both of them. When they had tasted the soup, Anne asked, 'May I see what intrigued our fierce lieutenant?'

Michou turned to the page and handed her the sketchbook. 'His portrait is unfinished. I'll complete it in a safer place.'

Anne studied the sketch. Michou had rendered the man in three-quarter profile – head thrust back, eyes opened wide, moustache bristling. His strong, determined chin tilted upward. A powerful, assertive nature seemed to be expressing itself, exactly the self-image that Maury prized. Little wonder that the sketch disarmed his suspicion.

'You were wise not to mock him,' said Anne to Michou. 'How will you proceed with the sketch?'

'I'll work mainly on the eyes. They tell me that he's ambitious, ruthless and deceitful – a man to be distrusted and feared.'

Three

David's Brutus

While his wife observed the demolition of the Bastille, Colonel Paul de Saint-Martin sat at his writing table and read reports from his lieutenants at Villejuif and other rural posts. Their message was alarming. Bandits were raiding flour mills, barges and carts of grain en route to the city, seriously disrupting the flow of provisions to the city markets.

He patted sweat from his brow, lest it drip on to the paper he was holding. At noon on this warm, humid Sunday, the air in his office was oppressive. He had closed the door for privacy, hung his blue coat on the back of a chair, and was working in shirtsleeves. Across the table his adjutant, Georges Charpentier, waited for questions. He had gathered the reports and knew the situation in the countryside better than anyone.

The colonel looked up from his reading. 'Georges, are these attacks random or systematic?'

'Systematic, sir. The bandits work in small gangs, get help from local desperate day labourers, carefully scout their targets, and strike at night. Sometimes they hit two or three estates at the same time. They also evade the traps we set for them.'

'How do they manage that?'

'They pay discontented peasants to warn them. Out of fear of reprisals, even friendly peasants aren't helping us as much as they used to. The bandits threaten to beat them, maim their livestock, and burn their buildings. Yesterday, near Villejuif, not far from your aunt's estate, bandits seized a grain cart and severely beat a peasant and his son.'

Saint-Martin felt a stab of anxiety. 'I'll warn my Aunt Marie to be vigilant and to look after my estate as well as hers.'

'Don't worry, sir. The countess is alert and resourceful, a difficult target for the bandits.'

The colonel tapped the reports neatly together and closed the folder. 'The highway patrol is doing all that it can.'

'So why aren't we successful?'

'Because the root of our problem is here in Paris, beyond our reach. As you know, my jurisdiction includes only the area surrounding Paris, not the city itself.' Saint-Martin paused to stress his point. 'To promote the cause of the Duc d'Orléans, a faction at the Palais-Royal try to restrict the city's supplies of grain in the countryside and blame treason and profiteering for the shortages. At the same time, they dole out small amounts of free food to win favour for the duke among the poor. When the people are fearful, terrified and angry, the duke's men then proclaim that the King is incompetent, and only the duke can restore order and save the country.'

'They're right about the King,' Georges remarked. 'But the duke is no better.'

'The duke's men know that,' Saint-Martin conceded. 'They think of the duke as merely their puppet – and their purse. They expect to govern through him, and they have a high opinion of their own ability.'

'Ah,' Georges murmured, 'that could be their downfall.'

This discussion was concluding when Anne returned from her visit to the Bastille. She had left Michou at her studio on Rue Traversine. Saint-Martin, Georges and Anne retired to the garden, a more comfortable place than the office for conversation in the summer.

'Shall I order food or drink?' she asked Paul, as a servant approached their table.

'Only a cool drink for me,' he replied, fanning himself.

Anne glanced at Georges. 'The same for me,' he said. She ordered lemonade for the three of them, a drink she had learned to enjoy a year ago during a winter vacation in Nice.

While waiting to be served, Anne described her morning visit to the Bastille and her worrisome encounter with Lieutenant Maury. 'No harm came of it,' she concluded, 'and Michou has sketched a faithful portrait of him.' She handed the sketch to her husband.

He held it up to the light. 'A cunning, passionate man, I would say, and rather darkly handsome.' He passed it on to his adjutant.

'A daredevil,' Georges remarked. 'Maury will always try to be the first man into the breach. I've never heard of him before the Bastille, but now I understand why the common sort love him.'

The lemonade arrived and the servant poured for Anne. It had the right blend of sweet and sour. She gave the servant a nod of approval. He withdrew after serving the men, and conversation resumed.

'Maury's popularity troubles me,' said Paul. 'A veteran sergeant in the French Guards, he mutinied, stole weapons from an arsenal, and attacked a royal fortress at the head of a mob. In any army worthy of the name, he would be court-martialled and shot. Instead "the common sort" call him a hero. He's rewarded with a lieutenant's commission in the National Guard.' Paul took a long draught of the lemonade, then glanced at Georges as if inviting a retort. 'What does his popularity tell us about the people's judgement?'

'It's not as bad, sir, as you seem to think. The people were right to approve Maury's deed, even if it was reckless.' Georges's tone was respectful but his throat taut. He continued in the same vein. 'The King's ministers had blundered. They pretended to honour the National Assembly and to accept recent reforms in this country, but at the same time they moved several thousand troops close to the city to intimidate its population while they retracted the reforms. To make matters worse, the city was only three days away from starvation. I'd say that the public had good reason to be fearful and angry and to arm itself. That's what the attack on the Bastille was about. Governor Delaunay was foolish to resist.'

Georges paused for a moment, twirled the lemonade in his glass, and searched the colonel's face for a reaction.

'Carry on, Georges, there's merit in what you say.' Saint-Martin expressed no irritation or pique, though Anne noticed his back was more rigid than usual. He usually encouraged his adjutant to speak his mind. Nonetheless, Anne was worried. Georges's sympathies lay with the people. He scorned the privileged and the rich. If he thought that Paul was baiting him, he might reply with harsh words that he would later regret. Paul might take offence and a rift would open between the two men.

Georges seemed to sense Anne's concern. He gave her a reassuring glance and continued in a more conciliatory tone. 'The French Guards should have protected the governor while in their custody. He deserved a fair trial. The public blather about the people's justice rings false. There needs to be an inquiry. If anyone is found guilty of his death, he should be severely punished.'

'Thank you, Georges. I'll keep your views in mind when I meet the mayor this afternoon.' Paul turned to Anne. 'He asked me to dine with him in his apartment.'

'May I ask why?'

'The mayor didn't tell me. Puzzling, isn't it?'

'Would you have time before dinner to visit Jacques-Louis David's personal studio? It's also in the Louvre on the top floor of the south wing. Michou has received an invitation and wants us to accompany her. David has offered to show us his paintings in progress for the Salon.'

Paul looked surprised. 'Why does she need us?'

'David slurs and mumbles his words. She can't read his lips.'

'How does she usually communicate with him?'

'Marc translates for her, but he doesn't want to see David's paintings now. He'll wait until they're exhibited at the Salon.'

Georges raised a hand. 'I happen to know about David's problem. As a young man he injured his left cheek in a sword fight. Lieutenant General Sartine sent me to investigate for evidence of a crime. We didn't pursue the matter – the wound seemed minor. But it left a scar. A large tumour formed inside the cheek, disfigured his mouth, and impaired his speech.'

'What a pity!' said Anne, trying to imagine the man's appearance.

Paul finished his drink. 'Monsieur David is a major figure in our art. I'm happy to spend a few hours in his studio. I'll go from there directly to Mayor Bailly's apartment.'

Early in the afternoon, Anne, Michou and Paul arrived at the foot of the stairway to David's studio on the top floor of the Louvre's south wing. They glanced at each other anxiously, mindful of David's reputation for angry, erratic behaviour. Michou signed to her companions, 'He's a great painter, but he's moody and excitable. I don't know how he's feeling today.'

Anne assured Michou that they were aware of the painter's temperament. They climbed the stairs, entered the studio's ante-room, and were seated in modern copies of antique chairs. Similar antique lamps lighted the room. Engravings of David's paintings hung on the walls. Anne recognized *The Death of Socrates* from the Salon of 1787. Michou commented on them with an easy familiarity.

'Your intimate knowledge of these pictures amazes me,' said Paul.

She smiled brightly for the compliment. 'I've been here often and studied them.'

'How have you come to know Monsieur David?' Anne was astounded that an obscure female deaf painter could make the acquaintance of one of the country's most popular living artists.

'Through my fiancé, Marc Latour,' Michou replied. 'He knows David, showed him my miniature paintings. He liked them and recommended them to his patrons. Marc and David think alike about the Royal Academy of Painting and Sculpture. As a member of the academy, David quarrels with its senior leaders – rigid, backward little despots, he calls them.'

'Hurtful words,' remarked Paul. 'What have the "despots" done to earn them?'

'They have annoyed him personally,' Michou explained, 'by recently forcing him to send away his young female students.' Michou's signing grew agitated, her expression scornful. 'As if those women would distract or corrupt the males.'

'Monsieur David has strong opinions, and not only concerning art,' Anne observed.

'Yes,' Michou agreed. 'Marc thinks that David wants to change the Academy like Lafayette and the National Assembly are reforming the country. He claims that artists should be free to determine their own rules, free from the government's control.' She paused, searching for the right signs. 'He thinks of the Academy, like the Bastille, as a symbol of despotism. Both should be torn down.'

'His strong views can be seen in his art,' Anne remarked. 'One of his paintings for the Salon promises to be controversial. It's called *Brutus returned to his home, after having condemned his two sons to death for joining in a conspiracy against Roman freedom; the lictors bring back their bodies so that he may give them burial.*'

'Why controversial?' asked Paul.

'It's extraordinarily violent. Michou thought you would want to see it. It won't be shown to the public until the Salon. But David is allowing a few selected viewers to study the painting and is interested in their reaction.'

After several minutes in the anteroom, Paul wondered aloud if this was a convenient time for the master to meet them. Michou explained that most of his students were away at dinner. So it was actually a good time. A conscientious teacher, David might have encountered an unexpected problem in a student's work.

A few moments later, their patience was rewarded. A servant opened the door and led them to David's office. He was at a table, studying a sketch off to one side. As the visitors entered, he turned to greet them.

Anne was prepared to see a disfigured face but was shocked nonetheless. The right side of his face was handsome, the left side was swollen. An ugly scar ran from the mouth across the cheek. The contrast was jarring. He must have noticed her reaction for he turned his head and partly concealed the cheek. No one commented. Within moments they overcame this initial difficulty and a normal conversation began.

Anne surveyed the office for clues to David's character. Her eyes lit upon a pair of iron shackles hanging on the wall. David followed her gaze and remarked, 'They come from the dungeons of the Bastille. One of my students gave them to me. Early on, he had joined in the attack and was among the first to enter the fortress.' David's voice rang with pride and approval.

Paul appeared irked. 'It's been many years since those shackles held a man's legs. The dungeons were empty. The attack aimed at taking the garrison's gunpowder, not a handful of witless prisoners.'

David flinched. Anne's mind raced to prevent a clash of opinions. She gave the painter a gracious smile and said, 'It's kind of you to show us the paintings for the Salon.'

'I'll ask one of the senior students to serve as guide, while I stand in the background.'

To observe Paul's reaction, Anne thought.

The studio was immense, its ceiling high. Dozens of easels held canvases at various stages of completion.

The visitors stopped briefly to view a few of his lesser paintings for the Salon, then went to the *Brutus*. While they gazed at the painting, the guide related the story of Brutus from the Roman historian Livy. A patriotic magistrate of the ancient Roman Republic, Brutus ordered the execution of his two sons for conspiring to restore despotic rule in Rome. Their part in the conspiracy was minor, and the law did not require their death. But because they were his sons, Brutus felt obliged to show them no favour or mercy.

Anne found the behaviour of Brutus to be excessively harsh and repellent. After studying the painting, she wasn't sure whether David approved or disapproved of the ancient Roman.

The Salon painting appeared fully sketched out on the canvas. David had completed the faces of Brutus and the grief-stricken women of his family. Their bodies and the setting remained to be painted. The guide reached to the side and uncovered a small painting on an easel next to the Salon painting. 'And this is the oil sketch with which he started.'

Brutus sat brooding with his back to the body of one of his sons being carried into the house.

'Look,' signed Michou, pointing to an obscure detail in the original oil sketch. The men leading the procession were carrying two heads on pikes. 'The sons of Brutus, punished like Monsieur Delaunay and his assistant. Odd coincidence, isn't it?'

'When did Monsieur David start work on this painting?' Anne asked the guide. 'Could the recent violent episodes in the city have influenced its composition?'

The guide appeared unsure and began to stammer. David stepped forward to take the question and pointed to the unfinished *Brutus*. 'Now in case you're wondering, madame, if the bloody events at the Bastille or the assassination of its governor, Monsieur Delaunay, inspired me, note that I completed the little oil sketch several weeks ago. That's when I began the full-scale painting. The story of Brutus has fascinated many artists.

For me the story is a powerful lesson in civic virtue. Livy told it in words; I've told it in paint. It's for the ages to judge whose *Brutus* is the most moving.'

After leaving David, Anne asked Paul, 'What are we to make of David's painting?'

Paul replied, his voice tentative, 'I don't see any political message. David is fascinated by the conflict in Brutus between his civic duty and his family. He omitted the oil sketch's gory details – the sons' heads on the pikes – because they detracted from the Salon painting's central moral issue.'

Anne shook her head. 'According to Marc, the painting reflects the people's assault on the Bastille in the name of Liberty. The "execution" of its governor and other officers was to prevent tyranny from returning to France. In plain words, the painting is a warning to the King's ministers and their partisans: they would meet a similar fate if they were to attempt to overturn the National Assembly and to restore despotic rule.'

Paul frowned. 'The ministers aren't simpletons. They would detect the warning if it were there. And they wouldn't allow his painting into the Salon.'

Anne persisted. 'The country's chaos may distract them, prevent them from carefully reading the painting's message.' She smiled at her husband, took his hand. 'For the little that it's worth, that's at least what I think.'

Four

A Dangerous Mission

Paris, Sunday, 19 July

They left David's studio together with lively impressions of *Brutus*, proof of its dramatic power. Anne and Michou went to Marc Latour's studio to show him the gold locket with the young woman's portrait. He might have an idea of its history and value and how to find its rightful owner. Colonel Saint-Martin went to his dinner appointment.

At the foot of the stairway to Mayor Bailly's Louvre apartment, the colonel was still preoccupied with David's painting. What would he do, were he Brutus in a similar conflict between duty and family? Or between the demands facing him as a provost in these troubled times and his abiding love for Anne, the elixir of his life? Thus far in the three years of their relationship he had not been tested like Brutus. For that he was grateful.

Suddenly, a young palace guard, his hand gripping the hilt of his sword, stepped out of the shadows and confronted Saint-Martin. He was taken aback. Then he recalled that he was out of uniform.

'Your papers, sir, and the nature of your business.' The command was crisp and firm.

Saint-Martin showed his papers and the mayor's invitation. 'I have an appointment with Monsieur Bailly.'

The guard gave him a searching glance, then stepped aside. 'You may pass, Colonel.'

Saint-Martin saluted. 'Well done, young man. I'll commend you to Mayor Bailly.'

When he had climbed a few steps, he had an afterthought. Did the mayor *really* need armed protection? Moreover, Bailly had told him, 'Wear a gentleman's plain clothing. You will attract less attention.'

Saint-Martin started up the stairs again, puzzled. Why should the mayor not wish to receive a royal officer in uniform? Perhaps this particular officer was the problem, a man thought to be close to the Baron de Breteuil, a distant relative. The baron personified the former autocratic system of governing that was now being challenged.

Saint-Martin granted that the baron's influence had made him a provost of the Royal Highway Patrol. In the past, the job was a sinecure for elderly retired army colonels. Six years ago, the baron insisted that the patrol needed young, vigorous leadership to become more effective, and he prevailed.

Midway up the stairs, Saint-Martin examined his conscience. Had this personal debt to the baron ever compromised the discharge of his duties? He could honestly say no. Under his command the highway patrol operated effectively and to general satisfaction. Lieutenant General DeCrosne, his superior, was pleased with his performance and often chose him for especially difficult assignments. Was that why Mayor Bailly had invited him?

Outside the mayor's apartment Saint-Martin loosened the kerchief from his throat. He was perspiring. A servant opened the door and showed him into the mayor's study. A table for two was set by a window overlooking the river.

This was truly a scholar's den, thought the colonel as he surveyed the large, bright room. Shelves of books covered one wall, astronomical charts and maps hung on another. A celestial globe, as tall as a man, stood in a corner. Before entering politics a few months ago, Sylvain Bailly had been a distinguished astronomer and member of the French Academy. His reputation for integrity and public spirit had propelled him into the mayor's office.

Saint-Martin wished him well but kept his expectations low. Accustomed to civil, scholarly discourse, Bailly was now being sucked into a whirlpool of competing problems. After two disastrous harvests, the city's 800,000 hungry, anxious men and women were clamouring for food, pillaging the markets and bakeries. Skilful demagogues urged them on, fed them with lurid tales of royal treachery and profiteering, stoked their anger, while dismantling the city's administration and undermining its system of provisions. These intractable issues would surely prove far more difficult to master than the movement of the stars.

'Colonel, I'm pleased that you could come.' The words sounded heartfelt.

Saint-Martin bowed. 'I'm honoured to serve Paris's first mayor.'

Bailly gestured to the table. 'We'll go directly to the meal and its purpose. There are so many claims upon our time that we must sacrifice the pleasures of a leisurely preamble.'

Bailly was a slender, dignified man, dressed in a plain black silk suit. Black, his habitual colour, enhanced his grave appearance and simple manner. At the table he rang for a servant and instructed him briefly. A few minutes later the servant placed a cheese omelette platter on a *réchaufé*, poured a light white wine, left a green salad on a sideboard and withdrew.

Bailly served the omelette, poured the wine, then met Saint-Martin's eye and remarked, 'You may be wondering about the purpose of this meeting.'

'True, the matter must be delicate – and serious.'

'Your mission is both. Former Lieutenant General Thiroux DeCrosne has sent you on previous missions and you always performed to his full satisfaction. This mission also falls within your jurisdiction as a provost of the Royal Highway Patrol.'

Saint-Martin registered surprise at the mention of DeCrosne. 'I assumed that he might have left the city by now to escape the mob's wrath. Among royal officers, he's perhaps the most likely scapegoat for all those who regard the law as their enemy.'

'No, DeCrosne is still here and has handed over to me his powers and his office at police headquarters. I should add that he did so with good grace and has given helpful advice to me in police matters. For safety's sake, he's a guest in my home in Chaillot.' Bailly offered the salad.

Saint-Martin served himself. 'Tell me about this special mission.'

Bailly drew a deep breath. 'How well do you know the royal intendant for the Paris region, Bertier de Sauvigny?'

'I've spoken to him on several occasions. He has dined at my table. In the course of a long career overseeing the needs of the Paris region, he has earned an enviable reputation as an unusually competent administrator and an honourable man.'

'I share your view. But yesterday four men from the Paris city council arrested him in Compiègne and charged him with profiteering.'

Saint-Martin felt a surge of scepticism.

'Yes, Colonel, this is a most suspicious and dangerous development. Those four men have no mandate for what they've done. Henchmen of the Duc d'Orléans, they have acted at his initiative. In recent days they have stirred up popular sentiment against prominent royal officers, accusing them of manipulating the grain trade in order to starve Paris and to enrich themselves.'

'What's the duke's goal?' Saint-Martin knew the answer, but he wanted to hear it from Bailly.

'He wants to take control of the royal government, exile or depose the King, and "save" the people from despotism and starvation. As the royal officer in charge of regulating the Paris grain trade, Bertier is portrayed by the duke as a living symbol of the King's ineptitude and his indifference to the people's suffering. Destroying Bertier is a way to further undermine the King's authority. In addition, Bertier has given a confidential, unflattering description of the duke. It was brought to his attention and has ruffled his feathers.'

'That shameful hypocrite! He trumpets his gifts of food to the city's starving poor. But my troopers tell me that his men systematically divert grain from the Paris markets and try to make the crisis worse than it already is. Bertier is their scapegoat.'

'Right. I fear that they will arouse a mob in Compiègne, as they have done elsewhere, and cause him harm. Therefore, I'm asking you to go to Compiègne and bring him back safely to Paris. We'll lodge him in a secure prison and conduct a proper trial to refute the accusations against him.'

Bailly rang for the servant. He cleared the table and brought in a raspberry compote. 'For years, I've picked these berries from my own garden. But then I was just an astronomer.'

Saint-Martin detected a hint of regret in the mayor's voice. Like Paris itself, he faced a troubled, uncertain future.

When the servant withdrew, Saint-Martin asked, 'Is this mission secret? Is that why we're discussing it in your apartment rather than at the City Hall?'

'Secret? Yes. You must take the duke's four men in

Compiègne by surprise. If they are forewarned, they will precipitate violence against Bertier before you can reach him.' Bailly smiled gravely. 'There are only two places in Paris where I can speak in confidence: in this apartment and in my home in Chaillot. Moreover, during the present unrest, you would not be safe in or near the City Hall, or wherever the duke's men influence the people.'

'Is the duke so bold, so powerful? And why should his men pay so much attention to me?'

'I regret to say, Colonel, that the duke is the richest man in France and uses his wealth ruthlessly to advance his cause. He thinks you may be in his way. After all, you are the protégé of the Baron de Breteuil, a man notoriously loyal to the King and the Queen. Breteuil is on his way to Switzerland. Some say that he will try to rally support for an attempt to restore full royal authority, or so-called tyranny.'

Saint-Martin took the last bite of the compote and bowed to his host. 'I thank you, sir, for dinner and for the warning. I'll be careful in Compiègne. And rest assured I shall return Bertier to Paris safe and sound.'

Five

Mystery of the Locket

Paris, Monday, 20 July

Early on a dark cloudy morning, after breakfast, Saint-Martin prepared to leave for Compiègne, fifty miles to the north-east of Paris. He and Anne walked, arm in arm, into the courtyard. Several troopers waited by their horses, pistols holstered, hands resting on the hilts of their sabres. They looked on benevolently and with respect while Anne and Paul embraced. Paul gave an order. They mounted and rode off in a clatter of hooves on the paving stones. Paul waved as he passed through the gate. Then he was gone. Anne felt anxiety clutch at her stomach. Would he return unharmed?

At midmorning, dressed in fine muslin gowns, Anne and Michou set off in a carriage for the showroom of Charles-Auguste Böhmer and Paul Bassenge on Rue Vendôme near the Temple. Yesterday, Marc Latour had studied the gold case and suggested that they show it to the two jewellers. In a tone of awe, he had said, 'They are among the few who might know the owner of this case. It's a masterpiece.' Anne had sent a messenger ahead to arrange the visit.

'How do I look?' Michou signed nervously. 'I hardly slept last night. These men are jewellers to the royal court at Versailles. I'm a small, deaf woman. They won't even look at me. What difference does it make what I wear?'

Anne took her friend by the shoulders and looked her in the eye. 'You're beautiful and intelligent, Michou. They will pay attention to you.' Anne meant what she said. Michou was petite – no shame in that. She also had a well-shaped figure, graceful movements, and a generous smile. Her large luminous green eyes were a striking contrast to her thick auburn hair, tied in a chignon at the nape of her neck. Deaf, abandoned at birth, neglected and poor for most of her life, she had nonetheless developed a remarkable artistic talent. In three years of friendship with Anne, she had gained self-confidence. But it still faltered in the presence of the high and mighty.

'Don't fret, Michou. These men may be the most prominent jewellers in Paris, but they aren't the best judges of human character. A trickster's elegant appearance, polished speech and refined manners could deceive them. That weakness recently brought them to the verge of ruin.'

A few years ago, Anne explained, the partners were caught in the scandal of the decade. Bassenge, the junior partner in the firm, had designed a magnificent necklace of hundreds of diamonds. The senior partner, Böhmer, had tried to sell it to Queen Marie Antoinette. She refused the offer – it was too expensive even for her, Madame Deficit, as her enemies called her.

A band of slick thieves persuaded the Cardinal Rohan, a rich worldly cleric, to buy it for the Queen to win her favour. During the transaction the thieves swindled the jewellers out of the necklace, broke it up, and sold the pieces in England. The cardinal was arrested, imprisoned in the Bastille, and put on trial. The scandal, distorted by her enemies, tainted the Queen's reputation. And Messieurs Böhmer and Bassenge lost 1,600,000 *livres* that they had invested in the necklace.

'You see, Michou, Messieurs Böhmer and Bassenge are not gods. They appear to have less common sense than you or I.'

Michou smiled. 'I'm not tempted to worship them – I see their feet of clay. But I fear them, and other wealthy, powerful men. They can so easily hurt me.'

At the showroom Anne and Michou were greeted by an attractive young woman in a fashionable striped, multi-coloured silk gown, her hair piled high upon her head and held together by silk ribbons matching the colours in the gown. She led them past glass cases of sparkling brooches, necklaces, earrings, and other glittering jewellery.

Michou signed to Anne, 'Paste diamonds?'

Anne nodded. 'If they were real, a company of soldiers would be needed to guard this place.'

Monsieur Böhmer was waiting in a small, elegant parlour.

Mirrors in gilded frames covered the walls. Pale northern light poured through two large windows and blended with soft, lively light from a crystal chandelier and from silver sconces between the mirrors. Anne tried to imagine the glory of the Queen's stolen necklace in this room.

If the jeweller still mourned the lost *livres*, he didn't show it. The coachman who brought Anne and Michou to the show-room had said with a hint of contempt that the jeweller was a German Jew from Saxony, suggesting a sly, greedy, ugly creature. In fact, Anne now discovered to her pleasant surprise that he was a handsome, cultivated gentleman. His French was excellent, only slightly accented. He seated them comfort-ably in upholstered chairs and asked what he could do for them.

'If you aren't too busy,' Anne began, 'you could help us discover the origin and value of my friend's gold locket. She's deaf; I'm speaking for her.' At a nod from Anne, Michou handed the locket to the jeweller.

At first he seemed taken aback. He might have hoped that the attractive wife of Colonel Paul de Saint-Martin had come to buy an expensive piece of jewellery. But he took the locket with a polite smile, laid it on a green velvet-covered table and began to examine it. He soon nodded his cautious approval. He leaned forward and caressed the smooth curved surface of the gold case. With a small magnifying glass he studied the engraving, then touched it lightly with his fingers. He examined the hallmarks on the back of the case with his glass. He opened the case and stared at the young woman's portrait.

Finally, he looked up and addressed Michou. 'You have a remarkable locket, Madame. The gold is of the highest quality. Offhand, I can't give you the goldsmith's name. His mark is unfamiliar to me. The case was made sometime before my partner and I came to Paris from the court of the King of Poland.'

He rang for a clerk, who led an elderly man into the room.

'My partner, Monsieur Bassenge. He will know the mark; he has worked with Paris old gold more than I.'

Bassenge examined the gold case and said, 'The master's mark is from Georges Dubé and son, goldsmiths on Rue des Orfèvres. Best in the business. The tax farmer's mark is from 1768.'

'Can you tell us something about the portrait?' Anne asked.

'Perhaps.' Bassenge turned his attention to the painting. 'Gouache on ivory, by a masterful miniaturist.'

'I know,' signed Michou. 'I too paint miniatures.'

Anne translated, and added, 'The Comtesse Marie de Beaumont is her patron.'

Böhmer glanced at Michou with new respect. He asked Bassenge, 'Who is the artist?'

'The painting is in the style of Pierre Hall . . . or even by him. A Swede, he came to Paris about 1766 and has become the foremost miniaturist in the city.'

'What's its value?' Michou signed and Anne translated.

Böhmer and Bassenge exchanged glances. The former replied. 'The gold case alone is worth at least a thousand *livres*.' Anne quickly calculated. That was twice as much as most artisans could earn in a year.

'I can hardly put a value on the portrait,' said Böhmer. 'The painter probably earned three hundred *livres*.' His eyes grew moist. The beauty of the piece apparently touched him. 'It must have meant much more than money could buy to the man who commissioned it and to its painter. It's a work of love.'

As they rose to leave, Anne asked Bassenge, 'Would you know where Monsieur Hall lives? He might tell us who commissioned the painting and the identity of the woman.'

'His studio is on Rue Favart near the Théâtre des Italiens. Ask anyone in the neighbourhood for the exact address. I understand that he's a gregarious man, attracts attention, should be easy to find.'

Böhmer accompanied the women to the door. 'By the way,' he said slowly and clearly to Michou, 'if you ever choose to sell the locket, Madame, please allow me to make an offer.'

Rue Favart was a short street, and the Swedish painter was well known. The coachman found the address without delay. It was about noon. Anne and Michou had neither an introduction nor an invitation, but a servant nonetheless admitted them into a small parlour. Anne introduced them and stated their business. 'We've discovered a fine miniature painting of a woman. Monsieur Bassenge believes it might come from Monsieur Hall's studio.'

'I'll ask if he will see you,' said the servant, and closed the door. A few minutes later the door opened and a middle-aged man in a painter's smock entered. The women rose to their feet. Anne sensed Michou's anxiety growing. Hall stood at the very peak of their profession. At this moment she must reckon herself near the bottom.

'Pierre Hall, Mesdames, at your service.' He was a corpulent man with a genial manner. His eyes danced from one woman to the other, making quick, shrewd estimates of their quality. He apparently liked what he saw, for he bowed graciously and motioned them to be seated. 'May I see the portrait? I'm intrigued that it might be one of mine.' His voice was warm and lively. Anne felt immediately at ease. Michou also relaxed and handed him the locket.

He took it gently, and gave her a brief, teasing smile. 'What do we have here?' He opened the gold case, gazed at the woman's portrait, and gasped softly. 'This is indeed mine; it is among the earliest from my Paris studio. It's one of my favourites, if I may say so.' He examined the hallmarks, closed the case, and studied the engraving. 'A perfect match, case and portrait,' he exclaimed. His expression changed; a question seemed to grow in his mind.

'Did you buy this locket?' he asked Michou, returning it to her.

Michou nodded yes, and then hesitated.

Anne cautioned her to say no more. Monsieur Hall was still mostly a stranger. Anne hastened to add, 'We'd like to know who commissioned it and the identity of the woman.'

Hall grew thoughtful. 'Since coming to Paris, I've painted hundreds of miniature portraits. My memory needs help. We should go to my records.'

Hall led them to a room whose walls were nearly covered with paintings and sketches. Pieces of sculpture stood on pedestals, tables and shelves. It was a rich and varied collection, including a terracotta bust of Hall himself. Michou gasped with amazement.

The painter chuckled. 'Monsieur Fragonard and other artistic friends gather here for an evening to enjoy a bottle of wine and to savour these beauties.' He waved grandly at his collection. 'You may do the same while I go through my records. A servant will bring you wine.'

A few minutes after he left, a servant came with glasses and a bottle of wine, poured for the women, and left. They sipped, exchanged glances of approval, and agreed that Hall must have an excellent cellar. Michou wandered about the room, then stopped at portraits sketched by Van Dyck and examined them closely. She raised her glass and saluted them. 'This may be as close as I'll get to heaven.' She paused, grimaced. 'How I envy Monsieur Hall, living close to such beauty.'

The painter returned with a file box. 'I've jotted down the information that you've asked for.' He handed Michou a sheet of paper. She passed it on to Anne. She glanced at it and stopped at a name. 'Who is he?' she murmured. The handwriting was cramped.

Hall leaned over her shoulder. 'The man who commissioned the portrait was a Monsieur Boileau, a prominent book dealer and publisher. He paid three hundred and ten *livres* and received the portrait in October of 1768.'

'And the woman in the portrait?' asked Michou.

'She's Monsieur Boileau's daughter Adelaide, eighteen at the time. He seemed extraordinarily fond of her, a shy, tender, lovely person. Our sessions in the studio come back to me now with perfect clarity. She sat for me several times. Her beauty was fragile, delicate, like the petal of a rose. I wondered how she could survive in our cruel world unless with the constant protection of her doting father.'

Anne asked, 'Did Monsieur Boileau have other children?'

'Yes, a son. He and his sister were twins. He came to one or two of the sessions. A bright, high-strung, brooding lad. His father said he wanted a portrait of the boy as a pendant to his sister's. But nothing came of the idea.' Stroking his chin, Hall reflected. 'I can't recall the boy's name.'

'Do you know what happened to the family?'

'I had no further contact with them. The question makes me wonder. Your friend apparently didn't buy the locket from Boileau or his children, did she?'

'No, she bought it from a Mademoiselle Palloy.'

Confusion spread across Hall's broad face. 'Really?' he murmured.

'The locket is cloaked in mystery,' Anne said. 'My friend and I are attempting to discover the truth.'

*   *   *

As they rode in the coach to Rue Traversine, Anne and Michou went over their conversation with Hall, and Anne filled in what Michou had missed.

Michou reflected, and then signed, 'I need to learn more about Monsieur Boileau and his family. The locket belongs to them.'

The two women were on their way to the town house of the Comtesse Marie de Beaumont, Anne's husband Paul's enlightened aunt. Michou had her own studio and an apartment on the second floor. Anne had a small apartment on the top floor and looked after the building while the countess was at her country estate south of Paris.

'Comtesse Marie might be able to help us,' Anne said. 'In the late 1760s she was active in Paris society and well informed. She and her friend the Comte de Savarin are expected at the town house today. We'll try to meet her.'

'I know little about the count. What kind of man is he?'

'A widower, reserved in his manner, but loyal, generous, and affectionate to his friends.'

'Does he work for a living?' Michou's eyes had a mischievous glint.

Anne smiled. 'For a count, he works hard. His job is to keep the records of the royal family and the aristocrats at the palace in Versailles. He also translates coded messages for the foreign office, and two years ago he helped Paul solve a murder investigation.'

Michou's eyes had begun to glaze over. 'What I really want to know is whether they're going to get married.'

'I don't know, Michou. The countess says only that they're good friends. I think marriage is likely. He's a widower; she lost her husband ten years ago. They're both almost sixty, healthy and vigorous, and enjoy each other's company.'

Michou nodded thoughtfully. 'Then I believe they would be happy together.'

When Anne and Michou arrived at the town house, Marie and the count were about to dine. Anne and Michou hadn't eaten all day and joined them at the table. For a moment the count seemed surprised, but he quickly gave the two commoners a welcoming smile. Anne easily forgave him.

As a lamb ragout was served and a light red Bordeaux

wine poured, Anne asked the countess, 'What brings you to Paris?'

'This evening's concert at the Tuileries. The virtuoso violinist Monsieur Saint-Georges will lead the orchestra of the Loge Symphonique.'

Anne enjoyed music. On stage at Sadler's Wells outside London, she had sung traditional English airs. Until she met Paul, she had had little exposure to serious music. But he had gradually won her over to his favourites: the Austrian composers, Mozart and Haydn. Now she was eager to increase her musical knowledge.

'Who is Saint-Georges? I've heard the name.'

'A fascinating young man, a handsome creole from our island of Guadeloupe in the West Indies. Plays several instruments and composes music.'

'Handsome, you say. Michou should sketch him. What will he play?'

The count replied, 'Joseph Haydn's Symphony Eighty-eight in G-Major. The orchestra first played it here last year to great acclaim, so they're repeating it this evening.'

Marie glanced at him fondly and added, 'The count is especially looking forward to the cello in the second and third movements. It leads the lovely melodies.'

Anne was aware that Savarin, among his many other talents, was a serious amateur cellist.

The countess asked Anne what she and Michou were doing.

'Trying to find the owner of a precious locket.' She turned to Michou. Her friend took the locket from her bag and handed it to the countess, who showed it to the count.

'How did you find such a valuable piece?' he asked, caressing the smooth gold surface.

Anne briefly told the story of the locket and her investigation thus far and asked, 'Do either of you recall Monsieur Boileau, a book dealer and publisher, active in Paris twenty years ago?'

Savarin replied, 'Indeed I do. For years I bought books from him. During the controversy between the King, then Louis XV, and the Parlement de Paris, Monsieur Boileau ignored my pleas to be prudent. He published pamphlets that attacked the King personally. In 1771 he was arrested and put in the Bastille. Before the year ended, he died of prison fever. The crown closed his business and took his property.'

Marie added, 'The Abbé de l'Épée also knew Monsieur Boileau and followed that incident closely. He could give you more details.'

'I'll speak to him,' Anne said, but she knew already that the locket had a tragic history.

Six

Fateful Journey

Compiègne–Paris, Monday–Wednesday, 20–22 July

L ate that evening, Colonel Saint-Martin and six troopers arrived in Compiègne – just in time. A small, noisy, ugly-looking crowd had gathered in the square in front of the municipal building where the local authorities were holding Bertier. A half-dozen frightened guards blocked the entrance and struggled to hold the crowd at bay.

As he entered the square, Saint-Martin recognized the four councillors from Paris in their well-tailored suits and fashionable hats. The rest of the crowd was dressed in rags. Some brandished knives. The representatives were leading the cries to hang the profiteer Bertier from the nearest lamp-post.

As the colonel and his troop drew near, the crowd turned towards them, mouths gaping. Its cries then subsided into a murmuring babble. Taken by surprise, the representatives gathered in a desperate conclave and temporarily lost contact with the crowd.

In that moment, the colonel ordered the crowd to disperse. His troopers slowly advanced towards the entrance, sabres drawn. The crowd melted away, leaving the four councillors pinned between the troopers and the guards at the entrance.

In a loud voice, full of authority, Saint-Martin addressed the councillors. 'You have no authority here. As provost of the Royal Highway Patrol for this region, I'm the magistrate in charge. Leave immediately.'

The four exchanged sour glances and refused to move. Their leader stepped forward. 'The prisoner inside the building isn't a common bandit, Colonel, but an enemy of the people. We must bring him back to the city ourselves to face the people's justice.'

Saint-Martin produced Mayor Bailly's instructions, but to no effect. The councillors claimed that the mayor had no authority outside Paris.

'If true,' the colonel retorted, 'then by your own reasoning you also lack authority beyond the limits of Paris. Therefore, you had no right to arrest Bertier in the first place.'

When the councillors still refused to move, Saint-Martin ordered his troopers to arrest them. As the troopers were about to seize him, the councillors' leader waved a hand of surrender, then hissed through gritted teeth. 'We will return to Paris and report to the people that you have allied yourself with their enemy. You will pay dearly.'

Under the icy stare of the colonel and his troopers, the leader and his colleagues marched off, chins high, shoulders squared, muttering that the colonel was a tyrant's minion and would soon feel the people's wrath. Lest the crowd return, Saint-Martin and his entourage moved into the municipal building for the night. They found Bertier calm and in good spirits.

Early the next day, the Paris councillors quietly left Compiègne. The immediate danger abated, Saint-Martin and his 'prisoner' were free to enjoy a day of leisure. Bailly had instructed the colonel to arrive in Paris late in the afternoon of the twenty-second. On the following day, the mayor and the city council would meet to hear the charges against Bertier and consider their response.

Saint-Martin used this opportunity to study his vilified companion and form his own opinion. They installed themselves and the troopers comfortably in the south wing of the empty royal palace. In his role as intendant of the area, Bertier had recently overseen its completion.

During long walks in the palace park and while playing chess in the evening, Saint-Martin confirmed his earlier, favourable impressions of his companion. At fifty-two, Bertier was at the height of his powers, a diligent, intelligent, masterful administrator of the most complex district in the kingdom. He was also a man of integrity and honour, motivated by a strong sense of duty.

'Why has the Duc d'Orléans attacked you so vigorously?' Saint-Martin asked while they were alone at the dinner table.

Bertier replied in a matter-of-fact voice, 'I've always been civil to him and respectful of his princely rank. But when asked in confidence to judge his character and ability, I have reported that he is lazy, self-indulgent, wilfully ignorant of affairs of state, and easily led by clever, unscrupulous men like his secretary, Choderlos de Laclos – cold, witty, graceless. These faults would matter less if the duke were not also rich, ambitious, ruthless and hungry for power. He has no respect for the traditional, sacred character of royal authority. Hatred for the present King and Queen consumes his spirit. In a word, he is not fit to rule this country.'

'A truthful assessment,' Saint-Martin remarked, raising his wine glass in homage to Bertier's candour.

'Unfortunately, my opinion has reached the duke's ears. He has concluded that I'm a significant obstacle to him becoming regent or King of France. In revenge, he faults me for provisioning the royal troops near Paris. He also blames me, rather than mother nature and our inefficient agriculture, for the present crisis in Paris's food supply.'

'But there's more,' the colonel noted. 'Pamphlets from the Palais-Royal denounce you and Monsieur Foullon, your father-in-law, as selfish profiteers, deserving death. The people are said to be starving because of you.'

Bertier smiled wryly. 'My system for supplying Paris works well under ordinary circumstances. Even with the catastrophic failure of the past two harvests, the system continues to feed the people, though they suffer shortages. The new harvest looks good and should provide an adequate supply of grain. Neither I nor my father-in-law personally engages in the grain trade. We haven't earned a sou at the people's expense.'

'So the pamphlets are full of lies?'

'Of course. They are meant to arouse fear and anger and thus serve the duke's cause.'

'Who writes them?'

'Laclos has hired several scribblers, most notable among them Jean-Paul Marat. But the one who especially attacks me and Monsieur Foullon is Hercule Gaillard. Years ago, I helped Inspector Quidor send him to the Bastille for crimes of slander and extortion. The pamphlets are his revenge.'

'Did you know that Gaillard's father, a book dealer named Boileau, died in the Bastille a decade earlier? Shortly thereafter, his son changed his name to avoid being linked with a convicted criminal.'

Bertier seemed surprised. 'I didn't know. My role was to persuade certain highborn victims to testify against Gaillard. I didn't go into his background. I see how it could aggravate his hostility.'

A servant entered the room and filled their glasses. When he left, Saint-Martin asked, 'Is it wise for you to return to Paris? My patron the Baron de Breteuil has moved to Switzerland; other prominent royal officials have left for England. I would not force you to return with me.'

Bertier smiled. 'I appreciate your concern, Colonel, and I recognize the dangers ahead. But only in Paris can I defend my honour. Mayor Bailly and the Marquis de Lafayette will ensure that I have a fair trial. I have no doubt that I shall emerge victorious.'

The next day, Saint-Martin and Bertier set out for Paris, prepared for battle. The six heavily armed mounted troopers accompanied the intendant's carriage. A coachman, a groom, and two trusted servants, dressed as commoners and armed, rode outside. The colonel and the intendant sat inside, their swords near at hand.

It was a grey, cloudy day. As they approached Paris, intermittent showers wet the city's tiled roofs and the streets. The weather depressed spirits that were already subdued. The ride to Paris had proven uneventful, thanks perhaps to Colonel Saint-Martin's precautions. But as they approached the city gate at Porte Saint-Martin, he felt his chest tighten. His companion also grew tense.

They were supposed to meet a detachment of National Guards at the Royal Highway Patrol post. The guards would have orders from Bailly and Lafayette to bring Bertier to the prison at the Abbaye Saint-Germain on the Left Bank. He should be safe there.

The carriage drove into the post's courtyard. About a dozen

guards were waiting by their horses. Their commander approached the carriage. The colonel stepped out and they saluted. The officer showed his orders, properly drawn up and signed. He was Lieutenant Maury from a barracks in Chaillot, Mayor Bailly's village just west of the city. Saint-Martin had immediately recognized him from Anne's description, the audacious 'hero' of the Bastille. Maury ordered two men to ride inside the carriage with Bertier, who gave his sword and scabbard to Saint-Martin. The remaining guards mounted their horses, some to lead the way through the city, others to follow.

During this exchange, Saint-Martin closely observed the lieutenant. Short and muscular, his face swarthy, he would likely be a temperamental Gascon. Though Maury behaved correctly, he spoke with a detectible tone of insolence, but not enough to earn a reprimand. His eyes shifted as if moved by some hidden deceit.

Can I trust the man? Saint-Martin wondered. On a sudden impulse he asked, 'May I ride in the coach with the intendant?'

The lieutenant bristled. 'My orders from our commander, the Marquis de Lafayette, state that my men and I are to escort the prisoner. We neither need nor want your assistance.' He mounted his horse. 'You have done your part, Colonel. We shall now do ours.'

'I should hope so, Lieutenant. I hold you honour-bound.' There was little more that Saint-Martin could do. The marquis would not allow a challenge to his authority. The National Guard was his creation and the cornerstone of his power in Paris. It was also inextricably wrapped up with his enormous vanity. Unfortunately, the National Guard was scarcely a week old and lacked discipline. Its ranks included men of highly dubious character and loyalty.

At a gesture from the lieutenant, one of the guards climbed up on to the carriage and took the reins from the coachman. He, the groom, and the two servants joined Saint-Martin standing on the paving stones. At that moment Bertier leaned out the open window. Saint-Martin raised Bertier's sword in a blessing and said, 'God be with you.'

Bertier replied with a brave smile. 'Colonel, look after my wife and my four sons.' As the coach began to move, he waved his hand and mouthed the word 'Adieu' in a haunting gesture of farewell.

The lieutenant gave a sharp command to the guards. The coach rolled out of the courtyard into slow-moving traffic on Rue Saint-Martin towards the centre of the city.

For a long moment the colonel stood silent. Then, feeling impotent anxiety beginning to stir within him, he turned to his two servants. 'Follow the coach from a safe distance until it reaches the prison. It will barely creep through the city's congestion. If anything goes wrong, report to me as soon as you can.'

The coach moved slowly towards its destination, the Abbaye prison on the Left Bank. A light rain continued to fall. To occupy his mind Bertier tried to make conversation with his guards. The older of the two was a surly, taciturn man, who averted his eyes from the intendant's gaze, probably intimidated by his high rank.

The younger guard, though shy at first, responded easily to Bertier's questions, identified himself as Joseph Mouton, and described his life growing up as a maidservant's son on an estate near Grenoble. Since arriving in Paris, he had joined the French Guards. Recently, he had followed Maury into the National Guard. At a glance Bertier could determine that the young man was intelligent and well-mannered. His speech was much superior to what could be expected from a servant's son. A patron's hand was at work, advancing the young man's education and his entry into the military.

Bertier complimented Mouton on his achievements, and the young man smiled with gratitude. Before they could resume their conversation, however, the coach came to a sudden halt. Bertier glanced out the window. They had reached Pont Notre-Dame at the river.

'Which way shall we go?' asked one of the horsemen in front of the coach. They had stopped to decide between two routes to the prison: straight ahead over the bridge, or to the right to the next bridge, Pont au Change, and then on to the Abbaye.

The lieutenant who was riding alongside the coach yelled out. 'Turn to the left. We'll go to the City Hall.'

The two guards in the coach with Bertier glanced at each

other, their eyes clouded with confusion. Mouton asked, 'Has the lieutenant received new instructions?'

The older man shrugged.

Bertier stiffened. He knew what he would meet at the Place de Grève in front of the City Hall – a mob thirsting for his blood. He would not yield easily.

Seven

Mob Justice

At midmorning Anne approached the institute for the deaf, eager to speak with the Abbé de l'Épée. On Monday she had followed the Comtesse de Beaumont's suggestion to ask him about Monsieur Boileau's imprisonment in the Bastille, years ago, and the fate of his children. The abbé was intrigued and promised to look into the matter.

Mademoiselle Françoise Arnaud, once one of the abbé's most talented students and now his assistant, met her at the door and brought her to the abbé's office and signed, 'He seems livelier than usual today, still very weak but alert and looking forward to meeting you. Your visit on Monday has rejuvenated him.'

'I'm pleased,' Anne signed. She owed him much. He had brought her to a personally rewarding profession, teaching deaf children. She took every opportunity to express her gratitude.

Mademoiselle let Anne into the office. The abbé was at his writing table. His body was shrunken and bent, but his eyes were bright. With a feeble gesture he showed Anne to a chair facing him.

'What can you tell me?' Anne asked.

'Yesterday, I consulted old correspondence and refreshed my memory. I knew Boileau, an honest, upright man, learned in history, religion and politics. We had long conversations when he delivered books to the institute. I shared the intensity of his convictions but warned him to be prudent. He sometimes spoke out with little heed to the consequences.'

'Why was he sent to the Bastille in 1771?'

'In a word, politics. After decades of dispute, the King suppressed the Parlement de Paris and the provincial courts. They had opposed his autocratic rule. In their place, he established a new system of higher courts entirely dependent on him. The public regarded his action as high-handed or despotic. Among those protesting the strongest was Monsieur Boileau. He published several anonymous pamphlets critical of the government. Police spies easily discovered that he was the author.'

'Surely other authors wrote against the government. Why was he singled out for the Bastille?'

Épée shook his head. 'In one of the pamphlets, the most popular, he attacked the King personally, called him a lecherous old fool, a courtesan's toy, a religious hypocrite, a lazy, self-indulgent and spiteful man wilfully ignorant of the principles of good governance. And he demanded that the King dismiss his mistress Madame du Barry, do penance for his sins, and lead a righteous life from then on.'

'I can understand how the King would take offence, though Boileau's portrait, I believe, was close to the truth.'

'In fact, the King was furious. He wrote a letter to Monsieur Sartine, the lieutenant general of police, ordering him to put Boileau in the Bastille's deepest dungeon. No trial, no amenities. After several months of bad diet, foul air, and dirty, crowded conditions, Boilcau caught prison fever, or typhus, and died. Meanwhile, the government closed his business and seized his property.'

As Épée told the story, he seemed driven by the memory of old battles for freedom of conscience. His voice grew strong, indignant.

Anne was too moved by his fervour to interrupt him, but finally she asked, 'Can you explain why Boileau hid the gold locket in a religious book?' She described the bundle that Michou had purchased at the Bastille.

'Contrary, I suppose, to the King's instructions, Lieutenant General Sartine must have allowed the prisoner to have a few books. He couldn't trust anyone in the prison, from the governor on down. So, he hid the locket as best he could in a book that others wouldn't care to read. When he died, his books were stored. Next of kin couldn't be found – or no one bothered to look for them. The books were forgotten, gathered dust.'

'What happened to his family?'

'His wife had died a few years earlier. Her brother adopted the twins. They took his name, perhaps because it offered better opportunity for advancement. Their father's name was in disgrace, certainly in official circles. I don't know what has since become of them.'

'And what name did they take?'

'Their uncle's, Gaillard. I think the boy was called Hercule.'

'Hercule Gaillard?' Anne exclaimed. 'Since talking to Monsieur Pierre Hall on Monday, I've suspected as much. How can Michou and I return the locket to such a trouble-maker?'

The abbé replied, 'You must find his sister. She has the stronger claim to the piece.'

Anne thanked the abbé and rose to leave. She reflected, then added, 'I begin to understand Gaillard's passionate attacks on the royal family. How far is he willing to go?'

From the abbé's institute, Anne went to visit Michou in the Louvre, where she was helping her fiancé in his studio. He was also a painter, but with the academic training that she lacked and a promising career ahead of him.

'Come, Anne, look at Marc's masterpiece.' Michou led her through the cluttered room to a large canvas stretched on a rough wooden frame fastened to a wall. Marc was standing on a scaffold and painting a rocky wooded hillside in the upper right-hand quarter of the picture. As Anne drew near, he laid down his brush and palette, climbed from the scaffold, and greeted her.

'What do we have here?' she asked, impressed by the painting's large scale. The main figures in the foreground seemed nearly the size of living persons.

'My version of the ancient legend of Coriolanus. With luck it will earn me membership in the Royal Academy of Painting and Sculpture – and immortal glory.' He spoke with a self-deprecating smile. Anne understood that this painting would make or break his career.

She studied the picture with help from Marc and Michou. The principal figures were nearly completed. In the foreground the bearded Roman general, with ancient armour, helmet, and sword, extended his arms in a yielding gesture to his mother,

Volumnia, kneeling before him. Nearby, his wife, Vergilia, and their two young children stretched out their arms towards him.

Michou pointed to the youngest of the children and signed, 'Today, I'm working on his face.' She excelled in the portraits of children.

A proud patrician general, Coriolanus had made enemies among common Romans and was exiled to a hostile neighbouring tribe, the Volscians, whom he had once defeated. He became the head of their army and vowed to take revenge on Rome. In the painting his family was persuading him to abandon his plan.

Anne felt uneasy. She had seen Shakespeare's version of the story on the stage in England and knew how it ended. The Volscians assassinated Coriolanus as a traitor for having abandoned the attack on Rome. Now, as Anne stood before the painting, she recalled Governor Delaunay's recent brutal assassination after surrendering the Bastille. More violence and betrayal were to come.

Marc roused her from these bleak reflections. '*Coriolanus*,' he explained, 'must be ready for the Salon here in the Louvre next month.'

Nearly every major artist – and many minor ones – would take part in this, the country's premier biennial exhibition. If Marc's painting were successful, he and Michou might soon marry.

'There's much to do,' Michou signed to Anne. 'We'll work late tonight.'

'After dark, Michou, the streets will be dangerous,' Anne cautioned. 'Don't try to go home to Rue Traversine. It's too close to the garden and arcades of the Palais-Royal where all the hotheads of Paris gather.'

'I'm not afraid of them,' Michou signed. 'Why would they bother me?' Petite and shy, Michou usually escaped notice wherever she went. For years she had lived and worked in the Duc d'Orléans' enormous complex of shops, theatres, and other places of business and entertainment. She was still at ease there despite the current unrest. 'I'll sleep in Marc's studio.'

Anne walked to the door. 'I would like to have stayed longer – your picture is fascinating – but I want to be home when my husband returns to the city. He's been away on a special mission for Mayor Bailly. It's confidential, so I'm not supposed to talk about it. I must go. It's only a little after three in the afternoon and most people are at work. Later, they'll be free to reflect on their misery and might take to the streets to protest.'

Marc raised a hand in warning. 'You shouldn't go home alone, Madame. It's even more dangerous for you than for Michou. I could send a servant with you. Rumours of random violence are flying about the city.'

His concern touched Anne. 'That's thoughtful of you, Marc. But Georges Charpentier, my husband's adjutant, is in the Louvre on police business and will meet me downstairs in a few minutes. We'll walk home together, safely, I'm sure.'

'I just came from the mayor's apartment,' said Georges as he met Anne in the Louvre's courtyard. 'There's word of another crisis. Bailly has hastened to the City Hall. A large, restless crowd has gathered in front of the building – many are armed and drunk. They are protesting the scarcity of food. Some say there's only enough bread to feed the city for three days. The duke's henchmen have slipped into the crowd and are calling for the death of hoarders and profiteers and treasonous royal officials.'

Anne took Georges's arm and they walked out of the Louvre. 'We should be safe,' she said as they turned left on to Rue Saint-Honoré. 'The City Hall and its rioters are a mile to the east.'

But when they reached the Place du Palais-Royal, the square in front of the duke's palace, they heard the ominous beating of drums, the high-pitched piping of fifes, the angry shouts of a crowd advancing. Frightened people on the street scurried westward to safety or sought refuge in the shops and side streets. Anne and Georges slipped into a fashionable jeweller's shop opposite the palace entrance.

The noisy crowd lumbered by like a crazed beast, chanting 'Death to the people's enemies' and thrusting pikes and swords into the air. Alarmed, the jeweller rushed to the front door, locked and barred it. His clerks swiftly closed the shutters, then seized boxes of the most precious stones and climbed up to the next floor.

Georges and Anne followed them. At a window overlooking

the palace square, she drew an opera glass from her bag and studied the crowd. A pair of men dragged a headless body, leaving a thin trail of blood on the paving stones.

'Look! exclaimed Anne. 'That's Simon, the man who passed out pamphlets at the Palais-Royal.' The short, thick-bodied, flat-nosed man lifted a head aloft on a pike. The mouth was stuffed with a small sheaf of wheat, an obvious allusion to the victim's alleged crime of hoarding grain.

Anne felt her gorge rising, took a step back, and handed the glass to Georges.

He glanced at her. 'Are you ill? Your face is as white as chalk.'

'The view from here is ghastly. But I'll be alright.' She pressed a hand to her chest. 'You see, I know the dead man, Monsieur Foullon. A few months ago, he came to us for dinner.'

Georges looked through the opera glass at the scene below. 'Mon Dieu!' he murmured. 'It *is* Foullon. He was a leading city merchant and former minister of finance.' He returned the glass to Anne. 'Stay here. I'll sneak out the back door and into the crowd and find out what's going on.' He handed his hat and sword to Anne, then pulled a clerk's smock over his uniform. 'I need to be a little less noticeable out there.'

He returned only a few minutes later. 'A band of the duke's men found Foullon hiding on a farm in the countryside, stuffed his mouth with that grain, and marched him to the City Hall. They hung him from a lamppost, cut off his head, and dragged his body here. They will go next to the Palais-Royal. The duke has allowed them to parade through the garden.' Georges pointed to a movement in the crowd. 'They're setting up a trestle table. Someone is going to give a speech. Lend me the glass again.'

'Who is it?' Anne asked.

'As I suspected, it's Hercule Gaillard. He has gone from writing pornographic tales about the Queen to assassinating a former royal finance minister.'

'I'm not surprised,' Anne remarked, 'considering how the crown sent his father to the Bastille.' Anne told Georges what she had learned from the Abbé de l'Épée.

Georges nodded. 'That experience would scar almost any man. Then several years later the crown put Hercule there as well. Yes, I can see why he might want to lash out at the King and his servants.'

'What would happen if he were to recognize us?'

'He would claim we were the King's spies and urge the crowd to massacre us.' He handed the glass back to Anne.

Gaillard walked to the table with a shuffling gait. His emaciated skin stretched taut over high cheekbones and a beak nose, broad forehead and sharp jutting jaw. His eyes, dark and sunken, glowed with fierce passion. He climbed on to the table and began to rage against the 'enemies of the people'. His arms slashed the air with furious gestures. Beads of saliva dripped from his mouth. The crowd hung on his words, cheered him on.

A frisson of fear shot through Anne's body. She was beginning to understand how this physically unimpressive, almost deformed man could bend a motley, desperate crowd to his will, fire their spirits with his convictions.

At the end of his speech, Gaillard seized the bloody pike and pointed to Foullon's head. 'Let all those traitors who would starve the people share his fate,' he shouted with a voice that could be heard over cannon fire. 'To the Palais-Royal now. Afterward, to the river, and we'll feed him to the fish.' Gaillard jumped down from the table, raised the bloody pike like an army standard, and marched off. Most of the mob followed him, dragging Foullon's body at their heels. Others dispersed into nearby wine taverns.

Spellbound, Anne and Georges stared out the window for several minutes, even after the last stragglers from Gaillard's grotesque band had disappeared and people emerged from the shops. Life in the Place du Palais-Royal resumed its normal rhythm.

Anne asked Georges, 'Tell me more about Monsieur Foullon. Why would the duke's men want to kill him and do it so brutally?'

'Foullon was a rich, elderly merchant, known to drive a hard bargain.' Georges spoke thoughtfully, as if recalling mixed impressions of the man. 'In the course of a long career managing royal finances, and promoting his own interests, he must have made many enemies. Even without a scrap of evidence, they would gladly accuse him of profiteering in the grain trade. The duke could use him as a scapegoat to undermine the people's respect for the government.'

Troubled, Anne searched her memory. 'Now I recall Monsieur Foullon more clearly. He was the father-in-law of Bertier de Sauvigny, the royal officer whom my husband is supposed to bring safely to Paris later this afternoon.' She shuddered, stared at Georges. 'What sort of reception will they receive?'

Georges grimaced. 'We'll find out. Let's disguise ourselves and visit the taverns near the river.'

From the residence on Rue Saint-Honoré, Anne sent a message to Paul on his way to Paris, reporting Foullon's death. She and Georges would try to warn the authorities at City Hall of Gaillard's threat to Bertier de Sauvigny. The message was a desperate effort, probably too late. Then, in great haste, she and Georges disguised themselves as visitors from Rouen in Normandy. Georges covered his bald pate with a short wig – he was supposed to be a simple merchant, Anne his niece. Both wore the rough-cut, unfashionable provincial costumes that they had used on similar occasions.

Their disguise included the provincial dialect. Anne's family was from Normandy but had fled to England to escape religious persecution. As a child she had learned the Norman dialect at home from the servants. Georges was born and raised in Normandy. His brother lived in Rouen, the provincial capital.

'Where are we going?' Anne asked as they walked towards the river.

'Members of the mob are refreshing themselves in wine taverns near the river. A half-hour has passed since we saw their spectacle on the Place du Palais-Royal. By this time, jugs of wine will have loosened their tongues. They might boast of their exploits and tell us their plans for further mischief.'

On the Rue des Orties, behind the Grande Galerie of the Louvre, Anne heard the high-pitched tones of a fife and the rattle of a drum. The sounds came from a large wine tavern, Le Chat Enragé. The sign over the entrance depicted a black cat, its lips drawn back in a frightening hiss, its fur bristling. Inside, to Anne's relief, was a decent mixed company, men and women from the neighbourhood of Saint-Thomas du Louvre and from the barges on the nearby river.

'I recognize those two,' said Anne, glancing towards the

drummer and the fifer who were performing for their drinks. 'They were leading Gaillard's crowd.'

'And they're about to take a rest,' Georges said. 'We'll sit with them.'

Strangers to the place, the musicians had chosen a table apart from other customers. Georges asked, 'May we join you and buy you drinks? We've enjoyed your tunes.'

To judge from their flushed faces and clumsy gestures, they had already emptied a jug or two. Their ragged appearance, and especially the accent in their slurred speech, betrayed their origins in Saint-Antoine, a district of poor artisans and the site of the Bastille. Anne imagined them playing for a meagre living in taverns and on street corners.

The wine was served. Georges steered the conversation to the recent mob scene on the Place du Palais-Royal.

'Were you there from the beginning at the City Hall?' he asked, feigning ignorance.

Yes, they said, and went on to describe Foullon's hanging and decapitation, the march to the Palais-Royal, and his graceless burial in the river.

'How much did Monsieur Gaillard pay you?' Anne asked directly.

'Six *livres* for each of us,' the fifer replied, unfazed by the question.

The drummer shook a small purse of coins. 'Just as much as Nicolas Coupe-Tête received, who cut off the old man's head.' Both men chuckled, then saluted each other and drank deeply of their wine.

'And we're not finished,' added the fifer. He raised his instrument and played a brief flourish. 'About an hour from now another of the King's men will dance to our tunes.'

The two men rose from the table, thanked Georges and Anne for the wine.

'It's time for us to get ready for work.'

'Where?' asked Georges.

'In front of the City Hall. The people are waiting, hungry and angry.'

The setting sun cast long shadows across the Place de Grève. At the main entrance to the City Hall a noisy, restless crowd pressed against a thin line of National Guards. 'We want bread,

death to profiteers,' they shouted. Well-dressed agitators urged
them on.

On the edge of the crowd Georges leaned towards Anne
and spoke into her ear. 'The crowd is trying to force its way
into the building and threaten the city council. We can't
possibly reach the Marquis de Lafayette this way.'

Anne understood that they had to warn the marquis,
commandant of the National Guard, of an impending attempt
on the life of a royal official. 'Is there another entrance that
we could use?'

Georges nodded and they set off for the rear of the building.
At a narrow door on the ground floor he looked around to
make sure no one could see them. 'A friend of mine, a guard,
told me about this one.' Georges reached into a crevice in the
wall and pulled out a key.

Once inside, they hurried up the back stairs to the first floor,
where the city council met and the marquis had an office.
When they reached the landing, they heard in the distance the
sound of doors bursting, an explosion of shrieks and shouts,
and the thunder of feet pounding on steps. Anne froze. The
crowd had broken through the building's main entrance and
would soon confront the city council.

Eight

A Brutal Scene

Paris, Wednesday, 22 July

Inside the City Hall Anne and Georges groped through a dark, narrow, empty passage. Beads of light trickled in through small holes in the wall. The air was musty, as if it hadn't stirred in decades.

'Where are we, Georges?' Anne asked, suppressing a feeling of panic.

'Fear not, Madame. You're not lost. I know the building from top to bottom. Years ago, when I worked for Lieutenant General Sartine – my master in the art of detection – I used to spy on the wealthy merchants who met here to plan ways to cheat the public and the King. This passage runs alongside the main hall where the new city council sits. The holes that you've noticed offered me various vantage points.'

Georges took Anne's hand and led her forward. She felt partly reassured. But soon she heard loud shouts and cries, the crash of falling furniture.

He squeezed her hand. His voice was low and tense. 'The mob has forced its way into the hall. It's too late to warn Lafayette, but we may as well see what's going to happen.'

They came to a circular stairway. 'This goes up to a mezzanine, a safe place for us to watch the action below. On festive occasions a band of musicians plays there.'

The door to the mezzanine was unlocked. They crept in and peered through the balusters. The hall was a large, elegant rectangular room two storeys high, illuminated by giant crystal chandeliers hanging from the ceiling and by silver sconces on the walls. The council of some sixty members formed a semicircle at the far end of the room. A score or more of bailiffs, clerks, and invited guests were attending the session.

A raucous mob was surging into the hall through the main entrance. Desperate bailiffs struggled vainly to stop the flow. Their shouts mingled with the mob's cries for bread, liberty, death to traitors. The mob pressed forward, threatening to force the council members back against the wall. Scanning the room with her opera glass, Anne detected Gaillard in the middle of the mob, urging them on.

Among the members of the council Mayor Bailly and the Marquis de Lafayette both tried desperately to keep a semblance of dignity and composure. The crowd soon enveloped them, rendering them powerless, unable even to move. Their mouths worked in futile protests and calls for order. With her glass Anne read the shame and humiliation on their faces.

The chaos went on for several minutes without any apparent direction or focus. Then Anne heard a new ominous sound, like an animal's deep-throated, angry growl. The crowd parted. His sword thrust high, an officer of the National Guard forced his way from the entrance up to the hard-pressed council.

'I know him, Georges,' Anne whispered. 'That's Lieutenant Maury, the so-called hero of the Bastille.'

Impaled on the lieutenant's weapon was a bloody object. The crowd quieted in gaping astonishment as he presented his trophy first to the marquis, who reeled back in horror, then to the mayor, who raised his hands to block the sight.

The soldier turned to the crowd, waved his gruesome trophy, and shouted, 'Behold the heart of a traitor, once the intendant of Paris.'

Anne and Georges quickly retraced their steps through the passage. Outside the building, feeling nauseous, Anne pleaded, 'Stop for a moment, Georges, I need to calm my nerves, clear my head.' She breathed deeply of the night air. 'The crowd was awful, worse than wild beasts. What have they done to Bertier? I knew him, he was a fine man. He often met with Paul, sat at our table.'

Georges gazed at her and said softly, 'I fear he's dead. Let's hope it was quick. Now we must find out what has happened. It was certainly criminal.'

They hurried around to the front of the building. In the Place de Grève excited men and women milled about, shouting, gesticulating. Georges drew Anne's attention to a carriage, still hitched to the horses and parked near the middle of the square. A detachment of National Guards kept curious onlookers at a distance.

Georges asked Anne, 'Are you willing to go closer?'

She nodded, and they worked their way through a maze of people coming and going. They reached a spot between two guards that offered them a clear view of the carriage. 'It comes from the intendant's stable,' Georges whispered in Anne's ear. 'It bears the insignia of his office.'

They pressed on towards the City Hall. A ring of soldiers created an opening in the crowd. In the light of their lanterns, Anne detected bloodstains on the wet paving stones at her feet. Her nose caught a faint whiff of gunpowder. She turned to Georges. He nodded. This was the place of execution.

'We just arrived,' Georges said to a bystander. 'Where's the body?'

The man shrugged. 'I've heard that they're dragging what's left of it through the streets to the Palais-Royal.'

A soldier glanced at Georges and moved as if about to question him. Fortunately, a comrade's call distracted him. Georges stepped back, beckoned Anne to follow, and they stole away to the edge of the square.

Anne nudged Georges and pointed to a young National Guardsman on a bench in the circle of light beneath a street lamp. He was bent over, head in his hands, groaning.

'I know him,' Georges whispered, after studying the young man. 'A newcomer, joined the French Guards about a year ago. I met him once at the Royal Highway Patrol post in Passy, visiting Lieutenant Harivel du Rocher, the commandant there. He's said to be the young man's secret patron.'

'Let's see what I can learn from him.' She approached the young man. He looked up at her, his eyes red. He might have been weeping. He started to rise, but she motioned him down and sat next to him. Georges stood off to the side.

'How are you?' she asked in a sympathetic tone. 'I don't wish to intrude, but I might be able to help you. I'm Madame Cartier, wife of Colonel Paul de Saint-Martin of the Highway Patrol.'

The young man glanced at her. 'I've actually heard about you – kind words, Madame, with respect. And I've also seen your husband, the colonel, late this afternoon.'

She stared at him in surprise. 'How could you?'

'I was one of the National Guards who met him and the intendant at Porte Saint-Martin.' He added, 'My name is Joseph Mouton.' His lips began to quiver. 'I rode in the coach through the city with Monsieur Bertier. A kind gentleman. He talked to me like a father.' The young man shook his head, unable to continue.

She put her hand on his shoulder, met his eye. 'What's the matter, Joseph?'

'I got sick out there.' He gestured towards Bertier's carriage in the distance. 'Lieutenant Maury cursed me, said he had no use for a girl, and dismissed me from service for the day. He told me to walk back to the barracks. He'd deal with me in the morning.'

Anne drew closer to him. 'Joseph, did you see what happened?' She raised a finger to her lips. 'Don't be alarmed. Speak softly.'

'Yes, Madame Cartier,' he murmured. 'I saw it all, God help me.'

'Then, it's no wonder that you became sick. What they did to Bertier should revolt every decent man. But this isn't where we should talk about it. Too many crazed people around us. Could we meet you in a more private place nearby? The Rose d'Anjou? It's a wine tavern at the flower market.'

Mouton thought for a moment, nodded, then said, 'I'll be there in five minutes. We should go by different routes.'

Anne and Georges arrived at the tavern first, followed within a minute by Mouton. They chose a dark, secluded corner. Georges ordered cheese, bread, and wine for Anne and himself, chicken broth for the young soldier. While they waited for their food, Anne studied him closely. He was breathing heavily, wringing his hands, staring into space.

Finally, without being prompted, he exclaimed, 'It was horrible.' He looked down at his plate, shook his head, unable to continue.

'Let's eat a little first,' said Georges, as the waiter arrived. He poured wine, served the broth. Meanwhile, Georges inquired about life in the National Guard barracks in Chaillot, leading the conversation towards Lieutenant Maury.

'He was my sergeant in the French Guards for several months.' Mouton gradually warmed to his subject. 'He's a brash, daring kind of man, rude in his ways, loves to gamble. He's easily provoked and violent when angry, but also clever and ambitious. Recently, he claimed that he would soon be a commissioned officer. None of us believed him. We thought he was dreaming. Common soldiers are rarely promoted. Still, within a week the National Guard replaced the old French Guards and there he was, a lieutenant.'

'Can you explain how he did it?' Georges asked.

'They say that he has powerful friends in a Masonic lodge.'

'Do you suppose that his friends also secured for him the mission to escort the intendant from Porte Saint-Martin to the Abbaye prison?'

Mouton nodded.

'When did you realize that Monsieur Bertier was in danger?' Anne asked.

'At Pont Notre-Dame Lieutenant Maury ordered us to turn to the left toward the City Hall. We knew that a crowd was gathering there.'

'How did you know that?' asked Anne.

'Early in the afternoon, Lieutenant Maury had led us to the Palais-Royal, said he had business there. While we waited for him, we saw the duke's men rushing through the arcades and the garden, handing out leaflets urging people to go to the City Hall and protest to the city council against hoarding and profiteering in grain.

'When we arrived at the Place de Grève troublemakers were already stirring up the crowd, urging them to break into the building and threaten the council.' He glanced over his shoulder and lowered his voice to a whisper. 'At that point, our carriage drove into the square. We let the intendant out and began to march through the crowd towards the City Hall.

'Agents of the duke were there – I recognized many of them from our visit to the Palais-Royal. They were waiting for Bertier. They shouted that he was a traitor and had profited in the sale of grain.

'I sensed trouble was brewing. We tried to move ahead faster. But the crowd pressed in upon us and forced us to stop.

We pushed back to give space to Bertier. Suddenly, a few paces from me, a short fat man with a smashed nose pulled a small pistol from his coat and shot Bertier in the left arm.'

The fat man must be Simon, Anne thought.

Mouton took a drink of his broth, then continued, 'The sight of blood seemed to infuriate the crowd. They cried out for more, and some of the duke's men drew knives. Despite his wound, Bertier seized a sword from a careless onlooker. For a short while, he fought off his enemies. "Vile assassins!" he shouted at them.'

Anne asked, 'Couldn't you and the other guards do more to protect him?'

'Frankly, we were afraid of the crowd, so we waited for orders from Maury. He had a strange look on his face. He told us to leave and guard the coach. He would take care of Bertier. We tried to obey, but we were trapped by the crowd and couldn't move.

'Meanwhile, to our surprise, Maury drew his sword and lunged at Bertier. He parried the thrust, called him "Coward! Common criminal!" But the duke's men joined Maury and renewed the attack, and the intendant fell.'

Mouton paused. With trembling hands he tore off a piece of bread, dipped it in his broth. The shaking was such that he could hardly bring the bread to his mouth.

Anne and Georges waited, encouraging him to take his time.

Mouton resumed in a low, halting voice. 'It was dreadful. The lieutenant went berserk. He cut the heart out of Bertier's dead body, stuck it on to the tip of his sword, and ran off with it through the crowd to the City Hall.'

Anne shuddered. 'We saw him display it inside the building.'

Georges asked, 'Didn't anyone try to stop Bertier's murder, or at least protest that he should be brought before a magistrate?'

'That's what I've asked myself, but I don't have an easy answer. Even I kept my mouth shut. The duke's men had a plan, acted in concert, paid out money to win support. Perhaps others thought as I did: if these men were prepared to kill the intendant of Paris, they surely wouldn't hesitate to kill me, if I were to interfere. Most of the people in the crowd were poor and desperate. Hunger and anger made them willing to lash out at anybody. God let the harvests fail, but they couldn't kill Him. So Bertier served as a convenient scapegoat.'

Georges asked, 'Could you identify any of his killers, besides Maury?'

'Yes, if I saw them again.' Mouton hesitated, thought for a moment. 'Monsieur Bertier seemed to know at least one of them by name, besides Maury.'

'Who was he?'

'An older man – thin, sloped-shouldered, sharp-faced. I've heard him speak in the Palais-Royal garden and insult the King and Queen. He stayed in the background and seemed to direct the killing. I believe his name is Gaillard.'

In the provost's office Colonel Saint-Martin sat anxiously at his writing table. His servants who had followed Bertier's carriage had just returned. Their story greatly disconcerted him. At Pont Notre-Dame the coach had stopped briefly. The servants drew close enough to hear the lieutenant give the order to change course. His soldiers seemed momentarily confused. But the carriage proceeded in the direction of the City Hall instead of the Abbaye prison. The servants followed the carriage part way to the Place de Grève. Unfortunately, the lieutenant noticed them and dispatched guards to seize them. They were detained for questioning but were eventually released and hurried home.

Had the lieutenant received new orders, Saint-Martin asked them. No, they replied.

Saint-Martin reflected on the servants' report. The lieutenant's behaviour looked like brazen disobedience and a serious risk to his career in the National Guard. The Marquis de Lafayette put a high value on his authority and would regard the lieutenant's action as a personal affront. Maury would run the risk of severe punishment unless he had previously received secret orders, and very likely money, from a higher, more powerful patron than the marquis. That person could only be the Duc d'Orléans.

What then had happened to Bertier at the Place de Grève? He was in mortal danger of the crowd throwing itself upon him. Would Lieutenant Maury protect him? Saint-Martin could not pretend to hope.

Saint-Martin was at least as concerned to know what Anne and Georges were doing. Since the fall of the Bastille and the social unrest that followed, the Place de Grève had become a dangerous place. Thousands of desperate people had gathered there. He was tempted to go there himself and search for them. But that would be futile. It was wiser to trust that they would return safely with news of Bertier.

An hour later, as the colonel glanced out the window, he saw Anne and Georges walk across the courtyard. He rushed to the door, opened for them, and led them into his office.

'Tell me what happened.' He seated them, but he remained standing behind his writing table.

Anne described to her husband the assassinations that she and Georges had witnessed: first Foullon's, then Bertier de Sauvigny's.

At the mention of the latter's death, Paul exclaimed, 'I feared as much, after my servants reported that Bertier's carriage had gone to the Place de Grève instead of the prison.' His eyes began to tear. He walked to the window, his hands clasped tightly behind his back, and looked out over the courtyard. His emotions threatened to overwhelm him. Finally he gained control of himself and said, 'I regret that I didn't do more to save him.'

Anne joined him at the window and put a hand on his shoulder. 'No one could have done better.'

Georges stood up. 'The crowd numbered in the thousands, many of them armed, gripped by a common, fanatical urge to blame someone for their misery and to punish him brutally, without mercy. Gaillard succeeded in making Bertier, unfairly, the target of their rage. Only a regiment of the King's Swiss infantry could possibly have saved him. And our weakened King dares not send his soldiers into Paris.'

'That may be true,' the colonel granted. 'Still, I owe it to Bertier to ensure that justice is done.' Drawn and pale, he glanced at Anne, gave her a quick smile, and returned to the writing table. 'It's too late now. But first thing in the morning we'll draw up a full report on what we know about the deaths of Foullon and Bertier de Sauvigny. I'll take it to Mayor Bailly and find out how to proceed. Already it seems clear that Monsieur Gaillard will be our chief suspect, the mind and heart of a murderous conspiracy.'

Anne added, 'And our own ruthless, implacable enemy.'

Nine

An Anxious Mayor

Paris, Thursday, 23 July

Clouds heavy with rain scudded over the Place de Grève at midmorning. In the anteroom to the mayor's office in the City Hall, Colonel Saint-Martin watched drops spatter on the windows, creating strange, shifting patterns that baffled the eye – like the recent chaos in the city.

His report on yesterday's horrific events was in the portfolio that lay on his lap. He used this waiting time to reflect on what could be done about them. Georges and Anne would pursue Gaillard, the chief villain of the piece. As long as the crisis in the food supply lasted, he could exploit the people's fears and their anger. The way to stop him was to insert spies into his circle, gather accurate information, and anticipate his moves.

'Colonel Saint-Martin, come in.' The mayor stood in the doorway, dressed in his usual black. A remarkably even-tempered man, he looked serious but not at all desperate or perturbed, in spite of the pressures on him. 'My clerk couldn't tell me the object of your visit, except that it was serious.' They seated themselves at his writing table.

'May I speak freely, sir?' Several paces away, two clerks were busy writing at a table. Saint-Martin surveyed the room. The ceiling's stuccoed mythological figures in high relief, a few with gaping mouths, could easily be fitted with peep-holes. Portions of the walls could be razor thin for overhearing conversations.

The mayor's back seemed to stiffen with chagrin. He resented the insinuation that his clerks might spy on him. Still no change registered on his countenance. 'I'm sure my clerks can be trusted.' His tone, however, was less than convincing.

Saint-Martin handed him an envelope. 'Would you glance at the enclosed report and tell me if you wish to act upon it?'

The mayor scanned the document. Again his attitude changed almost imperceptibly. 'I'll take it under consideration, Colonel.' He wrote a brief note and passed it over the table to Saint-Martin.

> Come to my home in Chaillot for supper at seven this evening. I can't discuss your report here.

The colonel said, 'I look forward to discussing it with you. I won't take any more of your time.' He bowed and left, even more apprehensive than when he entered. How could the mayor function in such an atmosphere of uncertainty and distrust?

At one o'clock in the afternoon, Anne, Paul, and a servant set out by coach to visit Bertier de Sauvigny's widow and his sons in their town house on Rue Vendôme. Saint-Martin had promised the intendant to look after his family. He now felt pressed to honour that promise. As a precaution, he had sent a messenger ahead to determine if Madame Bertier didn't wish to have visitors for the time being. The atrocious deaths of her father and her husband might have shocked the family too much.

Madame Bertier replied by the same messenger that a brief visit would be appreciated.

When Anne and Paul arrived at the town house, they found black festoons hanging over the gate. The porter who opened for them wore a black armband. A liveried servant, also in mourning, showed them into a parlour. Black drapes covered the window. Black ribbons hung from the sconces and from a crucifix on the wall.

Wearing a black silk gown, the widow entered the room with her eldest son, Antoine, a young man of twenty-one years. Their faces were pale and taut with grief, but they held themselves erect and greeted the visitors with perfect courtesy.

Anne and Paul expressed their condolences to Madame Bertier and her family on their loss. Anne added, 'It's difficult even to imagine losing both husband and father in such a barbaric manner.'

Madame Bertier thanked her for the sincere sentiment, then remarked, 'The assassins butchered and desecrated their bodies, but could not touch their souls. Both men served God and their King with unblemished honour. I hope and pray that my sons will regard them with pride and follow their example.'

Anne stole a sideways glance at the Bertier son and saw firm resolve etched in his face.

Paul signalled his servant, waiting in the background. He came forward with an object wrapped in a black velvet cloth. Paul removed the cloth and revealed a sword in its scabbard. He presented it to Antoine. 'This is your father's sword, given to me at Porte Saint-Martin as he left to confront his assassins. May it remind you to guard his memory.'

His voice breaking with emotion, the young man said, 'I'll never forget him,' and grasped the sword with both hands.

It was time to leave. Paul pledged, 'I'll do my utmost to bring the culprits to justice.'

'Please avoid desperate or futile measures, Colonel,' said Madame Bertier. 'In the present chaotic circumstances, neither Mayor Bailly, nor the Marquis de Lafayette, nor His Majesty Louis XVI can pursue justice for my husband or my father. Our rulers and magistrates are at the mercy of desperate madmen. I find redress in the likelihood that the assassins will sooner or later quarrel over money and power and slaughter each other.'

Anne said, 'I hope that you'll find the strength to lead your family out of this tragedy.'

'I must be strong for the sake of my sons. For their safety, we'll soon sell this house and move to the country.'

The visit was brief. In the coach on the way home, Paul turned to Anne. 'Before I came, I feared that Bertier's enemies might attack his family. I now feel more at ease, knowing that they will leave the city.'

'I also feel hopeful,' said Anne. 'Bertier's widow is a strong person, gracious in her manner but rock-like in her character. Nothing daunts her, not even this present horror.'

Paul shook his head. 'Unfortunately, she would leave the assassins to their own devices. I understand why, since the law is in such disarray. Nonetheless, I'll raise the issue with the mayor. I can't rest until they are punished.'

Promptly at seven, after a half-hour ride in the evening mist, Saint-Martin reached the gate to the mayor's property in Chaillot, a fashionable village west of the city. The mayor was known to walk the five miles from his home to his office in the City Hall.

A porter opened the gate immediately. Saint-Martin dismounted and gave the man the reins to his horse, a great white stallion.

'Take good care of him,' said the colonel.

'I'll remove the saddle, treat him to a handful of oats, and brush him, sir. He's a prince.' Saint-Martin pressed a coin in the man's hand and walked through a small courtyard to the house.

A substantial two-storey stuccoed building, it was suitable for a prominent scholar, but perhaps not grand enough for the mayor of the country's capital city. Bailly had a lofty conception of the mayor's responsibilities.

A servant took the colonel's damp hat and cloak and led him to Bailly's study. A small table was set for three.

'Will Madame Bailly join us?' Saint-Martin asked, glancing at the chairs.

'No,' his host replied, 'she has supped earlier. Since becoming involved in politics, I have had to give up certain family pleasures, as well as the regular rhythms of a scholar's life. Sometimes I must bring troublesome problems home to this table – like tonight. Otherwise, she and I eat together in peace and quiet whenever we can.'

At that moment, the former lieutenant general of police, Thiroux DeCrosne, walked into the study and greeted the colonel warmly.

'I see that you know each other well,' remarked Bailly. He turned to DeCrosne. 'I've told the colonel that you have been my guest here since the fall of the Bastille and the slaughter of its commandant.'

Saint-Martin bowed to DeCrosne. 'I'm sure that your experience as chief magistrate of the city must prove invaluable to Mayor Bailly.'

The men raised their glasses of red wine and saluted each

other. They sat at the table and a servant came with the soup course, a vegetable julienne.

The mayor addressed Saint-Martin. 'Last night's violence at the City Hall indicates that Monsieur DeCrosne is no longer safe even in my house. Tonight, I shall personally escort him out of the city and send him on his way to safety abroad. But before he goes, I want his opinion on your report.' The mayor glanced towards a file on an adjacent counter.

Saint-Martin waved towards the file. 'Many powerful persons will not like it. But there it is. I regret any difficulty that it may cause you.'

'The mayor and I have read your report, Colonel. Now give us the gist of it.'

'Yesterday,' Saint-Martin resumed, 'two prominent officers of this kingdom were atrociously assassinated – callously, in public, before thousands of witnesses. To my mind these crimes were unprovoked and unjustifiable. Disguised as spontaneous expressions of an oppressed people's wrath, they were in fact carefully planned and executed by partisans of the Duc d'Orléans, part of his broader attempt to undermine public confidence in royal authority and to bring himself to power.'

Bailly tilted his head slightly in a thoughtful gesture. 'Your analysis is plausible, Colonel, based on the eyewitness testimony that you have gathered. I can tell you that all of us in the City Hall last night were shocked by the brutality of the two deaths and distressed that we couldn't prevent them.'

'What steps will you take?' asked Saint-Martin evenly.

'I have asked that question of members of the city council, as well as the Marquis de Lafayette. Most of the councillors are unwilling to regard the deaths as the calculated work of conspirators and prefer to believe that hunger and fear of a resurgence of royal tyranny spontaneously drove a desperate people to this horrific excess. Others simply think that, given the public mood, there's nothing we can do.'

'Either way,' Saint-Martin observed, 'these crimes would remain unpunished.'

'Yes,' Bailly admitted, 'I'm afraid so. We must move on. There's so much to do. We are building a new, free society from scratch under very difficult circumstances. To investigate these assassinations would generate dangerous, divisive controversy, consume too much precious time, waste valuable municipal resources, and end with a prosecution that would certainly fail. The public mood is contrary, the duke's faction is too strong. Finally, the Marquis de Lafayette, commandant of the National Guard, is opposed.'

DeCrosne raised a hand. 'May I add a word here?' He spoke with a more earnest expression on his face than Saint-Martin had ever seen before. 'Those who would ignore not only the right of Foullon and Bertier de Sauvigny to a fair trial but also overlook last night's gross affront to the rule of law should consider the precedent they are setting. Future cabals of violent, discontented men will feel entitled to kill any public figures who stand in their way. Where will the killing stop?'

'I agree with Monsieur DeCrosne,' Saint-Martin remarked, 'but I have a practical solution to these issues. Allow me unofficially to gather evidence concerning these crimes, such as depositions by eyewitnesses and documents that are likely to be otherwise lost or destroyed. If the rule of law were to be established again, we would then have grounds for a successful prosecution. Or we could at least throw the bright light of truth upon these crimes and shame their perpetrators.'

Bailly turned to DeCrosne. 'Is the colonel's suggestion feasible?'

'Yes,' DeCrosne replied. 'In the missions that he has undertaken for me, he has demonstrated the skill and the discretion that such a difficult investigation would require.'

Bailly nodded, then cautioned Saint-Martin, 'As mayor, I can't take responsibility for the investigation or even acknowledge its existence.' He paused, reflecting. 'In addition, these crimes lie beyond your competence as provost of the Highway Patrol for the Paris region.'

A moment of silence descended upon the room while Saint-Martin weighed his options. Finally, he said simply, 'Then I shall proceed on my own.'

At this point, conversation shifted to the meal. A servant had arrived with a platter of baked salmon *aux fines herbes* and a white wine Italian sauce. The mayor informed his guests, 'This noble fish was caught in the Channel, packed in ice, and delivered here within three days. It honours our departing colleague, Monsieur DeCrosne.' White wine was poured and the glasses raised to the former lieutenant general.

For several minutes they enjoyed the fish. Then a servant knocked on the door and was called in. 'Sir,' he said, addressing the mayor, 'Lieutenant Harivel du Rocher is here, asking for you. Will you see him?'

Saint-Martin knew the lieutenant, the officer in charge of the Highway Patrol post in Passy, the next village west of Chaillot on the road to Versailles.

The mayor glanced at his guests. They shrugged, and said in unison, 'Send him in.' Saint-Martin wondered what sort of business brought the officer to the mayor's house in the evening. Another disaster?

Harivel was shown in, apologized for disturbing supper, and asked the mayor if he could leave his horse with him for twenty minutes. It had lost a shoe and gone lame. 'I must run a brief errand to the National Guard's barracks nearby in the village.' He added, 'I can walk the distance. It's not far.'

The lieutenant's cloak was wet, for it had begun to rain during supper. The village would be wrapped in darkness, save for the glow from occasional windows of houses along the road. The mayor's horses were resting in their stable.

Saint-Martin said, 'If you won't be long, you can take my horse. It can be saddled and ready to go in a few minutes. It's the white one; you can't miss it.'

'One of my servants,' the mayor added, 'will fetch the smith while you are gone.'

Harivel smiled gratefully and assured the colonel that he would return as quickly as promised.

When the lieutenant had gone, the three men resumed eating their supper. Bailly asked, 'How is the family of Bertier taking this disaster?'

Saint-Martin replied, 'Better than I expected. Badly bruised, but they will recover.'

Conversation turned to DeCrosne's plans. He explained that he would travel to England, where he had friends. When law and order returned to France, he would come back. The country might need an experienced administrator.

The men had begun the last course of the meal, a pear

compote, when the servant reappeared at the door with the porter.

'Sorry to disturb you, sir,' said the porter, eyes wide with alarm. 'But I distinctly heard a shot in the distance a few minutes ago. Now Colonel Saint-Martin's horse has returned with Lieutenant Harivel du Rocher still in the saddle. But he's wounded. Badly, I think.'

Ten

An Ambiguous Death

Paris, Thursday, 23 July

The dessert was immediately abandoned. Saint-Martin helped servants lower the stricken man from the saddle. He mumbled a few cryptic words while being carried into the house but then lost consciousness and died within minutes. He had been shot once in the back. There were no powder marks on his cloak.

The mayor turned to Saint-Martin. 'This murder is yours to investigate, Colonel.'

DeCrosne met the mayor's eye. 'And as my successor, the case is also yours to direct, sir.'

'My first,' Bailly admitted. 'I would be grateful for advice from both of you.'

While DeCrosne helped the mayor prepare a protocol for the case, Saint-Martin and the porter went out to the stable. They examined the horse and its saddle and found no trace of blood. Nothing else seemed amiss. The victim's shirt and coat had absorbed his bleeding.

Saint-Martin asked the porter, 'From which direction did the shot come?'

'From there,' he replied, pointing towards the main street that ran along the river.

'We'll walk there. It can't be far. Bring a lantern.' The rain had slackened to a drizzle. The air was warm and humid. The pavement glistened in the lantern's flickering light.

A small knot of people had gathered on the street, some of them in night dress. At the sight of a police officer, a few retreated indoors. None of the group would admit to having seen anything related to the crime. The shot had drawn them to their windows and on to the street.

The colonel and the porter searched the site, hoping to find the murder weapon or other evidence, but they found nothing. It was too dark. They walked another couple of hundred paces to the National Guard barracks. At the gatehouse a yawning young sentry stood in the weak light from a lamppost. Saint-Martin thought he looked familiar, but his face was partly shadowed and hard to discern.

No, he said, Lieutenant Harivel hadn't visited the barracks. Yes, the sentry had heard the shot at a distance but thought it might be fireworks. He didn't raise an alarm since it didn't appear to threaten the barracks.

'Why do you ask, sir?' The young soldier's voice had a worried tone.

'That shot mortally wounded the lieutenant.'

'Oh, no!' exclaimed the soldier. 'That can't be true. I was expecting him.' He leaned on his musket and began to sob. He tried to regain control of himself but the sobbing grew worse. The porter retreated a few steps. Saint-Martin put a comforting hand on the young man's shoulder. 'Did you know Harivel?' The vehemence of the soldier's reaction was puzzling.

He nodded, then glanced anxiously at the porter and whispered in a voice too low and hoarse for Saint-Martin to understand. He waved the porter off and repeated his question.

The soldier mastered his voice enough to say, 'Harivel's my father. He didn't want anyone to know, especially Lieutenant Maury. They were enemies.'

'I'm beginning to understand – I've met Maury. I recognize you now, the young guard, Joseph Mouton, who rode in the coach with Bertier de Sauvigny and who met my wife last night and described his assassination.'

'The same, sir.' Mouton wiped the tears from his eyes. Anger began to creep into his voice. 'You *will* find my father's killer, won't you, sir?' His jaw grew taut. 'By the way, Lieutenant Maury left the barracks early this evening and hasn't returned yet. Do you perceive my meaning, sir?'

Saint-Martin did indeed. He told the young man, 'Your father was one of my officers. I take his death personally. His killer will be caught and rigorously punished.'

*   *   *

Near midnight, Saint-Martin, DeCrosne, and Bailly gathered again in the mayor's study. The mayor and DeCrosne had postponed their departure by a day. The mood was sombre. They had just moved the victim's corpse to a cool room in the basement.

The colonel opened the discussion. 'I've determined that Harivel was shot while on his way to the barracks. Apparently there are no eyewitnesses or other evidence of the crime. My adjutant, Georges Charpentier, and I will begin a more thorough investigation tomorrow. And I'll speak with the Marquis de Lafayette, since the National Guard is involved.'

'What can you tell us about the victim?' DeCrosne asked the colonel. 'He's one of your men, isn't he?'

'I have inspected his post at least once a year, and I've met him on other occasions. He comes from an impoverished noble family in the province of Dauphiné, near Grenoble. As a young man, he joined the cavalry and earned a commission. He was an intelligent, energetic man, and carried out his duties to my satisfaction. He was married, but he and his wife lived apart. I'll contact her in the morning. According to Joseph Mouton, the sentry at the barracks, and his secret son, Harivel was at odds with Lieutenant Maury. But who isn't?'

DeCrosne leaned back, appraised Saint-Martin. 'The victim was about your age, Colonel.'

'That's true,' Saint-Martin admitted. He realized what his former superior implied. After all, they had worked together on many investigations.

'His appearance was also quite similar to yours in height, weight, and other respects.'

Saint-Martin anticipated DeCrosne's next thought. 'He was also wearing an officer's cloak similar to mine and riding my white horse.'

'So,' concluded the mayor, pointing to the colonel, 'the intended victim could have been you.'

Saint-Martin had suspected as much, when he saw the mortally wounded lieutenant hanging on the horse's neck. He felt vindicated when his companions reached the same opinion on their own. The attempt to kill him meant that Anne and others close to him were now in danger. The assassin would try again.

'Who might have wanted to kill you, Colonel?' asked DeCrosne.

'The duke's henchmen,' Bailly interjected. 'This morning, I warned the colonel that as a protégé of Baron de Breteuil, he has earned the duke's enmity.'

'I'll keep an open mind, gentlemen,' said Saint-Martin. 'By the way, young Mouton insinuated that Lieutenant Maury should be included among our suspects. He was away from the barracks at the time of the shooting. I don't know yet why he would want to kill me. A hidden hand could have directed him.'

Eleven

A Stubborn Marquis

Paris, Friday, 24 July

Anne had waited in bed until midnight for her husband to come home, increasingly concerned for him. He wasn't the kind of self-indulgent, inconsiderate man who would ignore his wife and carouse with comrades until the early hours of the morning. A good reason must have delayed him. She had finally fallen asleep alone.

When her maid woke her up, the sun was already above the rooftops, and his bed was empty.

'The colonel is working in his office,' the maid reported. 'As soon as you are dressed, he and Monsieur Charpentier will meet you in the garden for breakfast.'

When she arrived, Paul and Georges rose from the table and bowed. Paul looked fatigued, but he smiled fondly and embraced her. Meanwhile, Georges discreetly studied a distant rosebush.

The servant poured coffee and withdrew. Paul explained, 'I was in Chaillot until after midnight. Sorry, I couldn't get home earlier. Had to open an investigation. Slept a few hours in the office.' His voice trembled with emotion. 'One of our officers was murdered near Mayor Bailly's home. You've met him, Lieutenant Harivel du Rocher.'

'How dreadful!' Anne recalled the officer, a handsome, gallant man. Then the recent atrocities rushed to her mind. Did a mob assassinate him, like Foullon and Bertier? Could his death be related to theirs?'

'The killer was probably an individual or two. I can't say more. The night was dark, my probe was brief. Georges will continue the investigation today in Chaillot.'

A certain expression in Georges' face led Anne to suspect that Paul had confided more to him than to her. She met her husband's eye. 'You're hiding something from me, Paul. What is it?'

The two men glanced at each other. Finally, Georges spoke up. 'The victim was shot in the back on a dark road while riding the colonel's white horse.'

'I see,' Anne said, gazing at her husband. Her voice dropped and wavered. 'So you could have been the intended target.'

Both men nodded, eyes alert to her reaction.

'I'm truly sorry for the lieutenant. He didn't deserve such a fate, any more than Paul.' For a few moments, the air grew still. A sudden fear of losing Paul stirred her affection for him. She rose from the table and embraced him.

She stepped back and said to him, 'While you report to the marquis and Georges goes to Chaillot, I'll enlist Michou and Sylvie in a modest effort to study Monsieur Gaillard. We must learn where he lives, his daily routine, and who he meets. What have we to lose? Any eventual list of suspects will surely include him and his henchmen.'

When Anne walked into the studio on Rue Traversine, Michou and Sylvie were already at work. Michou was at her easel, painting in oil on a canvas. 'I'm copying the young woman's portrait in the gold locket and getting to know her. We might become friends one day and I'll give her the locket.'

Anne and Michou joined Sylvie at the table where she was going over a ledger of her friend's financial accounts. Their eyes widened with horror as Anne described the lieutenant's murder in Chaillot.

'How brazen they've become,' Sylvie remarked. 'Gaillard must be somehow responsible.' Then she reported on the agitation that he and his henchmen were creating in the garden and the arcades of the Palais-Royal.

'They talk constantly of traitors in the city,' she said. 'The people are in an uproar.'

'And not only in the Palais-Royal,' signed Michou. 'The maids who work in this house went out to buy bread early this morning and returned in a fright. Someone told them that a mob had hung a baker on Rue Sainte-Anne.'

'Has Gaillard struck again?' asked Anne.

Sylvie slammed shut the ledger. 'We can't just sit here and curse him. We must ask our friends and acquaintances to help us uncover his weak side, penetrate his secrets, and bring him down.'

One of the maids appeared at the door. 'A messenger from the Abbé de l'Épée is looking for Madame Cartier. He inquired first at the provost's residence and was directed here. He claims that his message is urgent.'

Meanwhile, Colonel Saint-Martin set out for the City Hall with a trooper at his side. In view of the threat to his life, he had promised Anne not to go out into the city alone. Today, Lieutenant Faure from the Villejuif patrol post accompanied him. As they rode in a closed, unmarked carriage through the city streets, Saint-Martin described the previous night's murder of Lieutenant Harivel du Rocher in Chaillot.

'If the assassin hit the wrong target, he may try again. Be alert to any suspicious or threatening behaviour on the street and in the City Hall. Our enemy is clever and ruthless.'

The two officers chatted about recent developments in the city. When they began to speak of the new National Guard, Faure asked, 'Do you know the marquis personally?' There was a hint of scepticism in his voice.

Saint-Martin recalled his association with Lafayette. They had first met during the American War, when they served in the French expeditionary army. Saint-Martin was stationed mostly in the northern colonies while Lafayette was active in the south.

'Yes,' he replied. 'In 1781, we came together briefly in the siege of Yorktown. After the war we've met occasionally in the salons of Paris and at reunions of veterans.'

Faure persisted. 'Thanks to his American exploits, he has a hero's reputation, but is he really worthy of it?'

'Reputation can be a faulty measure of a man,' Saint-Martin replied. Mixed impressions of the marquis came to his mind. 'In combat, he was courageous, daring, intelligent – General Washington's darling. He led the British into the trap that was Yorktown. But his thirst for glory, his hunger for power and his vanity sometimes impair his judgement.'

'Is he up to the task of policing Paris?'

'I don't know. His ideas on government are enlightened.

He's eager to transform our antiquated, poorly functioning institutions into a modern state that rests on the will of the people rather than on divine right or tradition.'

'A lofty ideal, no doubt, but is he practical enough?'

'Time will tell. Unfortunately, the duke's men sometimes outwit him. Two days ago, they tricked him into choosing Maury, the so-called hero of the Bastille, to take Bertier to the Abbaye prison. That's a discouraging sign.'

At the entrance to the City Hall, they left the carriage. Faure glanced over his shoulder. 'We've been followed, Colonel. Two men, one short and fat, the other tall and lean.'

'I know them, Gaillard's henchmen, Simon and Nicolas. We must take care how we leave this building. They may arrange a lethal surprise for us.'

This conversation made Saint-Martin feel uneasy about the future. The country was in crisis and lacked credible leaders. At this moment, the marquis and the mayor were the best at hand. In Paris, they had taken over the King's prerogative to grant favours, satisfy grievances, and rectify injustice. Thus far, they had accomplished little of substance.

The crowded, noisy chaos in the anteroom to the marquis' office heightened Saint-Martin's concern. Petitioners, place-seekers, and persons with all kinds of grievances besieged the marquis' clerk. He met everyone with a stony countenance. A few received appointments, the others were told to go away.

The colonel and his companion worked their way through the crowd up to the clerk's table. Saint-Martin introduced himself and Faure, and said evenly, 'I've come to report the murder of one of my officers last night near Mayor Bailly's home in Chaillot. The intended victim might have been me. An officer of the National Guard is a suspect. The marquis will want to see me.'

At the reference to murder, the clerk's eyes widened, his lips parted. 'I'll speak to the marquis,' he murmured, then quickly disappeared into Lafayette's office.

The colonel and his companion found a bench and prepared to wait. Saint-Martin's thoughts ran to the violent death that he was about to report. Its circumstances differed from Foullon's or Bertier's. A mob was lacking. Still it could have political significance. After all, Harivel was also a royal officer, although of low rank. Saint-Martin was of higher rank and perhaps the intended victim. He felt ill at ease, shook his head. He hadn't fully come to terms with the idea that someone might seriously plan to kill him.

Lieutenant Faure coughed softly, distracting the colonel from his reflections. 'Sir,' Faure said, 'I see problems ahead for this investigation. For a start, the city's police system has changed. During the past ten days, the superior officers, who used to instruct us, are gone. Lieutenant General DeCrosne is on his way to England. Baron de Breteuil is in Switzerland by this time.'

'True, we lack strong, experienced leaders,' Saint-Martin admitted. 'Mayor Bailly has taken the lieutenant general's place as the city's chief magistrate for criminal matters – and will soon move into his office at the Hôtel de Police. How he will carry out his new responsibilities is uncertain. He hardly knows yet what they are.'

Faure pushed on, doubt in his voice. 'What role will Lafayette play? Like Mayor Bailly, the marquis is nearly overwhelmed by the challenges of creating new policing for the city.'

'He will replace the police of the previous regime with his National Guard. But I grant that it's untested and undisciplined. Worst of all, the city's former twenty-five districts are now sixty. Each of the new districts has its own police bureau and battalion of National Guards and resists the idea of a strong central authority.'

'So who will oversee the individual districts and coordinate their police?' Faure shook his head.

'Nominally, the mayor and a police committee of the city council.' Saint-Martin smiled wryly. 'In fact, unless God intervenes, I expect confusion.'

Faure persisted. 'Last but not least, who will carry out the investigations?'

'Frankly, I don't know. Inspector Quidor and the other inspectors of the Criminal Investigation Department continue to work at the Hôtel de Police. But we can't count on them. Many of their spies have become unreliable or compromised and the public has grown hostile and suspicious.'

From his doorway, Lafayette himself interrupted this exchange. He invited the colonel and his companion into his office and seated them at his shining brown mahogany writing table. The office was spacious and well-appointed, and probably the finest in the City Hall. Two scribes standing at writing desks glanced at the visitors, then returned to their work. The marquis' stream of instructions and orders kept them busy.

After exchanging greetings, the marquis remarked to Saint-Martin, 'Your business appears urgent. Tell me about it.'

'Last night, one of my officers was murdered in Chaillot. The victim was on his way to a National Guard barracks. I would like your view on how to proceed.'

Lafayette leaned back, head tilted, attentive. 'Tell me more.'

Saint-Martin described in detail the murder of Harivel du Rocher, then added, 'The circumstances of the crime also suggest that the shot could have been meant for me.'

The marquis grimaced. 'I hope that you were not the target, Colonel. Do you have any suspects?'

'One of the persons we wish to interrogate is Lieutenant Maury.'

The marquis frowned. 'This is a serious matter, Colonel, especially as the victim was one of your officers, and a popular National Guard officer might be involved. You must pursue the killer. If requested, I could make a few National Guards available to help your investigation.'

After a few more exchanges, the colonel ventured to ask, 'Does mob violence in the city show any signs of abating?'

'Frankly, not yet.' The marquis sighed. 'The common people remain anxious, agitated, apt to burst into flames like dry tinder. A small spark can set them off. Early this morning, in Rue Sainte-Anne, near the Palais-Royal, a mob accused a baker of hoarding flour and profiteering in luxury bread. They hung him from a nearby lamppost. The local police bureau is investigating.'

A frisson of fear shook Saint-Martin. He had quickly calculated the incident's short distance from his Aunt Marie's town house, an area frequented by Anne and her friends and previously free of violence. The new police bureau's investigation inspired little confidence.

'That reminds me, Marquis, to ask about the deplorable incidents in the Place de Grève two days ago. What steps are being taken to apprehend the killers of Foullon and Bertier de Sauvigny?'

Lafayette looked uncomfortable and stirred in his chair.

'I realized, Colonel, that you would be concerned, since you knew Bertier and brought him safely back to Paris. When I briefly questioned Lieutenant Maury yesterday, he said that he had misunderstood my orders. He thought that Bertier should first have a hearing at the City Hall, then be taken to the Abbaye Prison. When the coach stopped in the middle of the Place de Grève, Bertier acted aggressively. The lieutenant claimed to have killed him in self-defence.'

Saint-Martin raised a sceptical eyebrow.

'I agree, Colonel, that Maury's version sounds implausible. Ideally, Bertier's death, as well as Foullon's, should be fully investigated. However, the people and the city council believe that the two men deserved to die, and that the substance of justice, if not the form, was achieved.'

'Does that mean, sir, that the matter is closed?'

'Yes, Colonel. And to try to reopen it would only generate massive, violent protests. I have neither the time nor the resources to devote to such a lost cause.'

'Am I correct in seeing the shadow of the Duc d'Orléans behind Bertier's death?'

'Possibly, but you had better keep your suspicion within these walls until you can offer convincing evidence to support it.' He leaned forwards, and measured his words. 'Do I make myself perfectly clear, Colonel?'

Saint-Martin's chest tightened. Anger surged through his body. He struggled to reply civilly. 'Yes, sir, you surely do.' On that note, the meeting ended.

To avoid the duke's men and any mob that they might have gathered on the Place de Grève, the colonel and his companion left the City Hall by a side door. Saint-Martin turned to Faure and murmured through clenched teeth, 'In Bertier's case justice was mocked, not served. I intend to find his killers and make sure that they are punished. The people, the city council, and the Marquis de Lafayette be damned.'

Twelve

More Mob Justice

Meanwhile, at the town house, Anne hastened to the parlour. 'An urgent message' from the Abbé de l'Épée spurred her on. Waiting for her was the young deaf brother of André Dutoit, still breathless, his face red from exertion. He must have run all the way from the institute. With a child's naive gravity, he signed, 'Madame, come with me to the abbé's office. He's worried. There's a serious problem.'

Anne took leave of Michou and Sylvie and gave brief instructions to the cook for dinner, then hurried with the boy out into the street. She feared that the old priest might be suddenly failing. He was nearly eighty, and his health was poor.

At the institute, she was shown into the abbé's office. He sat at his writing table, a blanket on his lap, though the room was warm. 'Thank you, Madame Cartier, for coming so quickly.' He wheezed when he spoke, his voice faint. But his eyes engaged hers with a sense of urgency. In his usual gracious manner, he gestured for her to be seated.

Anne's fears for his health lessened somewhat and she asked, 'What has happened?'

'At dawn today,' he replied, 'a mob killed Monsieur Louis Gagne, a baker, outside his shop on the corner of Rue Sainte-Anne and Rue Hazard.'

'How dreadful!' Anne exclaimed, recalling the incident reported by Michou. Immediately, the slaughter of Foullon and Bertier rushed to her mind. Was there no end to these atrocities?

'The baker's wife, Béatrice, is deaf. Years ago, she studied with me. I found work for her in that bakery. Eventually, she married the baker, five years older than she. They've been happy together and their business has prospered – until now. She was away from the shop at the time. On her way home, she learned that the mob wanted to kill her too. They accused her and her husband of hoarding flour and profiteering in the sale of bread. Desperate and in shock, she came to me, barely able to sign. For the time being, Mademoiselle Arnaud is caring for her. I doubt that anyone would dare to attack her in this building.'

'What would you like me to do?'

'Please learn Madame Gagne's story. Inquire in the neighbourhood. Find out if she's really in danger and how we can improve her lot.' He handed Anne a letter. 'This will recommend you to the authorities and to persons who know me. They might help you, if they aren't too frightened. You also know Inspector Quidor. Ask him what can be done for Madame Gagne. Our new district police have not been helpful. In fact, they have placed a watch on this building, more likely to arrest Madame than to protect her.'

Madame Gagne was resting in Françoise Arnaud's own small room on the ground floor of the institute. Mademoiselle Arnaud had at least temporarily reduced, if not banished, the woman's fears. She sat opposite Françoise at the table, and sipped from a cup of herbal tea. Her hands trembled. In her mid-thirties, plain-faced, eyes lustreless, she seemed utterly defeated.

She responded to Anne's greeting with a thin, fleeting smile. 'I know very little about what happened at the bakery this morning; I was at the central market. On the way home a neighbour warned me that a mob had hung my husband. They accused me, like my husband, of hoarding flour and profiteering. They told everyone that they had a rope for me as well as for him. I didn't dare return to the bakery, so I came to the institute. My son Robert and the maid Jeanne have fled, terrified. I don't know where they are.'

She explained with signs that her son, thirteen years old and deaf, was learning his father's trade. The maid was a few years older and also deaf.

She and her husband the baker operated the business together in leased premises on Rue Sainte-Anne. A competent but surly journeyman Jacques Duby worked with the baker. The deaf maid helped Madame Gagne with household chores, while she kept the books.

'Do you have any friends in the neighbourhood? Anyone whom I could contact for you?'

She shook her head. 'Because I'm deaf,' she replied, 'most people can't or won't try to be friends with me. They think it's too difficult. Monsieur Gagne was my best friend as well as husband. He learned to sign so that we could comfort and encourage each other, share our feelings. I spent my days at the bakery with him and my son. In the evening I just stayed at home with them.'

Anne felt a wave of pity for the woman. Now with the loss of her husband and the disappearance of her son, her sense of isolation must be nearly unbearable. Still, Anne had to leave the woman with at least a glimmer of hope. She promised she would assess the danger, then find the son and the maid. Meanwhile, Mademoiselle Arnaud would seek a safe place for her.

Anne returned to the house on Rue Traversine. Michou was working in her studio on a sketch. Her friend Sylvie de Chanteclerc was also there in a housecoat, sitting at a writing table, an account book open before her. Her friend André Dutoit was at her side, pointing to a problematic entry. Upon seeing Anne, she laid down her pen and smiled. André rose and politely bowed.

Michou left the easel and embraced Anne, then went back to her sketch. Anne stepped behind her and looked over her shoulder. She had previously sketched from memory the likeness of a man. It stood on an easel off to the left. Anne recognized Gaillard. She had requested the sketch yesterday. Michou was almost finished making a copy.

'A good likeness,' said André, himself a portrait artist. He had come to Anne's side. 'Note the difference between the original sketch and this copy.'

Michou added some shadow to Gaillard's eyes that made his expression more menacing. She leaned back and pointed out the subtle differences. In the original he appeared to be scowling. 'I've seen him often lately in the arcades and the garden. His face is so passionate, so dark with resentment and anger. As I did the copy, those qualities came to the fore, especially the anger.'

Anne translated Michou's remarks for André, for he lacked easy fluency in signing. 'Do you agree?' she asked him.

He nodded. 'She's right, especially for his public face. In the duke's palace, where I frequently see him in unguarded moments, I also detect a streak of cold calculation, mixed with malice.'

André's remarks encouraged Anne to include him in her plans for searching the duke's palace. That's where she hoped to find evidence of the crimes committed by Gaillard and his henchmen, such as the assassinations of Foullon and Bertier, the baker Gagne, and Harivel. As a curator of the duke's art collection, André could move about the palace rather freely. The duke also valued his organizational ability and used him as a general factotum.

Anne thought she heard him sigh. Though valued, he was poorly paid and treated like a lowly servant with little respect. He tried not to show his resentment. He dared not risk his job – he needed the money. He also felt obliged to conceal his affection for Sylvie from his superiors in the palace, since they loathed the Baron de Breteuil, her godfather. But on that point he need not be so concerned, for they took less notice of her after she rejected the privileges of her class and lived like a commoner.

He gave Michou a pat on the back, excused himself, embraced Sylvie, and returned to his work in the palace.

Anne left Michou to her work and sat across from Sylvie. 'How does André deal with the evil that the duke and his faction are causing in the country?'

'He closes his eyes and ears to it as much as he can. Despite its faults, his job is terribly important to him. He's the chief support of his family since his father recently had to retire from making cabinets. And he pays for his brother's instruction at the abbé's institute. Finally, he feels that he has to save money so that we can get married someday.' Her gaze drifted off to a distant point.

'Then it would be very difficult, I should think, to persuade him to help our investigation of crimes committed by the duke's people.'

'You are right. It would be difficult.'

'Well, I have other matters to discuss with you just now. I'm on a mission in the city. As you know, it's dangerous out there. The people are in such turmoil. You may have heard that one of Paul's troopers, Lieutenant Jacques Harivel du Rocher, was murdered last night in Chaillot. In fact, Paul may have been the intended target.'

Sylvie's hand flew to her mouth. 'Who would want to kill Paul?'

'Georges is in Chaillot now, trying to find out.' Anne paused to sharpen the young woman's interest. 'And there's more to report on the violence at the neighbourhood bakery.' She described her visit with the abbé and her plan to help the baker's wife.

Sylvie's brow creased with concern. 'I've been inside the shop a few times and met the family – decent, hard-working people. What can I do for them?'

'Would you be free and willing to go there with me this morning? I should have a partner or two.' Anne thought she could trust Sylvie. Last year they had worked together investigating the mysterious disappearance of prostitutes in the Palais-Royal.

'Thank you for asking, Anne. Yes, I'd like to join you. I've just finished examining Michou's accounts. They are in good order. Give me a few minutes to change into street clothes.' She closed the book and rose from the table.

Off to one side, Michou had been following the discussion out of the corner of her eye and was intrigued. Anne briefly signed an explanation.

Michou left the easel and signed, 'I want to go with you.'

'Good, I might need your skill at sketching. I'll also change while I'm here.' Anne cautioned the two women. 'We should go as domestic servants, not as ladies. Let's not call attention to ourselves.'

Standing before a mirror in her room, Anne reflected. It might be difficult to disguise Sylvie, an aristocratic young woman, born and bred to privilege, trained from infancy in fine manners and cultivated speech. She was also a striking beauty.

But she had abandoned the use of cosmetics and the wearing of elegant, fashionable gowns. Her hands were rough from cleaning Michou's brushes and other housework in Comtesse

Marie's town house, where she lived. Frequent exposure to the sun and rain in the garden of the Palais-Royal had tanned her smooth complexion. She was rapidly learning the language and ways of common people and gaining understanding of them.

A few minutes later, the women arrived together in the studio. Both wore plain grey woollen gowns, adorned with a few tattered coloured ribbons. In rough street French, Sylvie addressed Anne. 'Mam, will this do? I've added some grime to my face.'

'Nice touch, Sylvie,' replied Anne. 'I hardly recognized you. God willing, none of Gaillard's mob will either.'

As they were walking towards Rue Sainte-Anne just a block away, Sylvie asked, 'What reasons can we give to people for asking questions about the baker's hanging? They'll be shy of strangers. To say that we're merely curious could raise suspicions. People would walk away, fearful of getting involved in something dangerous or illegal.'

Anne patted her bag. 'I have here a letter from the Abbé de l'Épée, a priest well known and respected in the neighbourhood. It should disarm any suspicions that people might have about us.'

Sylvie countered. 'They're likely to ask, why don't we go to the local police?'

'We'll say that the police are too busy now. In fact, we'll approach the local police later, after we've talked to Inspector Quidor. His experience with them, I understand, has been discouraging. But I want to hear the story first from sources independent of the police. Then I can question the police better, recognize when they're lying to me.'

Sylvie persisted. 'People will ask what good can come of pursuing this matter. After all, the baker is dead. We can't help him.'

'We'll say that Madame Gagne, the baker's wife, needs to know what happened in case she has to defend herself or recover her property. I think most people will accept that line of reasoning. Now let's see what kind of man has taken over the bakery.'

At midmorning, the bakery on Rue Sainte-Anne had already reopened. The National Guardsmen were gone. Anne, Michou and Sylvie stood outside and observed the scene for a minute. A steady stream of customers entered the baker's shop and came out again with bread. It looked like business as usual. Anne stopped a young woman leaving the shop with a basket of bread on her arm and feigned ignorance. 'Is it true that a man was hung here early this morning?'

'I know nothing about it,' stammered the woman, glancing up at the lamppost. She scurried away.

Anne turned to Sylvie. 'Continue to talk to customers leaving the bakery. If you discover knowledgeable, trustworthy persons, ask for their views on the hanging. Michou and I shall go into the shop and pretend to be customers.' Anne signed to Michou, 'Make a sketch in your mind of the man in charge, Jacques Duby. He used to be the baker's assistant, a journeyman. Take care that he doesn't suspect what you're doing.'

'Is he dangerous?'

'He has profited by his master's death. That's all I know at this point.'

Inside the shop, Anne and Michou waited in a line with other women. Through an open door they could see two apprentices in the bakeroom, stripped to the waist, their backs glistening with sweat. One was bent over, kneading dough in a long trough, the other was shoveling baked twelve-pound loaves from the oven. Heat from the bakeroom spilled out into the shop.

At the counter in a baker's apron Monsieur Duby was serving customers. A young woman looked on, apparently learning the task. Duby was a short, wiry man in his late thirties. Unsmiling, sharp-eyed, he carefully counted the coins handed to him, addressing most of the customers by name.

As Anne approached the counter, the baker signalled to the young woman to take his place and he stepped back. For a moment he and Anne locked eyes, then he glanced at Michou. His eyes narrowed with suspicion – he must have realized that they were strangers, or even spies. He frowned but said nothing. Finally, he turned away and walked into the bakeroom.

The clerk at the counter followed his exit with nervous side glances, then asked Anne what she wanted.

'A small loaf,' she replied.

With trembling hands and a distracted air, the clerk gave Anne a loaf, but she dropped the coins that Anne gave her and appeared on the verge of crying. Anne offered her a reassuring smile, nodded to Michou, and led her out the door.

The street was too busy for conversation. Across the street from the bakery, they found Sylvie in a café, called La Vache Agile – the Nimble Heifer – and ordered coffee. Michou pulled a sketchbook and a pencil from her bag, reflected for a moment, and set to work on a portrait of the new baker.

Anne related her impressions to Sylvie. 'He knew most of the customers. Among them I sensed little if any good feeling towards him. It would be helpful to know what they really thought. And I wonder if he and his master had serious differences or quarrels. I'll ask the baker's wife when she recovers.' Anne stirred sugar into her coffee.

Michou looked up from sketching and added, 'Monsieur Duby displayed no sign of sorrow or grief, neither on his features nor in his shop. His clerk is newly hired, possibly less than an hour ago and badly treated. She's fearful of him.'

'Rightly so,' Sylvie remarked. 'The few neighbours who would talk to me refused to comment on him, other than to say that his bread was good. They also claimed that none of them took part in the mob's attack on Gagne, or witnessed it.'

Anne remarked sceptically, 'Then the mob must have been composed of strangers.'

'However,' Sylvie continued, 'one man ventured a guess that the new baker probably had friends in the local police bureau.'

'He's probably right,' Anne agreed. 'That might explain why their investigation was so brief. Within an hour they convicted the dead baker of crimes against the people and handed the bakery over to the journeyman, temporarily at least.'

Michou declared that she now had sufficient material for a good sketch of the new baker's features. She closed her sketchbook with a flourish. In her studio she would draw the final version.

She signed, 'In the shop I could observe him closely. He revealed aspects of his character that most people, like his customers, wouldn't notice, and he would rather keep concealed.'

Anne and Sylvie watched Michou's signs closely, encouraging her to continue. Her judgements on people were infrequent but sound.

'I don't like what I saw. He's a hard, resentful, bitter man. Still, that doesn't necessarily mean that he's a murderer.'

With that pronouncement still hanging in the air, she tucked the sketchbook under her arm and left the café for her studio.

Anne finished her coffee. 'Our investigation here has raised more questions than I expected. An acquaintance of mine who lives next door to the bakery might give us some of the answers.'

Thirteen

A Reluctant Eyewitness

Paris, Friday, 24 July

Anne and Sylvie left La Vache Agile, crossed Rue Sainte-Anne, and approached the shop of the seamstress Cécile Tremblay, next door to the bakery.

'I remember this shop,' Sylvie remarked. 'Been by it several times. It often seemed closed.'

'The owner works alone and might have gone to visit her parents in the country. She could also have been resting in her room above the shop.'

'How well do you know her?'

'I met Cécile during one of Paul's investigations nearly two years ago. She was then the personal maid of the Comtesse de Serre, who was murdered while riding in her country estate.' Anne paused for a moment, calling up Cécile from memory. 'She was about forty then, a bright, good-hearted, well-mannered widow, who smiled readily. She might appear withdrawn when we meet her. The Serre investigation and other personal trials have bruised her and made her cautious.'

'Have you kept in contact with her?' Sylvie asked, looking doubtful.

'Yes, in a way,' Anne replied. 'I continue to direct customers to her shop. But it's been a year since we've met.'

The shop was open and its mistress stood at the counter with a customer. When she left, Cécile looked up and recognized Anne. Her reaction was a curious mixture of pleasure at seeing her and apprehension about the purpose of her visit. Echoes of the murder investigation, Anne surmised.

Anne embraced the seamstress. She had aged a little in a year. Thin streaks of grey now ran through her dark brown hair. But she was still a comely woman, with soft brown eyes, a pleasing oval face and a slender, shapely body.

Anne introduced Sylvie and asked to speak privately.

The seamstress hesitated, studying Anne's face for clues as to the reason for the request. Finally she said, 'My mother, Laure, is upstairs resting in my room. But there's a room in the café across the street where we can be alone.'

In the café, Cécile acted as if at home, nodding to familiar faces. A dozen men and women, most of them elderly, were sharing jugs of wine while they played cards and chatted. The barman smiled as he handed her a key. 'Would you like something to drink?' Cécile asked the two women.

'Apple cider,' Anne replied. Sylvie added, 'The same for me.'

They settled into chairs at a small table in the back room. Anne faced Cécile; Sylvie sat off to one side. A few minutes into the conversation, Cécile seemed to feel obliged to offer an explanation to Anne.

'Since we last met, my father, Vincenzo, passed away and my mother moved to Paris. About the same time, the owner of this café and I became friends. His wife had recently died. He pays me for keeping the business records and waiting on customers. The seamstress shop could not support both Mother and me.' She paused, searched Anne's eyes for any hint of criticism. 'The owner is a kind man. We're living together and plan to get married.'

'I wish you well,' Anne said and took a sip of the cider. 'But now I must ask how much you know about the hanging early this morning on the corner, a stone's throw from where we sit.' Anne described Abbé de l'Épée's concern for Madame Gagne, the baker's wife. 'To help her I must find out what happened.'

Cécile stiffened, frowned. 'Neither I nor my friend the café owner can afford to become involved in the incident. We have no protection. Our businesses could easily be destroyed and ourselves with them.'

Anne put a little ice into her voice. 'Monsieur Gagne's death may have been premeditated murder. His wife also appears to be in danger. A deaf woman, she can hardly defend herself, has no one to turn to but the abbé. In addition, her property appears lost, or stolen from her, and she's reduced to penury. Finally, her deaf son has fled, terrified by the atrocious killing of his father.' Anne met Cécile's eye. 'At the abbé's urgent request, I'll do whatever I must in order to help this family.' Anne knew that Cécile was a yielding person and could be influenced or intimidated, but she was no fool.

Cécile bit her lower lip, her eyes cast down. She appeared to understand Anne's allusion to help given to her in difficult circumstances. In the Serre case she had faced a conviction for embezzlement of her employer's funds. In fact, her deceased husband was the thief, but she could also have been held responsible. Ahead of her were years in prison. Anne had saved her by securing certain incriminating documents and returning them to her.

Finally, she sighed deeply and conceded, 'I'll tell you what I know.'

Anne nodded to Sylvie, who pulled pen and ink and paper from her bag, then sat back, ready to take notes.

'The owner and I opened the café shortly after dawn. This morning's business began as usual. The deaf boy from the bakery came with a basket of fresh bread. He looked tired. I treated him to a cup of café au lait. Most of the customers were neighbours, except for three strangers together at a table. After a quick breakfast two of them left the café. A few minutes later, a noisy, angry crowd stormed through the street.

'I went to the door to see what was amiss. Men were chanting, "Death to profiteers." I recognized a local day labourer. So I asked, "What's happened?" His eyes were wild. I could smell drink on him.

'He said, "We're hanging the baker and his wife. Blood-sucking traitors. Our men have found sacks of contraband flour hidden in the bakery and receipts for hundreds of *livres* from the baker's sale of luxury bread at twice the legal price." He stopped, grabbed my arm. "Come, join us," he said.

'I pulled away and said, "I've got to tend to the café." I shut and barred the door. By this time, my friend had come out of the kitchen. I told him what was happening. We hurried upstairs. From the first-floor window we saw the crowd about to hang Monsieur Gagne.'

Her voice broke. Tears gathered in her eyes. 'It was dreadful,' she stammered. 'He struggled, said he was innocent, cried out for mercy. The crowd laughed, jeered him. They tied a rope around his neck, then hoisted him up.' She turned her face away and began to weep.

'Take your time,' Anne counselled. 'It must be unbearable to watch someone you know and respect being abused and killed.' Sylvie laid down her pen. The room became still.

After a minute Cécile recovered her composure. 'I was concerned about his son, so I rushed back downstairs. He was looking out the window, had seen everything, and seemed terrified. I sensed that he wanted to get away to a safer place. I let him out the back door.'

'Did he say where he would go?'

'No, and I haven't seen him since. We didn't have time to talk. The crowd broke up quickly. Some of them knocked on our door. When they started shouting and banging hard, we opened up the café and served them.

'Shortly afterward, the local National Guard marched up the street. The lieutenant in charge talked to some of the men in the crowd, then went into the bakery. Two guards pulled the dead man down from the lamppost. The others followed their leader into the bakery, took away sacks of flour and a box of paper that looked like receipts. In a few more minutes the guards were gone. The whole incident took less than an hour.'

Anne reflected on what she had heard. 'Can you recall the three strangers who came into the café when it opened? Did one of them look like this?' She showed Cécile the sketch of Gaillard.

'Yes, that's him. The sketch makes him look calculating and cynical,' Cécile remarked. 'And that's how I remember him from this morning.'

'Describe his companions.'

'One of them, the liveliest, was short and stout. His nose looked like it had been smashed flat, his eyes were narrow, small and black, his face round. Frankly, he looked like a pig. A mean, nasty one! Gaillard called him Simon. The other man was Nicolas, tall and thin. He had a cropped right ear and wore a stupid expression on his face – perhaps he was simple-minded.'

'Do you think the baker actually hoarded flour and intended to make an unfair profit, or could the evidence have been secretly planted in the bakery to incriminate him?'

Cécile thought for a moment. 'Since the bakery was next

door to my shop, I knew Monsieur Gagne and his family. He didn't seem greedy. I never heard that he took unfair advantage of anyone. Those sacks and the receipts must have somehow been hidden in his bakery without his knowledge.'

'Then the next question is, who would have done it?'

'I don't know. Unfortunately, Monsieur Gagne had a way of making enemies.'

Anne raised a sceptical eyebrow.

'Yes, the baker was a good man but given to speaking his mind, loudly, heedless of the consequences. Recently, he criticized the Duc d'Orléans and accused the duke's faction of fabricating a crisis. They manipulated the grain trade and instilled a fear of scarcity in the common people. The intendant Bertier de Sauvigny did all that was humanly possible to feed Paris. The men who killed him were rogues, paid cowards all. Gagne tried to persuade other bakers to adopt his views and unite. He claimed that the duke's faction was exploiting them.'

'So this morning Gaillard and his companions came here and plotted to kill Monsieur Gagne,' Anne concluded. 'Did anyone warn him to be more prudent?'

'Yes, his wife and I and others. We told him to keep to his baking or risk losing everything.'

'Unfortunately, your prediction came true.' Anne paused for a second, finished her glass of cider. 'What was the role of the journeyman Jacques Duby in this tragedy?'

'I really don't know,' Cécile replied. 'I haven't heard him quarrelling with the baker or complaining about poor treatment. The lot of a journeyman is difficult: low pay, lack of freedom. This Duby is a reticent man, the opposite of the baker. Who knows what evil might lie hidden in his heart. But he wasn't out in the street among those who hung his master.'

Another witness might help unlock that heart, Anne thought. In the meantime, she moved on to other questions. She learned that the two strangers at table with Gaillard served as the hangmen. The short man took the lead, seemed to direct the mob. Cécile could not say how the sacks of flour and the receipts came to be hidden in the bakery.

'What can you tell me about the National Guard lieutenant?' Anne asked. She described Lieutenant Maury.

'That's him, short and swarthy, with the moustache. He directed the guards' investigation. His manner seemed perfunctory, disinterested.'

Anne added, 'Perhaps he knew what he would find, already knew the answers to the questions that he asked.'

Cécile could say little about the baker's wife, other than that she appeared to be a decent woman, shy and deaf, who kept to herself.

Anne concluded that it was time to end the interview. She asked Sylvie to show her notes to Cécile, who read them, then asked, 'What use will you make of them?'

'Like pieces in a puzzle,' Anne replied, 'they establish certain important facts, such as Gaillard's presence near the scene of the crime. They might be important in a later judicial procedure. So, if you think the notes are accurate, I'd like you to sign them. Sylvie and I shall witness your signature.'

Cécile hesitated again, her eyes darkened with fear.

Anne sympathized with the woman, understood her anxiety. Just a few hours ago she had witnessed how ruthless Gaillard and his men could be. Still, Anne needed Cécile's testimony, so she pressed on. 'I've demonstrated in the Serre case that you can trust me with sensitive information. I won't use the notes in a manner harmful to you. My only concern is that justice be done for Madame Gagne. My husband and I will do everything in our power to protect you.'

Reluctantly, Cécile agreed. 'We'll return to my seamstress shop. I'll sign there.'

Fourteen
The New Criminal Justice

Paris, Friday, 24 July

Anne and Sylvie made their way to the Palais-Royal, bringing with them horrific impressions of mob frenzy and cold-blooded slaughter. They felt even more distressed that life at the site of the baker's murder had returned – if only on the surface – to its normal pattern. People wanted to believe that nothing untoward had happened.

The two women walked through the palace garden until Anne could point out Inspector Quidor at a shaded table outside the Café de Foy. He often spent a late morning hour there, observing humanity, receiving the gossip, the rumours, the news of the day. In his own words, he read the pulse of the city at its heart and took its temperature. Today, a nondescript man sat with him. When the inspector saw Anne and her companion, he dismissed the man and beckoned the women to join him.

'An informant,' remarked Quidor, glancing over his shoulder at the retreating man. 'He had little of use to tell me. I sense that the duke is paying him more than I am. And that isn't much.' The inspector rose, gave Anne one of his rare smiles, bowed his head to Sylvie with appropriate deference, and nodded them to a pair of empty chairs.

'What brings you two into the lion's den?' The inspector gave the women a conspiratorial wink. The arcades and garden of the Palais-Royal were the centre of the duke's attempt to unseat the ruling family.

'An errand of mercy,' replied Anne. She described her conversations at the abbé's institute. 'We must find out what happened this morning at the bakery, so that we can assist the baker's widow. Can you help us?'

'I'm not officially involved in the investigation,' Quidor remarked. 'But I'm familiar with the incident.'

He signalled a waiter and ordered fruit drinks for his female guests. When they were served and the waiter departed, the inspector raised his glass to drink to their health. They responded in kind. He said in a low voice, 'I'll begin at the beginning. At dawn, one of my agents woke me up, told me that a riot was brewing on Rue Sainte-Anne. We reached the bakery in less than twenty minutes, but the baker was already hanging from the lamppost.

'A detachment of National Guards turned me away from the site. Their commander, a Lieutenant Maury, said that my services were neither required nor welcome. He was conducting the investigation and would report to the local police bureau.'

'I know something about him,' said Anne. 'My husband told me that Lieutenant Maury commanded the National Guards who transported Bertier de Sauvigny to his death two days ago on the Place de Grève. A trustworthy eyewitness saw Maury, unprovoked, kill the intendant. Georges Charpentier and I watched him rush into the city council's hall with Bertier's bloody heart impaled on his sword.'

The inspector grew very still, his expression darkened. 'This Maury is a dangerous villain, new to me. I regret that my sources of information are not as good as they used to be.'

He saluted Anne again with his glass and drained it. 'I thank you, Madame. You have thrown a helpful light on the baker's case. Though it's out of my hands, I'll observe it closely.'

Anne asked, 'Is the widow Gagne really in danger of being assassinated like her husband? Are the police pursuing her as if she were her husband's accomplice?'

Quidor took a moment to reflect, then said softly, 'If the widow were to leave the institute, she would be assassinated. A bystander overheard the guards say they were looking for her.'

'Why should they bother about her?' asked Anne.

'They fear that she might contradict the charges against her husband, and perhaps demonstrate that Maury's evidence is spurious.'

'Then we know what we must do,' Anne remarked cryptically, not wishing to draw the inspector into what the police bureau might consider an illegal act. She signed to Sylvie, 'We'll have to shelter the widow from the police.'

Quidor smiled indulgently. 'Some day I'll learn sign language. Nonetheless, I understand perfectly what you mean and shall help wherever I can. Since the new local police bureaus are so jealous of their authority, I must be cautious. Provoking them could be dangerous for all of us. The people throughout the country are desperate and easily led into violence. Here at the Palais-Royal I often take their temperature. For the time being, it's feverish. A popular rogue like Maury could send a mob after us.'

Anne and Sylvie finished their drinks, thanked the inspector, and left the table. Out of the corner of her eye, Anne caught a glimpse of Quidor's nondescript informant. He had been observing them from a distance. He quickly turned away and disappeared into the crowd.

'He's curious, thinks we are domestic servants working for Inspector Quidor, and may follow us,' said Anne. 'We must throw him off our scent without making him more suspicious.'

Sylvie looked puzzled.

Anne continued, 'As merely domestic servants, we'll soon be of no interest to him. If he were to learn who we really are, he would cling to us like a leech.'

Mindful of being followed, Anne and Sylvie took a roundabout route to Michou's studio. On the way they entered the church of Saint-Roch and hid in a side chapel. The spy searched vainly for them. When he left, they slipped out a side entrance.

By the time they reached Michou, she had finished her sketch of the new baker Jacques Duby and was making copies. They brought her up to date on the investigation. Anne asked her to observe Gaillard and Maury in the Palais-Royal. 'Sketch Maury. I'd like to add him to our collection of rogues.' Michou agreed with a broad smile. Then, with her copies in their bags, and still posing as domestic servants, Anne and Sylvie set off for the new district police bureau.

The bureau was located on the ground floor of an old building in a cul-de-sac off Rue des Orties and had a temporary look. To judge from the smell of stale wine and tobacco, the premises had formerly been a tavern. Three magistrates sat on chairs on a platform raised behind the bar. To their right sat a scribe, using the bar as a writing table. A large ledger lay open before him. The proceedings were suspended for a few minutes, while several convicted felons were led out and an equal number of newly accused persons were brought in.

A bailiff showed Anne and Sylvie to chairs at the back of the courtroom in what passed for a public gallery. Opening the proceedings to the public was a recent novelty. It was now dusk, suppertime for most people, and a few left. Perhaps twenty men and women remained, chatting with each other as if they were in a popular theatre waiting for the entertainment to begin.

The magistrates looked variously bored, impatient and distracted. Their scribe bent over the ledger, weary, occasionally cursing his pen for the mistakes he made. To the magistrates' left, a pair of National Guards leaned against the wall, carrying on a whispered conversation.

The prosecutor beckoned individuals in turn to stand before the court and hear the charges against them. In a few cases, the magistrates asked a question or two. Otherwise, one of them merely read aloud the report of a police investigation. The three magistrates conferred briefly, then pronounced a sentence. Rarely did they set the accused person free. Most of the crimes seemed minor: battery, petty theft, prostitution and the like.

After Anne and Sylvie had waited ten minutes, the prosecutor presented the case of the baker Gagne, a profiteer executed by the people. A magistrate read Lieutenant Maury's report on the incident, followed by the police bureau's decision in the morning to ratify the people's will – that is, to convict Gagne posthumously and to place his bakery and other assets in the hands of his journeyman until more permanent arrangements could be made. The prosecutor asked the court to determine whether to further punish the dead man. The magistrates drew from the criminal code of the previous regime and sentenced his body to be burned on the Place de Grève at a date to be determined.

Anne could hardly believe what she was hearing. Gagne's body was to be burned, as if hanging was insufficient punishment. How perverse and bizarre! The people's will? Nonsense. Gaillard's will more likely. But this travesty of justice was sadly familiar to Anne. Her stepfather, Antoine Dubois, suffered a similar fate four years ago. Himself murdered, he was posthumously charged with suicide and the murder of his mistress. His body was later burned on the Place de Grève. The horror of his story stuck in Anne's memory.

Sylvie stared at Anne and whispered, 'Are you alright?'

Anne nodded. She felt hot, her cheeks flushed, but she drew deep breaths of air and recovered control of herself. Something had to be done. She needed to know the court's intention towards Madame Gagne, and she had to prevent the burning of Gagne's body and arrange for its proper burial. During the proceedings she had studied the members of the court. It had been created only a few days earlier for the district around the Louvre. Its members seemed scarcely to know each other, their own responsibilities, or the law that they were supposed to apply. If challenged, the court would stiffen its collective back. But its individual members might react more helpfully, if approached in a diplomatic way.

Fortunately, she recognized one of the three magistrates, a young lawyer, Pierre Roland. He came on business occasionally to Paul's office, and she had met him. He then appeared to be a reasonable, well-trained, learned man. During the past week since the fall of the Bastille, the wave of reform must have swept him up on to the judicial bench. To judge from today's proceedings, he seemed embarrassed by the court's slipshod performance, and he only reluctantly followed the lead of the other two magistrates in their enthusiastic but ignorant legal reasoning.

With the baker's case dispatched, the court's session came to an end, and the magistrates rose to leave. Anne told Sylvie to wait while she approached the young lawyer. He had drifted apart from the others.

'Sir,' she murmured with as much pleading in her face and voice as she could muster, 'I would like to speak to you privately on urgent business.'

Confused momentarily by her disguise, Roland finally recognized her. 'Well, Madame Cartier, this is most unusual.' He smiled wryly, then glanced over his shoulder, and spoke softly, 'But what *is* usual these days? I'll be at your husband's office in half an hour.'

Fifteen

A Jealous Soldier

Chaillot/Passy, Friday, 24 July

Early on that morning, Julien Pioche, a veteran brigadier from the Highway Patrol post at Passy, joined Georges at a medical doctor's clinic in Chaillot. The body of Harivel du Rocher lay covered on a surgical table. Georges stood at a discreet distance while Pioche approached his fallen comrade. When the doctor removed the cover, Pioche grimaced. He saluted the body in a gesture of respect, then said to Georges, 'I've served under Harivel for many years. All of us at the post thought he was a fair and honourable commander. To me he was like an older brother, a personal friend.'

Both men struggled to control their feelings of anger and grief. Georges felt deeply touched, though he did not know Harivel as well as Pioche did. An unspoken resolve bonded them to avenge Harivel's death, to see that justice was done.

After covering the body again, the doctor said, 'I found the ball near the man's heart.

He was shot in the back by a small pistol at close range. The angle of the ball's path through the body suggests that his killer was on foot and fired upward towards the mounted officer.'

Brigadier Pioche muttered, 'This was the deed of a cowardly assassin. He fired at a man's back from a dark, concealed place.' He added grimly, 'When we find him, he will regret ever having been born. He deserves to be roasted alive, torn apart by wild horses.'

'Punishing him is the easy part,' Georges observed. 'Finding him might be difficult.' His eye shifted to a military cloak hanging on the wall. He examined it, found the bullet hole, and shuddered. The body on the table could have been Colonel Saint-Martin's.

From the clinic Georges and the brigadier moved to the scene of the murder. Village watchmen and men from the Passy Highway Patrol had guarded it overnight. Colonel Saint-Martin's inspection of the scene hours earlier had been brief and in the dark. It needed to be examined more thoroughly in daylight. Harivel was shot on the main route between Paris and Versailles. Now, approaching midday, it was clogged with traffic. Even near midnight, when the crime took place, more than a few travellers would still have been on the road. Yet no one actually observed the shooting. Georges surmised that the killer must have had an accomplice to signal that the road was clear, that his victim was approaching.

On the south side of the road was the river's bank, lined with boats moored to wharves and docks. On the north side stood a high stone wall. Behind it was a narrow terraced estate of gardens and orchards that extended up a hill to a manor house. To the left and right of the walled property were two- and three-storey buildings facing the river with shops at the ground level and apartments on the upper floors. An alley ran up the hill along a wall on the east side of the estate. At the intersection of the alley and the river road was a street lamp that would throw a small circle of light on to the road while leaving the alley dark.

The two officers agreed that the killer had probably hidden in the dark alley. A signal from an accomplice alerted him to Harivel's approach. He shot as the officer came into the lamp's circle of light, then fled most likely up the alley.

Georges surveyed the scene, arms akimbo. 'In a few words, I'd say that the killing was carefully planned and executed. At least two persons were involved. The intended victim was most likely Colonel Saint-Martin.'

Though apparently no one saw the crime, someone might have noticed suspicious strangers in the village. Georges and his comrade planned systematically to visit the shops and residences in the area, beginning near the scene of the crime. Neighbours had already told Colonel Saint-Martin that they had heard the shot and one man added that he had seen the wounded horseman turn his mount around and return in the direction of Passy. The most promising place to start an inquiry was the wine tavern about a hundred paces east of the scene.

A large and busy shop, it sold wine over the counter and served wine and food to several tables. Georges knew the place from previous visits while travelling between Paris and Versailles.

'Were you working here last night?' Georges asked the portly man tending the bar. He had an air of authority and a vigilant eye. Georges showed his credentials.

'Until eleven,' the man replied. Led by Georges' questions, he explained that he had served many strangers, as usual, since much traffic passed between Versailles and Paris. In addition, he ventured to say, soldiers had come from the National Guard's barracks a short distance further east towards Paris. 'They left at about ten.' He hadn't noticed any suspicious behaviour.

Georges and his companion sat at a table, ordered coffee and discussed the case for a few minutes. This gave Georges an opportunity to raise a potentially sensitive issue. 'Tell me about Harivel. What kind of man was he? Why would someone want to kill him?'

A troubled expression came over Pioche's face. He hesitated, then spoke with carefully measured words. 'I don't know of any declared personal enemies or family rivals who would want to kill him or had even threatened him. He was a brave soldier, a conscientious officer, and proud of his family. Though poor, they had distinguished themselves in the King's service. His brother is a royal diplomat, a consul. I believe he serves in Morocco in North Africa.'

'Could Harivel's killing have a political cause, like Bertier's?' asked Georges.

'Possibly,' Pioche granted. 'Our commander was very much a King's man. He spoke out against the duke's vile scribblers and orators at the Palais-Royal who show the King no respect and would steal his authority.' He paused, then added an afterthought. 'And Harivel was also impulsive and wilful at times. He would court danger, take on risky investigations.'

Georges tilted his head, inviting an explanation.

'He'd been working on a secret, delicate case for the past month, on the side, as it were. Wasn't quite ready to talk about it.'

That could be a significant lead, Georges thought, and he made a mental note of it. 'Can you think of anything else that might have put his life at risk?'

'He's separated from his wife,' replied Pioche tentatively. 'I don't know the details, or whether she's resentful enough to wish him harm. I've never been introduced to her. Harivel was known to be fond of women and to have a way with them. Lately, he had become involved with a young married woman in Chaillot who lives in this neighbourhood.' Pioche shifted in his seat as if uncomfortable with this conversation. 'We should not speak ill of the dead, especially of one who was an esteemed comrade.'

Georges leaned forwards, nodded to encourage his companion to continue. 'Harivel is the central figure in a murder investigation. Everything about him is relevant, including his weaknesses and faults, and the dark corners of his life.'

'That's true,' conceded Pioche. 'I don't know if the young woman returned his affection. But I've heard that her husband, a lieutenant in the local National Guard, is a jealous man. His barracks is a stone's throw down the road from here.'

'Describe him.' Georges had begun to smell the anger of a cuckolded husband, a timeless motive for murder.

'He's about thirty and swarthy. Has thick, wavy black hair and a moustache. His body is short and muscular. I'm told he's hot-tempered and an excellent swordsman.'

'What are his political views?'

'I haven't heard him speak, but he was at the Bastille when it fell, helped tear down the walls. He keeps one of its keys in his room, says it belonged to Governor Delaunay. He was also involved in the killing of Bertier, the intendant of Paris, at the Place de Grève two days ago.'

'Aha,' said Georges. 'Speak of the devil. Lieutenant Maury. We have our eye on him. But for the time being we're not investigating his role in Bertier's death. We'll focus on Harivel's case. It's less politically charged.'

At this point, a waitress brought the men a pot of coffee. While she poured, Georges described the jealous lieutenant to her. 'Do you recognize him? Was he here last night?'

She hesitated, suspicion growing in her eyes. 'Why do you want to know?'

Georges identified himself and his companions as officers of the Highway Patrol.

Alarmed, she took a step back. He calmed her with a gentle smile and a coin.

'Yes, he often comes here,' she replied in a low voice, glancing over her shoulder. 'I saw him early in the evening with a few comrades from the barracks.'

'Could you hear what they talked about?'

'They were drinking wine and spoke loudly. Everyone could hear them. "People should stand up for their rights," they said, "defend the National Assembly against traitors." And so on.' The waitress described the scene in a disinterested voice, as if she had heard bar-room rhetoric from soldiers before. She moved on to serve another table.

Georges told his companion that he would wait in the tavern for the colonel to join him near noon. Pioche should visit other wine taverns and shops in the village and inquire about suspicious behaviour that might be linked to the murder. He gave him a copy of Michou's sketch of Gaillard. 'The devil's own agent, writes for the duke's faction and organizes their assassinations. Find out if hc was in the village yesterday.' The brigadier studied the sketch, then left the tavern.

While waiting for the colonel, Georges noticed that the waitress was sitting alone at a table with a glass of wine in her hand, momentarily unoccupied. 'Tell me,' he said, sliding into the seat facing her, 'did that brash lieutenant ever quarrel with this man?' Georges described Harivel.

'Yes, indeed, a few days ago. Loudly. About a woman. The men were at the point of drawing their swords when the barman intervened and separated them.'

At noon, Saint-Martin strode into the tavern, his jaw set firmly, his eyes dark and brooding. Georges was taken aback. This wasn't typical of the colonel, usually so self-controlled. The meeting in Lafayette's office had probably gone badly.

Georges gave him a welcoming smile and beckoned him to the table.

'The people's justice indeed!' exclaimed the colonel with pent-up fury. Nearby patrons glanced at him. He ignored them and added, 'Mob rule, if the truth be told.'

'Calm down, sir,' Georges whispered. 'What happened?'

'The marquis refused to pursue the deaths of Foullon and Bertier de Sauvigny. The people, he claimed, have convicted and punished them. Besides, a criminal investigation would stir up a hornet's nest of opposition.'

He took his seat at the table, signalled the waitress for wine, and began to recall the morning's visit to the marquis's office with Lieutenant Faure. He concluded, 'We shall find a way around Lafayette's objections. The men responsible for these atrocities must be convicted and punished.'

The waitress came with the wine. His wrath spent, Saint-Martin asked Georges for a report. The adjutant described his investigation with Brigadier Pioche thus far. 'Wherever we turn, there's Lieutenant Maury, like a bad penny, as the English say.'

Saint-Martin nodded thoughtfully. 'I see a prospect of hope. Your investigation of Harivel's murder might take us back to the Place de Grève and Maury's murder of at least Bertier.'

'Justice would be served for Bertier if Maury hangs at least once,' Georges opined.

'Have you reached a theory yet about the Harivel case?'

Georges nodded tentatively. 'Lieutenant Maury is known to have a hot temper. Harivel is said to have had a romantic interest in Maury's wife. So Maury killed Harivel in a fit of anger. A typical crime of passion.'

'Your theory is plausible. Do you have an alternative?'

'Yes. It's just as likely that the assassin mistook his target. He meant to kill you.'

'Then I shouldn't be surprised to find Maury involved in the case, especially if I were the intended target.' Saint-Martin smiled wryly. 'Remind me to ask the commandant why Harivel intended to visit the barracks so late in the evening. Then we'll speak to Lieutenant Maury.'

The commandant, a colonel, received them with cool courtesy in his office. After brief introductory remarks, Saint-Martin asked his question about Harivel's visit.

The commandant shrugged. 'I have no idea. Perhaps he kept late hours and simply felt the urge for a ride on a warm summer night.' He paused. 'He might also have planned to speak to one of our guards, pick up money from a gambling debt, or leave a message. My adjutant might help you there.'

Saint-Martin and Georges exchanged glances. They would follow up on the commandant's suggestion.

Saint-Martin continued, 'Some of your men were in that tavern close to the scene and near the time of Harivel's violent death. One of them, Lieutenant Maury, had a quarrel with Harivel. Will you allow me to speak to them?'

The commandant cocked his head sceptically. 'I don't see how any of my men could be involved. When I heard of a quarrel, I spoke to Maury. He said that Harivel's attentions had annoyed his wife. She complained to him. He told Harivel clearly and firmly to leave her alone. He obeyed, stopped seeing her. End of the matter. The quarrel was much exaggerated.'

Saint-Martin wasn't satisfied. 'Still, I believe that I should speak to the lieutenant and his comrades about their visit last evening in the tavern and a couple of hours afterwards. They might cast some light on Harivel's murder. This morning, the Marquis de Lafayette urged me to pursue this case aggressively, for it involves the murder of a senior member of the Highway Patrol.'

That reference to the commander of the National Guard worked its magic. The commandant sighed, called in his adjutant, and ordered him to gather the guardsmen and put them at Colonel Saint-Martin's disposal.

A room was found. The guardsmen were to be questioned individually. Georges sat to one side to observe and to take notes. The adjutant was invited to remain in the room.

Lieutenant Maury swaggered in, erect, wearing a well-tailored officer's uniform and a costly sword. He met Saint-Martin's eyes evenly and said with exaggerated respect, 'Good afternoon, Colonel. So we meet again.' He sat down, hands on thighs, head tilted expectantly.

Neither man alluded to the searing, bloody events of two days ago on the Place de Grève. but they lurked in the air like malign spirits. With a few routine questions, Saint-Martin learned that for several years Maury had served in the French Guards and had risen to the rank of sergeant. He claimed that because of his glorious role in the capture of the Bastille, he received a lieutenant's commission in the new National Guard. At present, he served without pay and provided his own uniform and weapons. He didn't live in the barracks but in a cottage nearby with his wife.

The reference to her led Saint-Martin to ask, 'Were you angered that Lieutenant Harivel courted your wife?'

'A little annoyed, I must admit, but not for long. She rebuffed him.'

'Really? I've heard that you and he quarrelled, came close to blows in the tavern.'

'An exaggeration. People enjoy making a mountain out of a molehill. We disliked each other and exchanged a few sharp words. That's all.'

'What did you and your comrades do last night after leaving the tavern?'

'We went to my home to play cards for a few hours. Then my friends left, and my wife and I went to bed. I was off duty.'

'How did you feel when you heard that Lieutenant Harivel had been murdered?'

'I didn't grieve. The man was an ignorant rustic with hardly a copper coin in his pocket, yet he claimed noble descent back to Charlemagne.' Maury spoke with studied nonchalance, but his voice and facial expression betrayed a bitter hatred.

To avoid a useless quarrel Saint-Martin said merely, 'Others have described him as a brave, honourable soldier who served his King well in the Royal Highway Patrol.'

Maury glared at the colonel, then at Georges. Finally, he snarled, 'They have their opinion. I have mine.'

Saint-Martin curtly dismissed the lieutenant. When he had left the room, Saint-Martin turned to the commandant's adjutant. 'Sir, could you suggest a person whom Lieutenant Harivel might have wished to meet briefly late last night?'

'I can't think of anyone in particular.'

'Then I'd like to speak to the soldier on duty at the barracks gate last night. I spoke to him briefly then. His name is Joseph Mouton.'

The adjutant thought for a moment. 'Yes, Joseph Mouton is working in our weapons room today. I'll send him to you.' The adjutant left the room.

While waiting, the colonel asked Georges, 'What do you think of Maury?'

'A potential suspect,' Georges replied. 'He had sufficient motive to kill Harivel. The conflict between the men was more bitter than he has let on. He also had opportunity for the deed. He was near the scene at the time of the murder. His alibi depends on support from his wife and friends, who might have been co-conspirators. We need to talk to his wife when he's not around. Also, his sudden promotion to lieutenant intrigues me. Unbeknown to the Marquis de Lafayette, a powerful, hidden hand was at work securing that commission and providing money for his expenses.'

Saint-Martin nodded agreement. 'That hand could also have guided the lieutenant to the target, whether it was Harivel or me.'

At that point, Joseph Mouton appeared at the door. 'I was told that you wanted to see me, sir.'

'Yes, I've thought of a few more questions since we spoke last night.' Saint-Martin motioned for him to take a seat. He was a sturdy lad, about eighteen years old, and spoke with a strong provincial accent. At first glance, his expression seemed candid, without guile. But his jaw clenched with stress and his eyes studied the two officers shrewdly, apprehensively. He was no fool.

Saint-Martin leaned back, pointed to Georges, who asked evenly, 'Why would Lieutenant Harivel of the Royal Highway Patrol want to meet you last night while you were on duty at the gate?'

The young man's eyes filled with distress. When he tried to reply, he stuttered so badly that Georges stopped him with a gentle gesture. 'Take your time, Joseph. The lieutenant's death must have come as a dreadful shock to you. We realize that you and he were close.' Georges motioned him to a chair. 'Harivel trusted you and put you to work for him. So tell us why he wanted to meet you last night.'

'We arranged that he would come once a week while I was on duty at the gate. I would give him a report and he would give me a task to do.'

'What did you think when he didn't appear last night?'

'At first I thought he had been called elsewhere unexpectedly.' He addressed Colonel Saint-Martin. 'But you told me that he had been killed. I was devastated.' The young man began to breathe heavily, started rocking back and forth. Georges waited quietly, his head inclined at a kindly, encouraging angle.

Finally, Mouton said, 'Lieutenant Harivel was like a father to me, kind and helpful. He wanted me to observe Lieutenant Maury and his friends, keep track of their comings and goings. Harivel said that they were dangerous men, had killed the intendant of Paris. They even threatened the King and Queen.'

'So you spied on Maury and reported to Harivel when you met, is that right?'

Mouton nodded.

'We know that he and Maury's wife were friends. Did you carry messages between them?'

'Yes, I felt sorry for her. Maury was cruel. He beat her. She would sneak away to meet Harivel in a nearby cottage. He was trying to help her. I would keep watch and warn them if anyone were to approach.'

Georges turned to his superior. 'I have no more questions, sir.'

'Nor do I,' said Saint-Martin. He addressed the young soldier. 'You've been very helpful, Joseph. We'll hold your comments in strict confidence.'

Georges showed the young man to the door. 'By the way, what is Lieutenant Maury's duty for today?'

'He's serving in the barracks until evening.' The young soldier saluted and left the room.

The other guardsmen, two non-commissioned officers identified by the barmaid, gave testimony consistent with Maury's and supported his alibi. Their background was similar to his: as French Guards they were involved in the attack on the Bastille. They joined the National Guard and were rapidly promoted.

When the last of them left the room, Saint-Martin leaned back and asked, 'Could Lieutenant Maury have suspected Harivel of investigating the assassinations on the Place de Grève, perceived him as a threat, caught on to his routine, and intercepted him?'

'Quite likely,' Georges replied.

'Then we shall pick up where Harivel left off. Since the lieutenant will be on duty in the barracks until evening, we shall visit his wife now.'

Sixteen

The Strongbox

Chaillot, Friday, 24 July

The cottage that Madame Maury shared with the lieutenant was halfway up the Chaillot hill that overlooked the river. Saint-Martin and his adjutant passed through a gate into a tiny front garden. While Georges stood back a few paces and watched the windows, the colonel knocked on the door. There was no answer. The colonel knocked again in vain.

'Sir,' Georges murmured, 'someone is inside, standing by a front window. She pulled the curtain aside to peek out.'

Saint-Martin addressed the window. 'Madame, we are the police. Open the door. We must talk to you.'

The curtain moved again. Then, seconds later, the door opened a crack, and Saint-Martin identified himself and Georges.

Like a woman at her wit's end, she fumbled with the latch. Finally, she opened the door. Her eyes were red, her cheeks creased and wet from weeping. The expression on her face was akin to terror. The men bowed politely, spoke gently, motioned her to a table, and they sat down.

Saint-Martin began the questioning. Yes, a few hours ago, while shopping for dinner, she had heard of Harivel's death. 'It was terrible.' That was all she could say. She stared at the floor, trembling, sobbing.

While waiting for her to gain control of herself, Saint-Martin surveyed her home. It consisted of a large single room with a cooking hearth at one end, a sleeping alcove in one wall, a large armoire against another. The table and a few chairs stood in the middle of the room. A sabre, a musket, and a pair of expensive duelling pistols hung over the mantel.

The windows were glazed, the walls neatly plastered, the floor tiled. That the room was also neat and clean was virtually the only sign of a woman's presence.

When she calmed down, Saint-Martin asked what she had done the night of Harivel's death.

'I was here all the time. After supper I knitted until about ten o'clock. My husband came home with friends. They played cards. I served them tea and biscuits. At midnight the friends left. My husband and I went to bed.'

Saint-Martin and Georges exchanged glances. The woman had spoken in a monotone by rote, as if she didn't expect the officers to believe her. The colonel studied her more closely. An attractive, shapely, well-groomed young woman, she had powdered her face but failed to conceal a swelling of her jaw. She moved painfully.

Another series of questions revealed that she was nineteen years old, eleven years younger than her husband. She had come to Paris from Chartres a few years earlier when her parents died. A married brother inherited the family property and had no use for her. In Paris she found work as a lady's maid until she met the lieutenant, then a sergeant in the French Guards. They had married a year ago.

She offered her visitors tea, but they politely declined, saying that they might return if they had more questions. At the door the colonel stopped, pulled Michou's sketch of Gaillard out of his portfolio, and showed it to the woman. 'Have you ever seen this man?'

She took the sketch in her hand and began to study it. At first her expression was merely curious. Suddenly it registered the shock of recognition, followed by confusion. Finally, she shook her head. 'No, I've never seen him.' Again she spoke with utter lack of conviction.

Saint-Martin smiled kindly, spoke softly. 'Was he here yesterday evening at about ten o'clock?'

She stiffened, lowered her eyes, nodded slightly.

'How long did he and the other men stay in the cottage?'

She lifted her hands to her face and mumbled through a torrent of tears, 'I can't tell you. He would kill me.'

'We'll leave you now. When you're willing to talk, you can contact us at the Passy Highway Patrol post.'

Outside the cottage, Saint-Martin said to Georges, 'So

Gaillard took part in planning the murder, but we don't know yet who his target was – me or Harivel.'

'Or if he pulled the trigger,' added Georges.

Saint-Martin and Georges walked up the lane from Maury's cottage to the top of the hill. Below them, the village stretched along the River Seine. Boats, large and small, scurried over the silvery surface like water bugs on a pond. On the opposite bank lay the vast field of the Champ de Mars and the gardens and buildings of the Royal Military Academy.

There was silence for a long moment while the colonel contemplated the academy. He had spent several of the unhappiest years of his life there, suffering from the taunts of bullies, distaste for the military curriculum, and homesickness. Finally, he drew a deep breath, turned to his adjutant, and commented, 'We seem to find Monsieur Gaillard wherever there's serious mischief.' Then his thoughts took another direction. 'What do you think of Madame Maury, Georges, aside from her languid blue eyes, clear skin, and gentle, yielding nature?'

'For a start, she has become virtually Maury's slave, completely cowed. He beats her, denies her money to spend on herself.'

Saint-Martin nodded. 'She's an educated woman, speaks good French, and almost certainly reads and writes.'

'But there were no books or writing materials in sight,' Georges remarked.

'True. And that's because he doesn't allow them. He may resent the fact that she's clearly from a social class superior to his.'

'I'd like to know what she really thinks of Harivel. Were those tears for him? He might have offered welcome relief from her brute of a husband.'

'Hmm, "husband" you say. I didn't notice a ring on his finger, though she had one. We should visit the parish priest. He might have useful information for us.'

They found the priest in his church and introduced themselves. He obligingly brought them into the sacristy and they took seats at a table. He opened the parish register. Maury's marriage was not recorded.

'Could they have been married elsewhere?' asked Saint-Martin.

'I don't think so,' replied the priest. 'She was unmarried when she arrived in our village three years ago and was inscribed in this parish. Subsequently, she could not be married anywhere else without the banns being published here. A braggart, like many of his kind, Maury comes from Gascony. I assume that he was baptized there. But to judge from what I've heard, he hasn't seen the inside of a church in many years.'

'So they are simply living together.'

'That's correct, Colonel, though she pretends that she's his wife. Probably raised in a strict religious family. She used to come to church frequently. He didn't seem to mind.' The priest paused, closed the register, and added, 'Then she seemed content enough with him. But recently he has changed, become angry, curses the clergy and aristocrats. I hear from people in the village that he's sometimes violent and abuses her. As a lieutenant in the National Guard, his fist reaches far. She's apparently afraid to leave him.'

'Then she'll be very reluctant to say anything to us that might displease him.' Saint-Martin thanked the priest and rose to leave. At the door, he pulled Michou's sketch of Gaillard from his portfolio. 'Have you seen this man?'

'Why, yes. I see him occasionally. Late yesterday morning as I was strolling along the river, he disembarked from a boat and walked to the barracks.'

Outside the church, the two officers sat down on a bench shaded from the mid-afternoon sun. Saint-Martin reflected on the priest's remarks while they were fresh in his mind. He turned to his adjutant. 'A spy in the mayor's office at the City Hall could have told Gaillard of my forthcoming evening visit to Bailly's home in Chaillot. Sensing an opportunity to kill me, he might have ordered an accomplice to follow me, while he took the boat here.'

Georges nodded, adding, 'From the time that Gaillard arrived in Chaillot, he had ten hours to pick the site for the murder, whether Harivel's or yours.'

'He could predict my movements – I was likely to return to Paris by the river road late at night – but could he know that Harivel would stop at the mayor's house and then ride towards the barracks?'

Georges' brow knotted with the effort to figure out a plausible answer. 'He couldn't predict that Harivel's horse would go lame at just that time and place. It looks like he was aiming at you.'

Saint-Martin smiled wryly. 'A sobering thought, and probably true. Well, let's talk to Madame Harivel now.'

Later in the afternoon, they visited Harivel's widow in Passy. Her home was a modest but elegant stone building of a recent simple classical design, consisting of a central two-storey block and two perpendicular wings. A liveried servant showed them into an anteroom in the present King's style.

Saint-Martin had met her on previous visits to the Passy patrol post. Now, while waiting, he described her to Georges. 'She comes from a wealthy merchant's family, born and raised in the village. Her domestic staff includes a personal maid, a cook and a pair of kitchen maids, a gardener and a groom. She's a cultivated woman: speaks several languages, sketches and paints, plays the pianoforte, and has travelled widely in her younger years. Now arthritis confines her chiefly to the village of Passy and her own home. She is frequently invited to the Princesse de Lamballe's nearby summer villa.'

'A remarkable woman!' Georges exclaimed. 'By what lapse of good sense did she marry Jacques le Harivel du Rocher, a poor, half-educated provincial aristocrat from Grenoble?'

'He was a diamond in the rough, handsome, a splendid figure of a man in his blue trooper's uniform, and charming as well. He had a glint in his eye for her, as for many other pretty women.'

'I see the picture,' Georges said. 'Harivel wanted her money and good looks; she wanted his noble title, his swagger, his attention.'

'Close to the mark, Georges. But they soon tired of each other. He moved into a wing of the house by himself, and they went their separate but amicable ways. While her health lasted, she entertained men and women of her own liking. Harivel threw himself into his work in the Royal Highway Patrol and devoted his leisure to good wine and loose women.

'When she became incapacitated, he attended to her, not

as a wife but as a friend, offered her sympathy with flowers and candied fruit, sought her advice concerning the prominent people he sometimes had to deal with.'

The servant reappeared and led them into the study, a small gem of good taste. Shelves of gold-embossed books reached to a ceiling painting of famous poets and philosophers of antiquity.

She sat at a brown mahogany tea table and invited the visitors to join her. They exchanged greetings. The colonel introduced Georges. A servant came with a tea service, poured, then withdrew.

'Early this morning,' Madame Harivel began, 'I was informed of my husband's death. I didn't care to view his body, a disagreeable sight. I want my lasting impressions of him to be at his charming best. We were never close or deeply affectionate. But I wasn't indifferent towards him, and in fact regret his passing, especially in its violence. I sincerely hope that his killer will be captured and severely punished. I assume that your visit has to do with investigating Harivel's death.' She paused, glanced from one man to the other. 'How can I help you, gentlemen?'

'Madame, we appreciate your cooperation,' Saint-Martin replied. 'Please tell us about your husband's affairs, especially those that might have been risky or dangerous.'

'You have probably heard that he was courting another man's wife. That *could* be dangerous, since the husband is Lieutenant Maury, a jealous man, given to violence. My husband confided to me that his interest in Madame Maury was professional, not romantic. He was hoping to get vital information from her concerning the lieutenant's nefarious activities.'

'Did he give you any hint as to the nature of that information?'

'No. He was pursuing a suspicion on his own. It was still too early to talk about it with me or with his men.'

'We know that he had a spy at the barracks who gave him access to Madame Maury. Did your husband speak about him?'

She smiled wryly. 'Joseph Mouton is his natural son, unacknowledged legally. Harivel told me about him only recently. I've met him on a few occasions. The young man was born on the family estate near Grenoble to a domestic maid. She raised him with my husband's support until age eighteen. My husband brought him to Paris and placed him first in the French Guards, then in the new National Guard.'

'How does the young man feel towards his father?'

'He seems fond of him, admires him. A spirited young man, he's wise beyond his years, clever as well. I haven't seen him recently, but I'm sure that he's distraught. I would expect him to attempt to avenge his father's murder.'

In a short while their conversation drifted away from the crime to Harivel's properties and his remains.

'I shall arrange for his burial. He made me the executrix of his will. His possessions are held in trust until his son is twenty-five.' She paused. 'I do have a question for you, Colonel. As his superior officer and an honourable man, would you examine the personal papers that he kept in a strongbox in his study? He told me a few days ago that they pertained to confidential police business. If anything happened to him, he wanted you to see them.'

Harivel's study lacked the elegant decoration of his wife's. It was dominated by a large writing table, covered with file boxes and loose papers. Maps, charts, and mounted weapons covered most of the walls. Two servants carried Madame Harivel into the room. She caught Georges' eye and pointed to a section of bookshelves.

'I've heard of your talents, Monsieur Charpentier. The strongbox is behind those shelves.'

Georges found a simple latch and pulled open the shelves to reveal a small closet. The box, mounted on casters, occupied most of the space and was locked. He rolled it up to the writing table and asked her for the key.

'I'm sorry, Harivel neglected to give me one. He may have expected you to wave a magic wand over the box.'

Georges bowed for the compliment, took out his tools, and in a few minutes opened the box. He and Saint-Martin began to examine its contents. Most noteworthy were a diary and a file box labelled 'Maury'.

Madame Harivel excused herself and was carried from the room. Saint-Martin and Georges set to work first on Harivel's diary. Saint-Martin learned that already as a French Guard, Maury had attracted Harivel's attention. The man was an unusually clever, capable soldier, but untrustworthy and more involved in gambling, politics, and the Masonic Order than seemed healthy.

Harivel had searched Maury's background. What he found seemed murky and aroused suspicion. Back in Gascony, several years earlier, Maury killed a man in a quarrel over a gambling debt. He escaped justice by pleading self-defence. Members of the victim's family contested the verdict and vowed revenge. Maury fled to Paris, where he continued to be involved in violent disputes over gambling.

Georges took a packet of notes from the file box, scanned them, and showed them to his superior. 'Colonel, these come from Maury's wife. Check this one, the last.' He handed the note to Saint-Martin.

> *July 22. My dear Harivel, my husband has just returned from the Place de Grève, his clothes covered with blood, a wild look on his face. Too much wine had loosened his tongue and rattled his wits. He shook a handful of gold coins before my eyes. 'My reward for butchering the Intendant of Paris,' he shouted. I don't want to know what he meant, but I'll pass this information on to Joseph. You will know what to do with it. Yours, M.*

Saint-Martin laid down the diary and studied the note. 'Joseph must have given it to his father that evening. Now we know that Harivel was secretly trying to convict Maury of Bertier's murder. This note is a major piece of evidence.'

Georges added, 'To judge from the bruises we saw on Madame Maury, Lieutenant Maury regretted his confession and beat her into silence.'

Saint-Martin picked up the diary again and resumed reading. There were many references to Maury's habit of gambling and his frequent need of money. His Masonic brothers usually were the ones who paid his debts. More often than not, it was Gaillard who passed him the money. It was also Gaillard who arranged for Maury and his men to escort the intendant Bertier supposedly to the Abbaye prison but instead to the Place de Grève.

In his last entry, Harivel asked himself what he should do with this information, but he recorded no answer. Saint-Martin passed the diary to Georges.

When he finished, he frowned, then simply repeated Harivel's question.

'When the time is right, Georges, we'll show it to the Marquis de Lafayette.'

Upon his return that evening from Passy, Paul found Anne waiting in his office. Monsieur Roland, the young lawyer turned magistrate, had promised to come shortly. Anne informed Paul concerning the baker's murder. 'Here's Cécile Tremblay's signed statement of her witness to the incident.' She handed the document to Paul. He had listened attentively.

Now he studied the statement and nodded with approval. He slipped it into a file box. 'Well done, Anne. This should help us build a case against Gaillard that will force Bailly and Lafayette to act. In the present chaotic circumstances, they are paralyzed by fear.'

'Is it so bad?' Anne asked.

'This morning, Lafayette told me that there'll be no investigation into the deaths of Foullon and Bertier. "The people have spoken," he declared. But he encouraged me to pursue the killers of Harivel.'

He glanced at the clock on the wall. 'If Gaillard were to learn that lawyer Roland was coming here this evening, he would take steps to prevent him. Have we perhaps compromised him?'

Anne replied in an apologetic tone. 'I thought of telling him to enter by the rear door, but I feared that I might offend him.'

The lawyer arrived on time, his manner apprehensive. He was apparently becoming aware of certain risks involved in this visit to Colonel Paul de Saint-Martin, a high-ranking officer of the old regime and related to that former agent of despotism, the exiled Baron de Breteuil.

Roland explained that he was elected a magistrate and accepted in a moment of enthusiasm for reform of the old system. True, dangerous factions were forming; respect for law was breaking down. But he was confident that Mayor Bailly and the Marquis de Lafayette would soon restore order. A rational, humane legal system could then rise out of the present shambles.

Concerning Madame Gagne, the lawyer explained that the prosecutor and Lieutenant Maury wanted to arrest her, but they hesitated to storm the institute. The abbé had many powerful friends in the present government, including Mayor Bailly and the Marquis de Lafayette. So she was probably safe there for the time being.

'What can be done to prevent the burning of Monsieur Gagne's body?' Anne asked.

'How much does that matter?' the lawyer asked. 'True, it's a barbaric, even absurd punishment. But, really, who is seriously harmed by it?'

'His wife is devastated,' Anne replied with heat. 'The insult to her beloved husband hurts her grievously.'

Roland flinched at Anne's rebuke, then reflected for a moment. 'Since a date hasn't been set, you may have several days to persuade the court to reverse its decision.' He met Saint-Martin's gaze. 'Or, you might even discover that the so-called people were misled when they passed judgement on the baker. In that case, the question of punishing his body would become moot. In the meantime, his body lies packed in ice in sailcloth in an old wine cellar beneath our police bureau.'

Paul felt heartened. The lawyer was casting doubt on the official investigation, as well as on the work of his own court.

'Colonel,' the lawyer added, 'what I've told you must remain within these walls. Otherwise I'll shortly be a dead man, or be obliged to deny everything I told you.'

Paul promised discretion on behalf of himself and Anne. In bidding the lawyer good night, Paul added, 'I hope that you'll move your fellow magistrates towards reason and sanity.'

Seventeen
Through Children's Eyes

Paris, Saturday, 25 July

Shortly after dawn, a gloomy grey mist hung over the city like a shroud. Men and women hurried to work, eyes cast down to the wet, slippery paving stones. With growing curiosity, Anne Cartier walked to the Gagne bakery on Rue Sainte-Anne. She wanted to examine the spot where the baker died. What was it like a day later? Had anything changed?

She sorely missed the advice and support of her male companions. Paul would again talk to the Marquis de Lafayette at the City Hall, and Georges would return to Chaillot, meet Brigadier Pioche, and continue their investigation of Harivel du Rocher's murder.

As she drew near, she met the strong scent of freshly baked bread. Against her will, her gaze shifted to the lamppost on the corner. She imagined the baker Louis Gagne hanging there, early on the preceding day, the excited mob mocking him and showing its contempt with obscene gestures.

She stood next to the lamppost, out of the path of the bakery's customers. They seemed to come and go more quickly than usual, with furtive glances to left and right. No casual conversations or friendly greetings. There was a distinct odour of fear in the air.

Anne pondered the mystery of Gagne's brutal death. Yesterday, Cécile Tremblay, eyewitness to the incident from across the street, had persuaded Anne that the baker and his wife had been falsely accused of profiteering and that he had been wrongfully killed by Gaillard and his henchmen. But how had they implicated Gagne? In what way, if any, was Duby involved?

Searching her mind for the answers, Anne inadvertently glanced up at the lamppost again. If she failed, the baker's widow would suffer the loss of her reputation and property and would remain a fugitive, an outlaw, in mortal danger.

'What's so fascinating about the lamppost, Madame?' A National Guardsman had approached her from behind. His expression was unfriendly, his tone threatening. The local authorities apparently felt that partisans of the Gagne family might protest the baker's assassination and seek to overturn the new arrangement in the bakery. Perhaps Duby requested police protection.

Provoked, Anne retorted, 'You must know, sir, that an innocent man was hung here yesterday.'

'Really?' he sneered. 'Gagne was an enemy of the people and deserved to die. Now move on before I lose my temper.' He pointed to the lamppost. 'I have half a mind to hang you up there, too. I hate impudent women!'

Anne glared at the guardsman, but choked back another retort. She left the bakery and made her way to the institute for the deaf. Gagne's missing son and the maid might have contacted one or more of their teachers or friends and indicated where they were hiding.

Mademoiselle Arnaud was at breakfast in her room. Anne joined her for coffee. Françoise had asked students to search for the missing young persons. Thus far, she had received no information about the boy. But one of the students had discovered the maid working in disguise in a millinery shop on Rue Richelieu.

As Françoise gave the address to Anne, she warned, 'You must take care.' She led Anne to a window overlooking the street. 'A spy is hiding in the ground floor of the building across from us. He has two or three associates. Yesterday, to test them, I went out wearing Madame Gagne's clothes. Instantly, the spy alerted one of his associates to follow me. He must also have contacted the police, but I returned to the institute just before they arrived.'

Anne took a sip of her coffee. 'I'll find a way to evade the spy and his men. They would terrorize the young maid.'

'They don't follow our students. Change clothes with one of them your size.'

*   *   *

In one student's gown and another's bonnet, Anne left the institute still apprehensive. Within a short distance she felt reassured that no one was following her. The millinery shop on Rue Richelieu had not yet opened for customers, but someone was moving about inside. Anne glanced over her shoulder. Still no spy. So she rapped on the door. It opened a crack. A frowning face appeared.

'Let me in,' Anne whispered. 'I have an important mission here.' She showed her the abbé's letter of recommendation.

The door swung open. 'I know the abbé. Quick, come in,' said the woman, a doubtful expression on her face. 'I'm not ready to meet the public.'

Anne slipped into the shop, explaining that she needed to question the young maid about her master's death.

The milliner shook her head. 'The girl is frightened, as well as deaf. How can you expect to learn anything from her?'

'I can sign and will treat her gently.' Anne offered her kindest smile.

The woman hesitated, searched Anne's face, then gave her a quick nod. 'I'm Madame Desrosier, the girl's aunt and the proprietor of this shop. When she first came to me, she was overwrought and couldn't explain what had happened. I put her to work in the shop. When I heard of Monsieur Gagne's death, I moved her out of sight of those who would harm her. Follow me.'

The maid was sitting at a table next to a rear window overlooking an interior courtyard. In front of her stood large wicker baskets of clothing. She was alone, head bent forward, sewing a patch on a pair of breeches. As Anne and Madame Desrosier neared her, she looked up, startled, apparently lost in her own thoughts. Suddenly, fear flashed across her face until she recognized her aunt and relaxed.

Anne had brought along sweetmeats, Madame Desrosier carried a pot of hot chocolate, plates and cups. The maid smiled with delight. Madame Desrosier presented Anne, and left. Anne signed a greeting, then she and the maid turned to the treats. After Anne had poured the chocolate, she signed to the maid that the Abbé de l'Épée was concerned about her, wished her well. 'Is there anything that we can do for you?'

'Tell me, is Madame Gagne still alive? Did she escape from the mob?'

Anne replied that she was hiding in the institute, accused of profiteering. 'We must discover the truth in order to save her. Can you tell me what really happened that morning in the bakery?'

The maid's brow creased with an effort to recall. She drank slowly from her cup, ate a candied apricot. Her eyes started to water as if she were going to weep. Finally, she calmed herself and began to sign.

'My bed was in an alcove in the rear of the bakery. In the middle of the night, I had to get up to relieve myself. I noticed shadows on the wall, coming from a lantern's light. Two men were moving several large sacks of flour into a storeroom for pots and pans, cloths, cleaning equipment. They piled up the sacks, then covered them with canvas, as if to hide them. That seemed strange. We had already received our shipment of flour for the day and we never put flour in that room.'

'Did you recognize the men?'

'I've seen them only once before and I don't know their names. One was tall and thin, the other was short and fat and had a flat, broken nose. They came to the bakery the day before yesterday and talked with the journeyman.'

Anne felt her heart begin to pound. According to Cécile Tremblay, those were Simon and Nicolas, the same men from the duke's palace who had hung the baker from the lamppost.

The maid went on to sign that she had hidden herself until the men left, then went back to bed. Shortly after dawn, she was cleaning utensils in the bakeroom. The journeyman was preparing a new batch of dough. Monsieur Gagne had just removed loaves of fresh-baked bread from the oven. A band of men armed with swords and pikes broke into the room, screaming. She fled into a dark corner, and they paid no attention to her. Some of the men roughly seized the baker and dragged him outside. The others went directly to the storeroom and 'discovered' the hidden sacks of flour.

'What happened to the journeyman?'

'Nothing. He continued to knead the dough. The men appeared to ignore him, though I noticed that the last one to leave patted him on the back. He seemed not to notice, kept kneading the dough. When everyone was gone, he sneaked up the back stairs to the baker's apartment. He wasn't gone long. As I left my hiding place in the corner, he came down the stairs and noticed me, tried to question me.

'But he couldn't sign more than a few words relating to baking. I didn't trust him, so I pretended not to understand what had happened. He slapped me hard, put his knife at my throat, and warned that he would kill me if I ever caused him trouble. Then he grabbed me by the arm and dragged me out of the shop. The mob threatened me too. Still, I managed to run away to my aunt's shop here.'

At this point, the maid seemed exhausted. Anne poured more chocolate and turned the conversation to sewing and other lighter matters. Finally, she questioned her about the baker's son and got a description. He was deaf like his mother but could read and write much better and was handsome.

'Did he have any friends or relatives to whom he could go?' Anne asked.

The maid thought for a moment, then shook her head. She signed that she didn't know the boy well enough. When the hanging occurred, he had been out in the neighbourhood delivering bread. 'I don't know where he might be.'

But a minute later, as they finished the sweetmeats and chocolate, the maid signed to Anne, 'I remember now. The boy used to mention a deaf acquaintance in another bakery to the north of the Palais-Royal.'

It was early afternoon before Anne found where the boy was hiding. At the bakery on Rue Saint-Marc near the Boulevard, the baker responded to her query with a suspicious look until she showed him the abbé's letter. The baker's wife overheard the conversation and objected. 'The boy will be our ruin, draw down on us the wrath of the mob who killed his father.'

'We can't just throw him out,' said the baker, exasperated. 'He'll be gone in a day or two. Go about your business.'

The wife threw up her hands in disgust and left, muttering to herself.

He turned to Anne and pointed the way. 'The boy's in the back room.'

The room served as an office. Pen in hand, the boy sat at a table, writing a message for the baker. He glanced at Anne with wary, intelligent eyes. She explained her mission. The abbé's letter lessened any suspicions that he might have had. He smiled and asked her to take a seat. Fair-haired and tall, he appeared remarkably mature for his thirteen years. He signed fluently.

'How is my mother?' was the first thing he asked.

Anne assured him that she was safe for the moment. But it was vital to clear her reputation as soon as possible. 'Tell me what you know about the death of your father.'

He lowered his eyes, rubbed his thighs, breathed deeply. 'I was in the café across the street, watching from the window when they killed him. I feared that they might come for me, so I fled out the back door and came here.'

'Did you notice anything strange going on in the bakery before the mob arrived?'

'Just before I left to deliver bread to our customers, I went to the room on the first floor where we kept our records. I help my mother manage the accounts. I wanted to check the list for the number of loaves that each customer had ordered. The journeyman came out of the room just as I was about to enter.'

'Were you surprised to see him?'

'Yes. He had no business there, alone, early in the morning. He frowned, seemed unhappy to see me, didn't offer any explanation. On the writing table inside the room, I chanced upon receipts from persons that I didn't recognize. I was in a hurry, so I decided to ask my father about them when I finished my deliveries.'

Anne pulled Michou's sketch of Gaillard from her bag. 'Do you recognize this man?' She handed the sketch to the boy.

He studied it and nodded. 'He was at a table in the café with two other men shortly before the trouble began.'

'That was Monsieur Gaillard, a dangerous man. Was one of his companions short and fat with a smashed nose, and the other tall and thin with a cropped ear?'

'Yes, Monsieur Gaillard gave each of them some money – under the table.'

Anne hesitated, studied the boy's face, then decided it was best to tell him. 'That was blood money. Those two men are the villains who actually hung your father.'

'Yes, I know. While I was looking at the scene from the window, I recognized them.' He signed slowly, carefully. 'And I hope one day to see them hanged.'

'Do you feel safe here?'

He shrugged. 'The baker's wife wants me to leave. So I'll change my name and look for another job tomorrow. Meanwhile, tell my mother that I'm safe and that I hope to see her soon.'

'Before I leave,' signed Anne, 'tell me about those mysterious receipts. They were probably planted among the bakery's business papers in order to incriminate your father. In whose hand are the bakery's genuine papers written?'

'For more than a year, I have written all but the briefest. My father and mother write poorly.'

Anne thought for a moment, then signed, 'Give me the names of persons to whom you or your parents have recently written. I'll try to collect samples of your handwriting to compare with the incriminating receipts. I also need samples of Gaillard's handwriting as well as the journeyman's. An acquaintance of mine at Versailles, Comte Savarin, might be able to prove that the receipts are forgeries.'

The boy wrote down a list of names and gave it to Anne. 'If you could sneak into our office files, you might find messages between my father and the journeyman concerning their contract, messages written or at least signed by themselves. Their signatures are also on the contract. Signed copies are in the files of the Bakers' Guild.'

Anne thanked the boy for his suggestion, urged him to be cautious and to continue to hope. As they parted, they both struggled to hold back tears.

Out on the street, Anne tried to think how she might get past the baker Duby and sneak into the office. She couldn't come up with a plan. In her imagination, he always caught her.

Eighteen
An Encouraging Proposal

Paris, Saturday, 25 July

After leaving the boy, Anne was about to go out into the street when she felt a stab of caution. Though she was still in disguise, one of Gaillard's spies might nonetheless recognize her and suspect that she was visiting Gagne's boy. She must not risk giving away his hiding place.

She edged back into the bakery's shadowed doorway and peered at the busy, passing scene before her. Since coming to Paris and working with Georges and Paul, she had gradually learned how to discern persons intent on crime or serious mischief, even in a crowded street: hooded, shifty eyes, bodies poised to act for no apparent or legitimate reason. Of course she couldn't always be certain. But now she detected no danger.

As she made her way towards the police bureau near the Louvre, she focused her mind on Gagne's incriminating receipts for the purchase of flour. Where would they be? Cécile Tremblay had seen National Guardsmen carrying boxes of files out of the bakery. Most likely they were now kept somewhere in the police bureau. Anne timed her arrival there to coincide with the end of the day's session. Somehow, she would arrange to meet the sympathetic magistrate Pierre Roland.

Hindered by rain showers, she arrived just in time. The magistrates were dispatching business quickly, their eyes on the clock on the opposite wall. With a discreet wink, Roland acknowledged her sitting in the back of the room.

When the session ended, they crossed paths and she slipped a note to him proposing to meet again at the provost's residence as soon as possible. He should come in disguise to the rear door into the garden.

He stepped aside and covertly read the note. Anne lingered at the door. He opened it for her, leaned towards her. 'I'll come to you shortly,' he murmured, and added with a thin smile, 'The rear door suits me perfectly.'

Anne found her husband in the garden. He had gathered a small bouquet of yellow roses for her. The afternoon's brief episode of rain had ceased but had left beads of moisture on the velvet-like petals. He had chosen her favourite colour and, as was his custom, had cut away the thorns from the stems. His thoughtfulness touched her; she embraced him warmly.

She arranged the flowers in a vase and set it on the garden table where she and Paul often escaped in the summer from the city's stench, noise, and congestion. While preparing the vase, she related to him the information she had gathered from the baker's maid and from his son, eye-witnesses to major aspects of his murder.

'I'm encouraged,' said Paul. 'The pieces of the puzzle are coming together. We may soon have a case to put before our frightened leaders, strong enough to force them to do justice.' His brow furrowed as he paused to reflect. 'I see reason for concern, however. Our enemy, Gaillard, will surely attempt to block this investigation. The more success we have, the more desperate he will become, and the harder he will strike.'

Soon Roland arrived, having taken the precaution of wearing a plain brown woollen suit and a wig. They sat together at the table with a jug of cool cider, far from any prying ears. Anne repeated her conversations with baker Gagne's maid and his son.

She added, 'They support the testimony of another eye-witness, Cécile Tremblay, in the café across the street from the bakery.'

Roland listened attentively. At her conclusion, he remarked, 'I am now convinced that the initial investigation of the incident was hasty and superficial, excessively influenced by pressure from the mob.'

'What can be done?' Paul asked with a hopeful lift of his voice.

'I could persuade my colleagues to allow me to look at the

case again with an eye to strengthening the grounds for our verdict. Even now, indifferent to the merits of the case, they realize that the mayor will examine our work before it goes to the city council for review. Any neglect or careless reading of the evidence, any failure to interrogate potentially serious witnesses, would reflect badly on us, the magistrates.'

He met Anne's eye. 'Do you think that I could question Madame Gagne at the institute? You would be present to translate for me and to reassure the woman that I wouldn't harm her.'

Anne nodded. 'You should come disguised as you are tonight. A spy watches the institute from across the street. We don't know for sure to whom he reports, possibly to Monsieur Gaillard, a very dangerous man, a suspect in several serious crimes.'

Roland raised a concerned eyebrow. 'I'll watch my back. He and I have shared a table occasionally in cafés in the Palais-Royal. A forceful speaker, an angry man, a bitter critic of the royal government and its servants, favourites, and hangers-on. Works for the Duc d'Orléans, I'm told.'

Paul agreed in general terms with Roland's perception of Gaillard. 'His campaign of violence and intimidation is most likely directed by Choderlos de Laclos, the duke's secretary, a master of intrigue. The duke himself has no stomach for the brutal details of this reign of terror. But he doesn't object since it's being carried on to advance his cause.'

Roland finished his cider and remarked. 'You both have been very helpful.' He prepared to leave.

As an afterthought, Anne suggested to him, 'Would you like to question the baker's maid and his son, and Madame Tremblay? I could try to arrange a safe time and place.'

'If possible, yes.' He settled back in his chair.

'There's more,' Anne continued. 'The handwriting of the incriminating receipts also deserves careful study.'

Paul added, 'It's possible that Monsieur Gaillard's scribe wrote the messages, but more likely that Gaillard would do it himself.'

Roland shook his head. 'I'm ashamed for my court that such a study has not been attempted, or even suggested. We deplore the arbitrary ways of the old system. But in the new system we have little sense of how to administer justice fairly and competently. In our defence, I have to point out that we were elected and the court established hardly a week ago, almost from scratch. Our facilities and our procedures are still primitive. Among other deficiencies, we lack the skill for an expert handwriting analysis. But I do have access to the baker's papers.'

'I know a man at the palace in Versailles who can read them,' suggested Paul. 'Comte Savarin, who unravels difficult coded messages for the Foreign Office. Part of his work involves handwriting. I've used him before.'

'Then come to the court first thing tomorrow morning, Colonel. Because it's Sunday, the building will be empty and locked. I have a key. The baker's papers are lying unguarded in a clearly labelled box on the basement floor. We haven't even begun to store evidence properly. I'll give the papers to you, and you can pass them on to the count. Hopefully he will work on them quickly. They won't be missed until the case moves to a higher level.'

Roland outlined the other steps that he wanted to take. He would not only secure the receipts but also samples of handwriting from the baker's business associates. He would find a pretext for examining the contract and any correspondence between the baker and his journeyman. He could allege the need to determine the legal basis for any eventual transfer of property from the baker to the journeyman.

Roland concluded, 'I must also find out from whom the flour is said to have come.'

'This is very promising!' Anne exclaimed. Roland's measures should bring about a revision of the verdict against the baker Gagne and also the return of his property to his widow. The abbé would be pleased.

Cautious as usual, Paul's reaction was more restrained. 'Again let me warn you,' he said, as they rose from the table. 'Watch out for Gaillard. He has money to spare, operates frequently undercover, and is clever and ruthless. He surely knows that we are trying to upset his plans. We can expect to hear from him soon.'

Nineteen

Great Fear in the Country

Château Beaumont, Sunday–Monday, 26–27 July

At breakfast in the garden room of the provost's residence, Anne gazed out the window. A light rain fell gently on the rose bushes. Their blossoms bent low under the water's weight. The city's usual raucous sounds were muted, even more than usual on a Sunday. Anne savoured this peaceful moment.

Georges came to the door. 'May I disturb you, Madame? I saw you sitting there. Thought I'd catch up on the news.'

'Please join us. The colonel has just been called to the office. When he comes back shortly, we'll have coffee together. While we wait, I'll tell you about last night's meeting with Roland the local magistrate.' She went on to describe Roland's plans to revive the Gagne investigation. She concluded with a sense of satisfaction, 'We've proved to Roland that the initial investigation was seriously flawed.'

'Sounds encouraging. You've accomplished more than I did yesterday in Chaillot. Brigadier Pioche and I searched all the village shops and taverns in vain for clues to Harivel's death. He and I will continue tomorrow, perhaps with greater luck. He has his eye on a few suspicious houses in the countryside where the killers might have hidden.'

The colonel entered the room, waved to Georges, and took a seat at the table. 'You can pour the coffee now, Anne. I'm sorry but there's been a change of plans. A message came from Aunt Marie. I won't be meeting Monsieur Roland this morning.'

'What's happened?' Anne passed him a cup of coffee, then served Georges and herself.

'Marie sent a servant to report that trouble is brewing at Château Beaumont. She asked if I could come immediately. Bandits are threatening her estate and mine. She didn't give further details. The situation must indeed be serious or she wouldn't ask.'

'You must help her,' Anne offered, mindful of how much she owed Marie, her first friend and mentor in Paris.

Paul nodded gravely. 'I said that I'd come. I've also sent word to the Highway Patrol in Villejuif to report to Beaumont. I'll need them. And I'll take Lieutenant Faure along. He's still in Paris.' He turned to Georges. 'I want you to meet Pierre Roland at the police bureau and pick up the baker's receipts for handwriting analysis. Roland seemed to think there wouldn't be a problem. But it might be prudent to bring a pair of pistols.'

Anne waved a hand. 'Roland hasn't met Georges. May I go along to introduce them to each other?' She wanted to stay involved in the baker's case and look after his family's interests.

Paul smiled indulgently and gave Anne a teasing bow of the head. 'Of course, that would be helpful. You could reassure Roland. Meeting Monsieur Charpentier for the first time could be unsettling.' Paul paused, dropped his playful tone. 'Gaillard surely understands the importance of the baker's files. Why isn't he guarding them more carefully? Roland might be walking into a trap.'

'I agree,' Georges said, glancing at Anne. 'We'll be alert – and prepared.'

On the way to Beaumont, Saint-Martin and Lieutenant Faure discussed the recent upsurge in violence in the countryside. Posted in Villejuif, the lieutenant was close to the problem and could describe recent attacks on grain convoys in disturbing detail.

Saint-Martin leaned back in the coach and reflected. The countryside had been in crisis for at least the past two years. Disastrous harvests had aggravated the fundamental problems in the country's agriculture: the soil was rich and potentially productive, but the cultivation of it was inefficient. Most peasants were ignorant, bound by tradition, and oppressed by heavy taxes. They could barely eke out a living on their own small tracts. They had no incentive to improve their work on the estates of the privileged classes.

Lieutenant Faure broke into these reflections. 'Colonel, you've been to England. Is it true that their agriculture is more productive than ours and the countryside more peaceful?'

Saint-Martin confessed that he wasn't an expert. 'But I've travelled through the southern counties and I've also read the learned Arthur Young. I understand that English land-lords have a powerful voice in the central government. So they've been able to consolidate their lands, evicting poor tenant farmers. This harsh measure allowed landlords to introduce more efficient methods of cultivation and breeding of livestock.'

'Where do the evicted farmers go?' Faure's mind had a sceptical cast.

'Many stay on in the countryside as poor day labourers. Others seek work in London and some emigrate to the colonies.'

Faure became indignant. 'The poor in England resemble sheep. Ours lately have begun to act like wolves.'

During the past couple of months, while royal authority declined and the drastic effects of the previous failed harvests were still being felt, the public fell into the grip of a strange great fear. Rumours spread like wildfire that hordes of crazed peasants were roaming the countryside, looting and burning chateaux and killing their masters.

Thanks to factual reports from his troopers, Saint-Martin could discount most of the rumours. But the real situation was nonetheless worrisome. Bandits, or men posing as such, robbed shipments of grain on the rivers and on the highways. Peasants violently resisted attempts by their masters to increase rents and fees at the mills.

'What are we to expect at Château Beaumont?' Faure asked.

'A few days ago, my aunt mentioned that strangers had come to the village on her estate and were attempting to subvert her authority. They were also seen agitating the peasants on my estate nearby. She expects an attack on one or more of our farm buildings or on a shipment of grain from our granaries. In reaction to her report, I've urged her to spy on the agita-tors to discover their plans.'

'Those rogues will be armed,' Faure pointed out. 'Four troopers are riding behind us. Is that enough?'

Saint-Martin nodded. 'Before we set out this morning, I ordered several more troopers to come from Villejuif. They'll hide in wooded areas near our barns. By nightfall, we'll be ready to deal the bandits a crushing blow.'

The coach turned off the highway into a shaded driveway. Château Beaumont soon came into view. 'Home again,' the colonel murmured. He had grown up here, and it was here that he'd first met Anne. He must now defend it.

Marie came out of the house as he and Faure descended from the coach. Erect, determined, she strode towards them.

'Thank you for coming, Paul.' She searched his face, then murmured for only him to hear, 'I'm pleased that you've brought Lieutenant Faure. But where are the rest of your men?'

He smiled. 'I've placed some of them in the woods near your granary. The others are hiding near mine. Faure will join them. They're ready to spring into action.'

Over tea in Marie's study, he explained his strategy. He would catch the agitators in the midst of an illegal act and put them in prison. Then the countryside would quiet down.

'How much support have those strangers gained in this area?' he asked.

'Many of the poorest and most desperate peasants listen sympathetically to their harangues. But only a half-dozen local men have actually joined them. I have inserted a reliable spy into their secret discussions. You know him, Philippe Gigot.'

Saint-Martin frowned. 'Can you trust him? He's one of your most severe critics, blamed the violent death of his wayward daughter on you.' Lucie Gigot, a pretty girl, had run away to the Palais-Royal in Paris and had fallen into bad company.

'Yes, at first I was suspicious when he warned me of a growing conspiracy. But he explained that he and the other more prosperous tenants stood to lose a great deal if the granaries and the carts were destroyed. He granted that he and I still had our differences, but we should work together to protect this estate. Its grain was among the best in the Paris region. Millers paid a high premium for it, because it was stored under optimal conditions and allowed to age properly. Gigot spoke with genuine pride. I was touched.'

'I see,' said Saint-Martin. 'The conspirators trusted him because they thought that he and you were enemies.'

'Correct. So he met with them, pretended to agree, and reported their plans to me. They intend to set fire to our granaries and to the grain wagons parked nearby.'

'When?'

'Tonight, at midnight. The sky will be overcast; the buildings and the wagons will be shrouded in darkness.'

'Will the rogues be armed?'

'The local men carry clubs and knives, their leaders have knives and pistols.'

'Do their leaders include this man?' Saint-Martin showed her Michou's sketch of Gaillard.

'I have seen him. Yesterday, I disguised myself in a peasant woman's clothes and visited your estate. The risk was small. I'm not well known there. He was studying your granary.'

'What role does he seem to play in the conspiracy?'

'My spy tells me that he hides in the shadows, doesn't take part in the secret discussions, but works through two assistants. His local allies have little or no contact with him.'

Saint-Martin finished his tea. 'It will be difficult to catch him – or, if caught, to hold him for trial. Still, we might capture his assistants in the act. And they could be persuaded to testify against him. We must plan now. There's no time to lose.'

As midnight approached, Saint-Martin had his forces in place. Lieutenant Faure and two of the troopers, supported by his estate steward and several trustworthy armed servants, concealed themselves at the approach to his granary. At the Beaumont granary, Saint-Martin led the defence, aided by the other two troopers and several loyal servants. The Villejuif troopers remained concealed with their mounts in the wooded background, prepared to chase any fugitives. The countess insisted on being present at her granary, armed with a pair of pistols.

Water had been placed in both granaries in case the rogues succeeded in starting fires. Traps were laid at possible exit routes. The rogues would come down to the granaries by the main cart roads and might attempt to steal carts already loaded with grain for the next day's trip to the market. When they reached the granaries, the defenders would set off rockets to illuminate the sky. Trumpets would send signals to attack. The countess had thought out these measures days ago.

A few minutes past midnight, Saint-Martin heard footsteps, then saw a pair of donkeys loaded with firewood. He counted four men as they passed. They approached the granary and began unloading the wood. The spy Gigot had said that the two operations would be synchronized and would begin at the lighting of flares. One of the rogues hitched a donkey to a grain cart and began to drive up the road.

A flare was lit. In the distance a flare responded. At that moment Saint-Martin set off a rocket, and another rocket went off in the distance. A trooper blew a trumpet call, and the defenders advanced upon the rogues. In minutes, three of them were caught and put in chains. A few small fires were extinguished.

'Where's your leader?' Saint-Martin demanded of the three.

They looked at one another and shrugged in unison.

'Here he is,' came Marie's voice out of the darkness. She urged the man forwards, two cocked pistols at his back. The donkey followed with the grain cart. 'I was waiting for them on the road.'

In the early hours of the morning Saint-Martin sat down with the countess at the writing table in her study. He stretched out his legs, suppressed a yawn. 'It was a good night. I think we caught them all – eight of them, including their two leaders.'

'I'm gratified,' she said, raising a glass of port to her lips. 'None of the villains were my tenants. Except for the two leaders, all of them were day labourers from this area.' She took a sip and put down the glass. 'I recognize them. Desperate men, they've had very little work for the past two years.' She took up a pen, gathered paper, and prepared to take notes.

He signalled to a trooper by the door. 'We'll hear their stories now. Bring them in one by one, beginning with the most docile and intelligent-looking of the local men.'

The trooper returned with a shaggy young man, shackled

hand and foot. He shuffled up to the table and remained standing, the trooper, alert, an arm's reach away.

'Your name?'

'Jean Noir.'

Most likely fictitious, thought Saint-Martin. 'Home?'

'Don't have any. I live anywhere there's work.'

'Why did you try to burn the granaries and the carts?'

'To punish the rich who steal from the poor.'

'Suppose I were to turn you over to the poor. Do you think they would thank you? In fact the granaries and the carts serve the area's poor farmers as well as their rich masters. You're trying to ruin everyone's livelihood. Without the granaries and the carts no one could bring grain to the city markets. But that's what your masters intended, wasn't it?'

The young man cast down his eyes, chewed on his lips.

'If they had the chance, the poor whom you claim to serve would beat you to within an inch of your life.' Saint-Martin changed direction, caught the young man's eye. 'How much did the strangers from Paris pay you?' The troopers had searched the men and found six *livres* in coin on each of them.

The question appeared to take the young man by surprise. He hesitated, then mumbled, 'Six *livres*.'

Saint-Martin showed him the Gaillard sketch. 'Do you recognize him?'

Noir nodded. 'Can't say that I know him, but I saw him a few times. Our leaders spoke to him. It looked like they took orders from him.'

Saint-Martin told the trooper to take the man away and bring in another. The subsequent interrogations were similar to the first.

Then the most promising of the two leaders was brought into the study. A crafty, insolent man in his thirties, he had the rough hands and weather-beaten skin of a day labourer. He also appeared remarkably calm, as if he expected a higher authority than the colonel to free him.

After the preliminary questions, Saint-Martin showed him the Gaillard sketch. 'On several occasions you were observed talking to this man. What was his role in your attempt to burn the granaries and the carts?'

'He had no role. Burning them was our idea. He gave us money for a construction project and told us how to carry it out.'

'How often have you done such projects for him?'

The man hesitated for a moment. 'This was the first time.'

'You're lying. For at least a month, my troopers have been investigating dozens of incidents similar to this one – all aimed at obstructing the grain trade and causing panic in the city. I see your hand at work. Now that you've been caught *in flagrante delicto* and will be lodged in prison, I expect many witnesses of your crimes to testify against you. Don't count on your patron to save you.' A hint of anxiety crept into the man's eyes. Saint-Martin ordered the trooper to lock him up in the chateau's basement, separately from the others.

Saint-Martin pursued the same line of questions with the second leader, as insolent as the first, and received similar responses. He was also sent to the basement to await transport to the city prison, the Châtelet, later in the morning.

Dawn was breaking in the east when the interrogations ended. Saint-Martin stood up, stretched, and drew a deep breath at an open window. His aunt continued writing for a few more minutes, then laid down her pen, dried the last page, and added it to the neat pile before her. 'Your report for the magistrates is complete, Paul. It's also well written, if I may say so myself.'

She rose and joined him at the window. Together they quietly watched the mist rise in a distant meadow. Birdsong lifted their spirits. 'I'm so grateful, Paul, that this estate will continue to be a beautiful, as well as a peaceful, place.'

'I agree with all my heart,' he said. But he foresaw severe storms in the country's future and wasn't at all confident that Château Beaumont could avoid their destructive force.

Two grain carts, carrying the prisoners and guarded by troopers, passed before the window on its way to the city. Paul turned to his aunt. 'The magistrates in Paris will drag the truth out of them. In a couple of weeks, when they and others like them are finally confined in the Bicêtre or, better yet, in the naval prison at Brest, we'll have no more violence in this part of the country, and the poor of Paris will receive their grain.'

Marie objected. 'But you still must deal with Gaillard. He will try again to ruin you, to kill you.'

'No doubt he's a dangerous enemy, especially with the duke

behind him. I must find a way to penetrate into the Palais-Royal, to uncover strong evidence of Gaillard's crimes. In the meantime, I want you to feel more secure. Your tenants have proven to be loyal. Gigot is now on your side. For his services I'll give him the money that I took from Gaillard's rogues.'

'For safety's sake, Paul, as long as Gaillard runs free, I'll keep my pistols loaded and close at hand.'

Twenty

Endangered Witnesses

Paris, Sunday, 26 July

After seeing Paul off to Château Beaumont, Anne and Georges walked to the local police bureau situated in a blind alley near the Louvre. As they approached the building, Anne sensed that something had gone wrong. Two National Guardsmen stood by the door in casual conversation. Pierre Roland was nowhere in sight. A few women dressed for church loitered at a distance.

At the sight of Georges' uniform the guardsmen straightened up, their eyes wary.

'Have you seen the magistrate Pierre Roland, Messieurs?' he asked directly. 'We were expecting to meet him here.' Anne took a few steps back. The guardsmen seemed distracted by her presence.

'They took him home a few minutes ago, said they would call a medical doctor,' replied the older of the two guardsmen.

'What happened to him?'

'Two men assaulted him. A pair of thieves, I suppose. That was as much as he could tell us. We found him lying here, bleeding from the head. No one in the neighbourhood seems to have seen or heard anything, or so they claimed.'

Georges joined Anne and they walked a few more paces away. She said, 'Surely someone in these buildings watched the incident. But they don't trust the police, whether new or old, not even you. To get involved as a witness can only lead to grief. Perhaps such persons would speak to me.' She pointed with a shift of her eye to the women in the distance.

Georges nodded. 'Go talk to them. I'll have a conversation with the guards and with men of the neighbourhood.'

But before Anne could reach the women, they moved away. The bells of Saint-Thomas du Louvre had begun to ring, announcing the early Mass. An older woman came out of the building next to the police bureau. From her agile, bird-like movements and her sharp, inquisitive glance, Anne sensed that she probably spent many of her waking hours looking out the window at activity on the street and might have observed Roland's misfortune.

'Madame,' Anne began, 'could I walk you to church? I'm a friend of Monsieur Roland who was assaulted here. Could you tell me how it happened?'

The woman searched Anne's face with a shrewd gaze, then said softly, 'Come along, my dear. First we need to get better acquainted. Then I may tell you what I did or didn't see.'

The walk to the church was too short. Anne was hard put to explain her interest in Roland without compromising herself. The woman might draw her out, then betray her to Gaillard for a gold coin or two. She might also have seen nothing of interest but would invent a tale in hope of a reward. In the end Anne took a chance and told the truth – the Abbé de l'Épée had requested that she try to help the baker Gagne's wife.

'The abbé gave me this.' Anne showed the woman his letter.

At the entrance to the small church, they stepped aside and the woman scanned the letter, then returned it. 'Thank you for being honest with me. I admire the abbé and have heard him speak about his work with the deaf and know people he has helped. He writes well of you. Still, I must be careful about whom I meet and what I say. Otherwise I could be badly hurt, like Monsieur Roland and the baker Gagne. I'll pray for guidance. See me after the Mass. If I agree to help, I'll give you an address for our meeting and you may follow me there.'

The woman entered the church. Anne waited a few moments, then went in with others. There was nothing for her to do but wait. It was a said Mass and finished in less than an hour. Anne sat in the back, where she could observe the woman and discern marks of her character. She was a cautious, shrewd person, to be sure, but capable of compassion for Madame Gagne. Still, Anne's heart beat fast as the worshippers moved towards the door, the woman among them.

As she passed Anne, she murmured, 'Bertrand. Fifteen Rue Fromenteau.'

That cryptic message gave Anne what she needed to know. Rue Fromenteau was only two minutes' walk away. Anne followed the woman at a safe distance through the streets to a decrepit three-storey house, then up the stairs. The woman opened the door and beckoned Anne to come in.

'I'm Madame Thérèse Gille,' she said with a smile. A woman of Anne's age and appearance approached. Madame Gille signed a greeting and they embraced. 'And this is my daughter, Madame Adrienne Bertrand. We usually meet here for tea on Sunday morning. You are welcome to join us today. We should sign because, as you can see, my daughter is deaf – and years ago, was one of the abbé's students.'

Amazing, Anne thought. Madame Bertrand could be the mirror image of herself: tall and slim, blonde hair and blue eyes. The young woman explained that she lived with her husband in this small room. During weekdays, she sewed for a nearby milliner. Her husband, also deaf, worked in the royal printing office in the Louvre. On Sunday mornings he played boule in the Tuileries garden with other deaf artisans.

A table was set with a tea service, a plate of sweet biscuits, and a bowl of plum preserves. The mother had learned to sign. A conversation ensued. Anne learned that Madame Gille and her daughter had worked in the wine tavern for a few years before it became a police bureau. During weekdays, Madame Gille continued to clean and do odd jobs in the bureau. In the evenings, mother and daughter cleaned rooms in the duke's palace.

Anne asked the mother, 'Tell me more about your connection to the palace.'

While the daughter cleared the table and cleaned the dishes, Madame Gille told Anne that her husband had been a liveried servant in the Palais-Royal. 'He was a tall, handsome man. Adrienne takes after him. I was a cleaning maid.'

They had lived in cramped quarters in the palace. When he died, the widow and her daughter were evicted from the palace without a pension but allowed to work there part-time at night. They both took outside day-time jobs.

'I'm shocked,' said Anne, 'by how poorly the duke has treated you. After all, he's said to be the richest man in France.'

'I'm sure he is,' Madame Gille agreed. 'But he spends his wealth to satisfy his carnal urges and to advance his political ambitions. He ignores the just claims of his faithful servants and gives to the poor only to win favour with the public.' Her throat grew taut, her lips tightened, as she hissed, 'He's a lecherous fraud. God help France if he ever becomes its King!'

'What do you think of Monsieur Choderlos de Laclos and the duke's other advisers?'

'Parasites! They encourage his worst instincts to please him, while they feather their own nests. There's scarcely an honest man among them.'

'Is Monsieur Gaillard any better than the others?'

She rolled her eyes. 'He's cruel and insensitive towards women, rude and arrogant towards anyone whom he considers beneath himself.' She paused for a moment, struggling to calm herself. When her wrath seemed spent, she remarked, 'I've said more than I should. If the duke or his men knew, they would crush me.' She met Anne's eye. 'But you will be discreet. I trust a woman who enjoys the abbé's confidence.'

'Have no fear,' Anne reassured her, certain that she could be persuaded to search Gaillard's office. Anne then led her to relate what she had seen early that morning in front of the police bureau. 'I was brushing my hair at the window, as I usually do, while getting ready for church. A man walked up to the police bureau just below me. I recognized him, Monsieur Roland, one of my favourite persons.'

'Have you met him?' asked Anne, surprised at the unlikely suggestion of familiarity.

'Not really. But in the afternoon, when I've nothing else to do, I sometimes attend the proceedings at the police bureau from the visitors' gallery and watch him and the others at work. I also observe them going in and out of the building, talking to each other in the street. Early in the evening, when everyone has gone home, I clean the bureau and try to figure out what kind of persons they are. In my imagination Monsieur Roland is a gentleman, someone I could trust. I don't like the other magistrates – too calculating and full of themselves.'

'So what happened to Roland this morning?'

'He was beaten.' She shook her head, saddened. 'I was

surprised to see him, because the bureau is closed on Sunday. He walked up to the door and took a key from his pocket. Two men approached him from behind. He turned around and they talked for a few minutes. He seemed to grow angry, shook his head, and turned back to the door. While he was putting the key in the lock, one of the men hit him with a club on the back of his head and he fell.'

'Why didn't you or anyone else raise the alarm?'

'I recognized the two ruffians, very bad subjects. I've heard that they work for the duke and have protection. They hurt people who try to meddle in their business.'

'Is one of them short and stout and has a flat nose?'

She nodded. 'And the other is tall and slender. Simon and Nicolas, they're called. I never see one without the other. They come occasionally to the bureau. People, including the police, are afraid of them.'

Anne concluded that Madame Gille was of a divided mind: resentful towards the duke, yet fearful of his long, malignant reach. Her cooperation was uncertain.

Anne left the woman at her daughter's home and found Georges in a café on Rue des Orties.

'No luck,' he said. 'The men I talked to were close-mouthed and fearful. What did you learn?'

'An eye-witness account of the attack on Monsieur Roland.' Anne related the gist of her conversation with Madame Gille.

For a moment Georges was thoughtfully still, then he said, 'Gaillard thinks we're gaining ground in the investigation. He's now pushing back, disabling our allies. Let's visit Roland at home and hear his tale. The beating may have made him less cooperative. We'll see. I'm not optimistic.'

'If Roland refuses, perhaps Madame Gille can help us, despite her fears. She could lead us to the baker's papers in the police bureau, even insinuate us into Gaillard's den in the palace.'

Roland's apartment was on the first floor of an old but substantial building on Rue Saint-Nicaise, a short distance from the police bureau. A well-groomed maidservant examined the visitors doubtfully, took their names, then seated them in a small anteroom and left.

A few minutes later, Roland's wife entered the room in a white silk housedress. A handsome woman, she had soft, pampered hands, which she clasped nervously. 'I was expecting your husband, Madame Cartier.' She spoke in a high, strained voice, her expression apprehensive. Perhaps Anne's common woollen gown confused her. She would have expected a colonel's wife to dress more fashionably.

'My husband is on a mission in the countryside,' Anne explained. 'His adjutant, Monsieur Charpentier, and I were hoping to meet Monsieur Roland at the police bureau to pick up a box of papers – hardly a dangerous business. We were surprised and sorry to hear that he has been injured.'

Madame Roland ignored their remark and spoke sharply. 'He is resting now and cannot have visitors. The doctor gave him a sleeping potion.'

'How serious is his condition?' Anne asked.

'He has received a hard blow to the head and suffers from a mild concussion, but no broken bones. With rest he should fully recover in a few weeks. That was the doctor's opinion.'

Anne expressed her relief that his injury was less serious than she had feared. 'Monsieur Charpentier has a question for you.'

Georges voiced his regrets. 'An eyewitness gave us a description of the incident, including the two assailants. We know them and will help your husband, should he wish to prosecute them. Has he told you why they attacked him?'

Her lips began to quiver. She met Georges' eye. 'This message, addressed to my husband, was slipped under the door.' She drew a small sheet of paper from her bodice and handed it to Georges.

He read it, frowned, and passed it to Anne. The brief message contained a threat.

> Monsieur, you must resign from your position in the police bureau and refuse to cooperate with any investigation into the death of the baker Gagne. If you fail to obey our instructions, you and your family will feel the people's wrath.

To judge from the careful script, it probably came from the hand of a scribe. Still, under analysis, it might reveal its author.

'May I keep it?' Anne asked, holding up the paper.

Madame Roland grimaced, waved it away. 'You may have it.' She struggled to control herself. 'You will understand why I must ask you to leave now and not come back.'

Anne and Georges exchanged glances. For the time being, no more could be done there.

Out on the street Anne said, 'Come, Georges, we must hurry to Cécile Tremblay.' Anne set off in the direction of Rue Sainte-Anne. 'Simon and Nicolas will surely try to silence her or force her to denounce the deposition that she gave me.'

On a Sunday, the seamstress's shop was closed, but the café, La Vache Agile, was open for business. 'We may find her here,' Anne whispered to Georges as they entered the bar room. At first, they could hardly see. Their eyes needed a few seconds to adjust from the bright sun outside to the café's dim interior. They approached the barman behind the counter. He recognized Anne from her previous visit.

'Do you know,' she asked him quietly, 'where Madame Cécile Tremblay could be found?'

Without answering her, he glanced across the room. She followed his eyes. Simon and Nicolas sat in a dark corner, watching them. The barman held up an empty glass, as if inspecting it, and murmured, 'Those two rogues have just asked for her. I don't think she would want to meet them. She and her mother, Laure, have gone to the garden of the Palais-Royal. I expect them back any minute now. Perhaps you could intercept them.'

Anne whispered to the barman, whom she trusted, 'We'll persuade them to live elsewhere until dependable National Guardsmen can patrol this street.'

They had hardly left when Cécile and Laure turned the corner on to Rue Sainte-Anne. Anne and Georges reached them before they could be seen from inside the café.

Anne briefly explained to Cécile that Simon and Nicolas were waiting in the café. 'Do you want to avoid them? If so, I suggest that we all go to the countess's town house nearby on Rue Traversine. You can wait there safely until the rogues leave the area.'

While Anne spoke, Cécile's eyes grew wide with anxiety. Laure stared at her, confused. 'What's going on?' she asked her daughter.

'We'll do as she suggests, Mother. She'll explain when we get there.'

They reached the town house without incident. In the parlour, Anne said, 'If you had entered the café, you would have recognized Simon and Nicolas as the men who hung the baker Gagne from the lamppost.'

'Why would they want to speak to me?'

'To force you to deny having seen them. They want no one to witness against them, should the baker's murder go to trial.'

'What do you suggest that I do?' Her voice filled with fear.

'Wait here for an hour until they leave. Then we'll go together to your home, pick up the things you need, and return here. Stay as the countess's guests for a few days until the National Guard can provide for your safety.'

Wild-eyed, Cécile glanced around the room, stared at the door. She breathed a deep sigh. 'We have no choice. We'll do as you say.'

Twenty-One
A Desperate Measure

Paris, Sunday, 26 July

At six o'clock Anne and Georges finished moving Cécile and her mother into the Rue Traversine town house. Exhausted by the stress, the two women retired to their room. Georges had earlier returned to the café and found that Simon and Nicolas were gone. They had finally realized that the seamstress and her mother had avoided the confrontation planned for them. As the two villains left the café, they had given the barman a message for Cécile, threatening her with vengeance if she tried to obstruct the people's justice. Georges picked up the message but kept it in his pocket and didn't pass it on to Cécile.

Anne and Georges were still at the town house, discussing the message, when Michou, Sylvie and André Dutoit returned from an afternoon walking in the Bois de Boulogne, the great wooded park west of the city. They had wanted to escape briefly from the rabble-rousing orators in the garden of the Palais-Royal.

The five formed a congenial circle at a table in the front parlour. Anne described the incidents of the day, from the attack on the magistrate Roland at the local police bureau to the attempted intimidation of Cécile and her mother at the café.

She concluded, 'We must stop Gaillard. His men act with impunity and cause chaos in the city.' She signed a summary of her remarks to Michou.

'How shall *we* do that?' asked Sylvie, glancing doubtfully around the circle of friends.

'By gathering strong evidence of their crimes and laying it before Mayor Bailly and the Marquis de Lafayette. Even as fearful as they are, and as uncertain of their responsibilities, they will be forced to arrest Gaillard and his men.'

'And where shall we find such evidence?' Sylvie persisted.

Georges replied, 'Probably in Gaillard's office in the Palais-Royal. We know from past contact with him that he collects all kinds of documents for possible use in extortion. He's also a writer, most likely keeps a journal. He must hide the journal and his papers in his office.'

Sylvie gave him a wry smile. 'And so all *we* have to do is enter the office and find them.'

'Correct,' Anne said, avoiding Sylvie's provocation. 'A difficult, but not impossible task. Georges will tell us how to do it.' All eyes turned to him.

Georges acknowledged each of them with a slight bow of his head. 'Except for Madame Cartier, you may not know that I thoroughly studied the palace many years ago when I spied on the duke's father for the Lieutenant General Sartine. I know all its rooms. However, I don't know precisely who occupies them today.' He turned to André Dutoit, who had thus far been a detached observer of the conversation. 'Young man, you work in the palace. Could you tell us, which room is Gaillard's office?'

André looked uncomfortable, shifted his weight. He was reluctant to take part in the investigation. Georges gazed at him with an expectant smile. Finally, he said, 'It's on the second floor near the centre of the building directly above the art gallery. His view is to the Camp of the Tatars and the palace garden beyond.'

'Can you tell us anything about the room?'

'Gaillard keeps it locked at all times. Visitors enter through an anteroom and meet his clerk. During the warm summer months, Gaillard opens his windows, but he locks them if he's gone for any length of time. Next to his office is a private sitting room with a bedded alcove, where he usually sleeps. During the day he might rest on a couch in the office.'

'How do you happen to know his arrangements so well?' Georges asked, eyes wide with amazement.

André shrugged off the compliment. 'He occasionally calls me into his office to run errands. I make the most of those opportunities. As an art student, I'm trained to notice details. After I've been in an interesting room like Gaillard's, I enjoy creating it again in my imagination.'

'Young man, you will be a gold mine of information for us again, as you were two years ago. You helped us foil Gaillard's attempt to steal compromising letters between the Queen and Comte Fersen.' Georges smiled benevolently, then frowned with an afterthought. 'At the time, we concealed your role. Apparently, Gaillard still doesn't suspect you. Is that correct?'

'Yes, it is,' he replied. 'But I feel very nervous when I'm near him, as if he might suddenly accuse me of betraying him.'

Georges nodded sympathetically. 'Rest assured, you will be safe. All I want you to do is to keep track of his use of the room. Try to predict when it will be empty. Tell Sylvie.'

Anne asked, 'Even if it were empty, how would you enter?'

'I would come down by rope from the floor above. That side of the palace is pitch-black at night. The windows are easy to unlock.'

'I should add,' said André, 'Gaillard keeps a large pet dog in his office.'

'Hmm,' muttered Georges, rubbing his chin. 'The dog would object to a stranger coming through a window. Too risky. We must find a different way in.'

A servant brought a tray of food and drinks to their table. For a few minutes, the companions focused on the meal. The afternoon's walk in the woods had left them hungry and thirsty. After a glass of wine, André relaxed and spoke to Georges. 'This might be of use to you. Late on Saturday evening, I was ordered to serve refreshments at a party in the palace for the duke's guests. Near midnight, I was relieving myself in one of the commodes behind a drape when Gaillard and Laclos met outside. Their voices were angry. Lieutenant Maury had apparently asked for money, much more than they were willing to pay. He had also failed to do a job for which they had paid in advance. When they complained, he had threatened to expose them.'

Georges turned to Anne. 'Do you sense an opportunity for us?'

'Yes,' she said. 'But how can we exploit it?'

It was late on Sunday when Anne and Georges left their companions at the town house and walked towards home on

Rue Saint-Honoré. Sylvie and Michou had warned against going out on the street. With the breakdown of the old system of public order, thieves and cutpurses were emboldened, especially after dark. André had agreed to stay the night at the town house rather than return to his room in the Palais-Royal. But Georges and Anne had demurred.

'There's safety in numbers, even for just two of us,' said Georges. 'And our route is better patrolled than elsewhere in the city.'

Nonetheless, they had hardly entered Rue Saint-Honoré when Anne began to feel anxious. She turned around suddenly and saw a man slip into a doorway.

'We're being followed, Georges.' She gripped his arm. 'It's later than we realized. I believe the clock in the parlour may have stopped.'

They took a few more steps, then Georges swung around. 'I saw him. A single person. Could be from a band of cutpurses or part of an ambush, perhaps in that interval between the streetlights.' He pointed towards a dark area that lay ahead.

Rue Saint-Honoré was better lit and usually busier at that hour than most of the city's streets. But at that moment, the street appeared to be deserted, all the windows closed and shuttered. A dog howled in the distance. Anne imagined bandits lurking in the dark doorways and alleys to the left and to the right.

As they reached the outer edge of lamplight and were about to plunge forward into darkness, Anne gripped Georges again and whispered, 'I hear someone coming towards us.'

Instantly, Georges tensed, clenched his fists.

'Hallo!' said a man. 'What are you two doing at this late hour of the night? Honest folk are in bed.' A National Guardsman unshuttered a lamp. Another guardsman also came out of the darkness. Both men were armed with pistols and sabres and carried clubs. Their demeanour was stern and suspicious. They drew closer and carefully studied Georges, then Anne.

Georges handed them his papers and explained that they had visited friends and lost track of the time.

'Charpentier, Royal Highway Patrol. Why aren't you in uniform? How are we to know that you are what your papers say?' And, without giving Georges a chance to respond, the officer turned to Anne. 'Who are you, Madame?'

Anne showed him the abbé's letter.

Probably illiterate, the guardsman struggled with it. An expression of irritated incomprehension spread over his face. He looked up at her. 'Are you married to this man?' His tone reeked of prurient curiosity.

'Why do you ask? Is it any of your business?' Anne regretted her impertinent retort almost as soon as the words left her mouth. But she resented being taken for a prostitute.

The guardsman's face hardened. He passed the abbé's letter to his comrade. 'Shall we take them to the police bureau as suspicious persons? After a night with the rats in one of our basement cells, they might be more cooperative.'

The comrade read the letter, searched Anne's face. 'You're the provost's wife. I've heard of you.' His gaze was respectful. He turned to his offended comrade and said, 'They don't look suspicious to me. Let them pass. Why make trouble for ourselves?'

Anne sensed that the more reasonable guardsman was disposed to be helpful, so she asked him in her most deferential manner, 'Would you please escort us to the provost's residence? We are being followed. I think a trap has been laid for us on the way.'

Georges added, 'We would pay you for the service.' He jiggled the coins in his pocket. The guardsman put out his hand, and Georges gave him a coin.

'We'll see you safely there.' He flourished his club. 'We met a pair of villains loitering on the road ahead and ordered them to move on. I'll wager that they were waiting for you two.'

Anne asked, 'Was one of them short and stout and had a flat nose? And the other tall and thin?'

'You've described them precisely,' replied the guardsman.

'Then, sir,' she said, 'you win the wager. They're known to us and intend to do us harm.'

She and Georges exchanged glances and relaxed. This episode could have ended badly. In the future it might be prudent to follow Sylvie and Michou's advice.

Twenty-Two

A Mysterious Disappearance

Passy, Monday, 27 July

Early in the morning, Georges took the river road towards the Highway Patrol post in Passy. As he passed the National Guard barracks in Chaillot, he thought of Lieutenant Maury and the angry conversation between Laclos and Gaillard over his threat to expose them. Georges made a mental note to mention the incident to Brigadier Pioche, now in charge of the local investigation into the death of Lieutenant Harivel.

As soon as Georges arrived, he and Pioche sat down to cups of tea at the writing table in Harivel's office and chatted. Pioche's eyes were sad, still grieving. The murdered man's presence was strong. Engravings of scenes from his ancestral province of Dauphiné hung on the walls. His pen and ink stand rested on the table. A plaster bust of Louis XVI stood on a corner shelf.

'I've changed nothing here,' said Pioche, surveying the office. 'It wouldn't feel right. He left so suddenly.'

'I agree,' said Georges, and allowed a moment of silence out of respect. Then he asked, 'How far have you come in your investigation?'

Pioche spooned sugar into his cup and replied, 'I've focused on Lieutenant Maury, our chief suspect. I've had him followed closely, hoping that he would do or say something to incriminate himself.'

'Have you had any success?' Georges had noticed unusual eagerness in the officer's voice.

'I haven't come any closer to solving the case, but I can report a major new development.' Pioche took a sip of his tea. 'At about eight o'clock on Friday night, one of my spies came to the office and told me that Maury had started gambling at a table in the wine tavern near his barracks.'

'Who were his companions?'

'Other junior officers in the National Guard, stationed at the Chaillot barracks.'

'How much do you know about them?'

'They share a passion for gambling and have previously served together as dragoons in the French Guards.'

'Friends of Maury?'

'Acquaintances only. I engaged a trustworthy female spy to wait on them and pay attention especially to Maury. I observed from a distant table. From time to time, she brought information to me.'

Pioche poured more tea into their cups and offered Georges a shot of brandy. He declined, added sugar instead. Pioche dribbled the brandy into his tea, then leaned back and resumed his story.

'When I arrived at the tavern, the officers were already drinking wine with abandon, casting dice, and wagering small sums. At first, Maury won more than he lost and his spirits were congenial. But eventually his luck turned bad. Drinking more wine seemed to make matters worse.

'As his losses mounted, he insisted on increasing the wagers. By eleven o'clock, he was drunk and deeply in debt. His comrades would give him no more credit. His mood turned ugly. He cursed them all to hell and upended the table, sending glasses and bottles, dice and coins crashing to the floor. For a moment he gazed at the wreckage, then gave out a resounding belch, and staggered out of the room.'

'Incredible!' exclaimed Georges. 'That's similar to his wild behaviour on the Place de Grève, when he killed the intendant, cut out his heart, and carried it into the City Hall on the point of his sword.'

'Yes, there's an ugly pattern of violence in his life. Before coming to Paris, he killed a man.'

'And we know that he beats his wife,' Georges added.

Pioche nodded. 'After he left the tavern, I grew concerned for her, so I followed him home and watched from behind a hedge. At the door he fumbled with his key, dropped it, and couldn't find it in the dark. He pounded furiously on the door, and shouted to his wife. She refused to open, probably realizing that he was drunk and angry. He cursed her, threatened her with a beating.

'I was at the point of stepping in to protect her when I saw her slip out the back door and run up the hill, presumably towards the little cottage, the secret lair that she had shared with Harivel. I don't know exactly where it is.

'Meanwhile, Maury broke down the front door. Discovering that his wife had fled, he howled like a madman. For several minutes, I could hear him cursing and smashing furniture. Finally, he grew tired and collapsed. I peeked through the front window. He was lying unconscious on the floor, frothing at the mouth.

'I realized that when he woke up the next morning his temper would not have improved. If his wife returned, she ran the risk of a beating from which she might never recover. She and I are not acquainted, so I told the young National Guardsman Joseph Mouton, who knows her well, to take her to the village priest. He could find her a safe house for the time being.'

'Did you know that Mouton is Harivel's son?' Georges asked.

'I suspected as much, but I didn't know for certain.'

'What happened next?'

'Early the following morning I assigned a spy to watch Maury's movements. The lieutenant rose late, walked to the barracks to try to borrow money from fellow officers. Unsuccessful, he stormed out and went to the tavern. There his creditors confronted him, but he refused to pay them. A sharp argument ensued that soon went beyond the gambling debts to other grievances against him. One of his comrades called him a cheat for failing to honour his debts. Another charged that his butchering of Bertier on the Place de Grève was a shameful, cowardly deed, a disgrace to the officer corps of the royal army.'

'That could lead to a duel,' Georges remarked. 'I didn't realize that his fellow officers held him in such contempt. Perhaps they concealed their feelings out of fear of his anger.'

'And out of respect for his patron, the duke,' Pioche added. 'I expected Maury to challenge at least the most offensive detraction, but he didn't – at least not to my knowledge.'

Georges mused out loud, 'I would expect all involved would want to avoid publicity. A duel is risky, a capital offence.'

Pioche countered, 'Where royal officers are concerned, however, it's sometimes tolerated.'

'True,' Georges granted, 'but even then the survivor risks exile or a setback in his career.'

'Perhaps not in this case,' Pioche insisted. 'Under cover of the present turmoil in public affairs, the officers involved might hope to conceal the duel from the public and the authorities.'

He paused for Georges to comment. But he waved him on.

'My spy followed Maury into Paris to the Palais-Royal, where he disappeared.'

'Since then, has there been any sign of him?'

'I think not. He never returned to the barracks on Saturday night. According to my spies, no one saw him on Sunday. We will continue to look for him today.'

'You should also question his gambling companions. They may already have perfected their alibis. Don't overlook Joseph Mouton. He may not be as guileless as he seems. If he believed that Maury killed his father, he might have sought revenge. With so many ardent, well-armed enemies, Maury may have come to a bad end.' Georges paused for a moment of reflection. 'It's a pity. I had begun to hope that Maury might expose the role of Gaillard and Laclos in the recent assassinations and answer to a court of law for his own crimes.'

While Georges was in Passy, Anne visited the abbé's institute to find out how Madame Gagne was doing. Françoise Arnaud's report was encouraging: the baker's wife had proven to be resilient, had in fact assumed the cook's duties when she suddenly took ill. Anne went to the kitchen and found Madame Gagne sitting at a table, chopping vegetables.

As Anne approached, the woman brightened, then signalled a kitchen maid to prepare a pot of tea for the visitor. Anne picked up a knife and set to work on a pile of carrots. When she finished, the tea was poured. Between sips, she described her meeting with Jeanne the deaf maid and with madame's son Robert. She was clearly relieved that they were well, but missed her son's company.

'Until we arrest the men responsible for your husband's death, your son is probably best off at a safe distance from the bakery.' The boy's mother breathed a resigned sigh of acceptance.

The compromising papers from the Gagne bakery had intrigued Anne since breakfast. 'Where might I find samples of messages in your husband's own hand?'

'At the Bakers' Guild. He applied for membership several years ago. I helped him compose the application, but the writing is in his own hand.'

'I'll visit the guild this morning. But before I go, tell me more about the journeyman Jacques Duby.'

Madame Gagne responded that his true character was hard to discern. On the surface he appeared to be a dependable baker, yet she sensed that she couldn't really trust him. Still, his habits seemed better than many of his class. At least he was clean and sober while baking.

'Where did he used to live?' Anne asked.

'In an inn on Rue Sainte-Anne, a short distance from the bakery.'

'What do you know about his life, his acquaintances?'

'Very little. We didn't communicate well. He doesn't sign and won't learn. He also slurs his words and speaks much too fast for me to read his lips. The syndics of the Bakers' Guild should know more about him. They sent him to us.'

Anne next visited the Bakers' Guild office on the Quai des Augustins and sought out one of the older, more experienced syndics. He read her recommendation from the Abbé de l'Épée and became quite forthcoming. 'The abbé's a good man, really cares about people. You're fortunate to work for him.'

The reach of the abbé's reputation often amazed Anne. She knew that the royal court and upper-class philanthropists, like the Comtesse Marie, attended his presentations, visited the institute, and read his books. But she wasn't sure that master bakers would know him.

The syndic showed her to his office. She explained her mission to aid the Gagne family and to investigate Duby.

'I knew the master baker Louis Gagne quite well,' the syndic said. 'His death shocked me. I also sympathize with his widow and their son. They appear to have suffered a serious injustice. I can't imagine that he would hoard or profiteer in his trade. I often inspected his shop and bakery. They were always among the best managed. I placed Duby there last year. Madame Gagne had asked for a skilled, dependable, hardworking journeyman.

That's Duby.' He paused, searched Anne's face. 'Why are you concerned about him?'

Anne carefully weighed her response. She sensed that the syndic would deplore the violence sweeping the city in the name of reform and would have an open mind about the journeyman. Still he might be fearful of the possibly dangerous consequences of helping her. So she replied in a tentative voice, 'I have reasons to believe that he may have conspired with others to bring about Gagne's death. It has greatly benefitted him. He has shown no remorse. Would you tell me what you know about him?'

He frowned, then reached for a file box. 'I do have some information on Duby.' He drew several papers from the box, scanned them quickly to refresh his memory, and laid them aside. For a moment he was thoughtfully silent. Finally he said, 'Monsieur Duby came to our guild from Rouen six years ago. He was a journeyman baker there for another six. That's a long time in servitude to various masters for a man as cunning, as skilful, and . . . as ambitious as Monsieur Duby. He's thirty years old with few if any prospects for advancement. He's also poor – no savings that I know of – and no connections to masters willing to help him. In a word, he must be desperate. I can easily imagine that he might betray his master in the hope of taking his place.'

'Is there anything that the guild can do to prevent him?'

The syndic shook his head. 'The present revolution in the city has greatly shaken the guild's authority. If I were to attempt to investigate Monsieur Duby formally, he would urge his fellow journeymen to deceive me, or even to hang me from a lamp-post. The guild will probably have to give him Gagne's licence.'

Anne's heart sank. Her efforts on behalf of the widow were likely to be in vain. 'Then I must do something to stop him. How can I find evidence of his crime?'

'I can at least give you a suggestion,' he replied with a gentle smile. 'If Duby betrayed his master, he did not act alone. Others were involved and are potential witnesses against him. For a start, you might question the most recent women in his life. Duby is neither kind nor faithful towards his female partners, or so I've heard. If he has wronged one who knows his secrets, she might be willing to speak to you more than to me or to a police inspector.'

'I thank you for the advice, sir. Where should I begin?'

'At the inn on Rue Sainte-Anne, where he used to eat and sleep.'

Later in the morning, Anne persuaded Sylvie to join her investigation. They disguised themselves as domestic servants in plain grey woollen dresses and went to Duby's inn. On the ground floor was a neighbourhood wine tavern, with private rooms in the back and a stairway to the upper floors. At the counter to the left of the entrance, women were buying wine by the jug for the midday meal. To the right several baker boys had gathered at a long table, heavy with loaves of bread and jugs of wine.

They had already begun to drink. Distinctive enough in their grey tunics and white cotton bonnets, they also proclaimed their trade with the powerful scent of sweat, an inescapable by-product of many hours of heavy exertion in the brutal heat from the ovens. To judge from bits of their conversation and the lines of fatigue on their faces, they had just come from a long night in various bakerooms of the district.

At small tables in the room sat young women who presumably worked in the bakeries as scullery maids or shop girls. They bantered with the men between draughts of wine. A few local domestic servants kept to themselves without attracting undue notice. Anne and Sylvie felt at ease in the room and sat at a small table near the men.

The men's food was served, along with more wine. They ate and drank with serious mien and little conversation. Occasionally one or another would cast a glance at Anne and Sylvie. Even in the role of a scullery maid and with grime on her face, Sylvie was a fetching morsel to tired, tipsy baker boys.

The meal finished, most of the men left the table, some going out on to the street for fresh air and cheap entertainment. Others climbed the stairs. They had a few hours of leisure before retiring to sleep until midnight, when they would return to work. Anne heard that they slept three or four men to a bed in small, cramped rooms.

Two of the men remained at the table, engaged in a friendly debate over the relative merits of kneading dough with hands or feet. From time to time, they cast furtive glances at Anne and

Sylvie. Finally, they screwed up their courage, rose unsteadily from the table, and approached the women. Though sex was on their mind, their manner remained respectful and polite. The two women received them coolly but didn't rebuff them.

'May we join you for a drink and a little conversation?' asked the older of the two. Both now reeked of onions and garlic, as well as sweat.

The women ignored the stench and allowed them to pull chairs up to their table. When the men realized that conversation was all they were going to get, they actually relaxed and smiled, happy to enjoy a few minutes of female company. They appeared to be a decent pair, journeymen in their twenties.

After a measure of trust had been established, Anne steered the conversation to the Gagne bakery. 'How is Monsieur Duby doing?' she asked in a neutral tone. 'It's been four days since he took over.'

'As well as can be expected,' replied the talkative one. He no longer smiled. His voice carried a hint of displeasure.

The other man, a gloomy, reticent type, added, 'We really know little. He doesn't talk to us any more. Fancies himself a master, though he doesn't have a licence yet.'

The talkative man added, 'First thing, he moved out of the inn into Master Gagne's rooms, even wears Gagne's clothes, though they fit him like a scarecrow.'

'Since Gagne's family has fled, who works for him?'

'He hired a young girl he met in a brothel to sell the bread. But she can barely read and write.'

The gloomy man added, 'For the bakeroom he's hired a stranger as a journeyman. He wouldn't hire one of us who knew him.'

Throughout this conversation the two bakers continued to fill their cups from a jug of wine. Their voices grew louder, and angrier, the more they discussed their former companion. They obviously resented his good fortune. Anne grew concerned that other patrons of the tavern might overhear the conversation and carry it to unfriendly ears. But she had one last question.

'He needs to get married,' she offered in a half-serious tone. 'Shouldn't he look for a baker's widow to run the shop and keep accounts, a woman like Madame Gagne?'

The talkative baker replied earnestly, 'He had one, Yvonne. She was with him for years. Reads, writes, and reckons. But she's poor, has no family. Duby sent her away, says he'll marry a wealthy master's daughter.'

'What's become of Yvonne?' Sylvie asked.

The men shrugged their shoulders. The talkative one remarked, 'We saw her yesterday in the Palais-Royal. Someone said that she has no prospects. She sleeps in a bakery on Rue Richelieu, carries bread to customers.'

Anne now had the lead she was looking for. She got the name of the bakery, then she and Sylvie bid their companions a friendly goodbye.

Late that afternoon, they found Yvonne in a dingy café near the central markets. She was close to Duby's age, a few years past thirty, and a comely woman. But her recent misfortune had aged her appearance. Fatigued and dispirited, she slumped over a table, staring into a half-empty glass of wine. Anne and Sylvie set about winning her trust. Anne asked, 'May we have a word with you, Madame? It might be to your advantage.'

The woman looked up with a sceptical eye. Still, she showed a flicker of interest.

'And who might you be?'

Anne introduced herself and Sylvie. 'We just came from the office of the Bakers' Guild. The syndic of the guild spoke well of you and suggested that we meet.'

Yvonne sat up, took a drink of the wine, stared at Anne over the rim of the glass. 'The syndic and his guild think only of the masters' interest and couldn't care less about the likes of me.'

'Usually, that's true. But you have something that might be useful to the syndic and to the masters.'

'And what might that be?' Her voice dripped with sarcasm.

'Pieces of a puzzle.' Anne set out to interpret the mind of the syndics. 'You know important facts behind the murder of the baker Gagne. This crime is like a dagger in the hearts of the masters. If it remains unresolved and unpunished, it threatens all of them. Journeymen throughout Paris will be tempted to hang their masters. Like us, the leaders of the guild also suspect that journeyman Duby took part in the crime in order to usurp his master's position.'

Yvonne put down the glass. Her eyes, now fully alert, regained their lustre. 'Why should I be concerned? For all I care, the masters can go hang themselves.'

'You are asking what's in it for you? A fair question. If your information is useful, the masters must pay you for it. I'm talking about a reward. You and the guild both win if the case is solved quickly and fairly.'

'I have a final question for you two ladies.' She pushed her glass aside, tapped on the table, and met Anne's eye. 'Why are you and your friend involved in this? What's in it for you?'

Anne pulled the abbé's letter from her bag and handed it to Yvonne. 'I'm working for Madame Gagne, who has lost her husband, her business, and her home.'

Yvonne scanned the letter and sighed. 'I know her. A decent sort. That bastard Duby has cheated both of us, stolen more from her than from me. I'll share with you all that I know. And may Duby burn in hell.'

She led Anne and Sylvie to a large bakery near the great merchants' church of Saint-Eustache. 'Wait outside,' she said and hurried into the shop. A few minutes later, she came out carrying a bag. 'My treasures,' she said with a sardonic smile. 'We'll go into the church. It's cool and private there. But we must watch out for the sexton. He tries to prevent the homeless and the hungry from gathering here.'

'I'll stand guard and warn you if he comes,' said Sylvie.

Anne and Yvonne found a secluded corner in a side chapel and pulled a couple of chairs together.

'First, Madame, let me tell you my story.' She had been Duby's partner for several years. Since he was nearly illiterate, she had managed his affairs – that is, kept his meagre accounts, wrote his messages, petitions and requests, read the news to him, and shared his bed when he hadn't another woman for the night. He kept her in thrall by promising that, when he became a master baker, they would marry. She would manage the shop while he baked.

'However,' she hissed, 'when he took over the Gagne bakery four days ago, almost the first thing he did was to send me away. He hired his latest slut, a beautiful, young, ignorant country girl, to sell bread from the shop. She can hardly count to ten. Then he declared that he would soon marry a well-dowered master's daughter or perhaps a rich widow.

'But he wasn't so sure of himself. I knew damaging things about him. From his dictation, I had written the false messages and receipts that implicated Gagne in hoarding and profiteering. Unbeknown to Duby, I had also kept copies of them, just in case they might prove useful in holding him to his promise. I had begun to distrust him.'

'Why didn't you confront him at that time?'

'I was afraid. He said that powerful, ruthless men, like the Duc d'Orléans, were protecting him. If need be, he could call the mob to his defence. The Bakers' Guild could do nothing; it's a toothless lion. And Duby threatened to cut my throat if I ever accused him.' She shuddered. 'Telling you all these things may be stupid of me. He has a long reach.' For a few moments she sat silently, wringing her hands.

'But I've come too far to quit. Duby's involved in a harebrained scheme. The police will uncover it eventually.' She reached into the bag and pulled out a small pack of papers. 'Look at these. They'll make him pay for cheating me.'

Anne scanned the papers, recognizing receipts for several hundred-pound sacks of fine white flour, together with messages to unnamed buyers promising them loaves of luxury bread at prices high above the legal limit.

Yvonne pointed to the pack. 'These are exact copies of the originals which Duby hid in the little bakery office where records were kept. The police were supposed to discover them and may have them somewhere.'

'Let's be clear. You said you wrote the originals as well as the copies.'

Yvonne hesitated, becoming aware that she might have confessed to aiding and abetting a serious crime.

'If you cooperate,' Anne assured her, 'you'll escape arrest. The police will regard you simply as a scribe, obliged to write under Duby's dictation. It's well known that he's virtually illiterate. Subsequently, you refrained from exposing him because he threatened to kill you.'

Yvonne nodded grudgingly. 'Yes, I wrote all of them. God help me.'

The last step in gathering evidence was to account for the sacks of flour that were illegally hoarded. The maid would testify that she saw strangers sneaking them into baker Gagne's storeroom while the bakeroom was empty. So Anne asked Yvonne what she knew.

'Duby didn't involve me in that part of the scheme,' she replied. 'But I overheard two men, Simon and Nicolas, tell Duby that they would hide two sacks of high-grade flour in the bakery's storeroom.'

'Had you seen those men before?' Anne asked.

'Yes. On one occasion when I was with Duby at the inn on Rue Sainte-Anne, we met them. He left me for a while and spoke with them at another table. Afterwards, I asked what they talked about. He replied, "Oh, just business." I noticed that they gave him money.' She paused, and a hard, sly look came over her face. 'Do you think that the magistrates will hang him?'

'It's too early to say,' Anne replied. 'But the evidence against him is growing stronger. I now feel more confident that justice will be done – and you might receive a reward.'

Twenty-Three

Death of a Lieutenant

Paris, Monday, 27 July

Monday morning, near noon, Georges and Pioche visited the barracks in Chaillot and discussed Maury's disappearance with the commandant. Together with several soldiers, they had spent the previous day in a vain search for the lieutenant. No one would admit to having seen him. That seemed ominous. Loud and aggressive, he was the kind of man who had to be noticed.

While Georges was in the middle of a sentence, a young boy burst into the room. Breathless, wide-eyed, he exclaimed, 'I've found a soldier's body.' The boy had been picking berries in a wooded area above Chaillot.

Led by the boy, the three officers immediately ran to the site. Maury's body, dressed in his uniform, lay face up in thick growth a few paces from a small clearing. A sword was stuck deep into his chest in a grotesque theatrical gesture.

The commandant examined the sword's hilt. 'That's his own weapon, expensive, elaborately engraved. He was very proud of it, showed it off at every opportunity.'

Georges bent down on one knee next to the body. To judge from its condition, Maury had died late Saturday night or early Sunday morning. The brush in which he lay was barely disturbed; there was no sign of struggle.

'He has been killed elsewhere, then brought here – carried rather than dragged.' Georges leaned over and studied the wound. There was little blood on the uniform, mostly spots near the sword. He seemed otherwise unscarred.

Georges rose to his feet, brushed specks of dirt from his knee. 'Maury was already dead when the sword pierced his heart.

The surgeon who is to examine the body will probably discover that he died from a gunshot wound.'

The commandant agreed that Georges and Pioche should continue with the investigation. After all, Maury was a suspect in the death of Lieutenant Harivel. The body was brought to the barracks and a surgeon summoned.

Georges and Pioche then called on Madame Maury to inform her of the discovery. She had found refuge in the home of an elderly woman near the church. She was frail and hard of hearing and couldn't grasp why they had come. But eventually they made her understand that they needed to speak to Madame Maury. A maid brought her to the parlour where the officers were seated.

'Monsieur Charpentier,' she exclaimed. 'What brings you here?'

Georges couldn't decide whether her surprised expression was genuine. 'We bring you news of your husband. We found his body.'

When the officers had earlier inquired about her husband's disappearance, she hadn't seemed surprised or concerned. 'This happens occasionally,' she had said. 'He goes off without telling me.'

Now, when they brought news of his violent death, she tried to seem shocked and distressed. 'Oh, how dreadful,' she whimpered, a pained expression on her face. But her eyes – dry and shining with gladness – betrayed her true feelings of profound relief. Given Maury's history of brutality towards her, Georges was hardly surprised.

'I have a few questions for you, Madame Maury.' He sent Brigadier Pioche out to question the maid.

'Were you legally married to the lieutenant?'

She glanced at her ring. 'We lived like husband and wife, but he wanted to be free to marry another woman.'

'One who could bring him a large amount of money. Am I right?'

'Yes,' she replied softly. 'He was unlucky at gambling, always in debt.'

'A final question.' Georges leaned towards her, caught her eye. 'Madame, where were you on Saturday night?'

'Here, of course. I slept till dawn.'

He had heard enough. 'We'll speak to you later, Madame.' He called Pioche, then he and the brigadier left the house.

On the way to the Maury cottage, Georges asked his companion, 'What did you learn from the maid?'

'She put her elderly mistress to bed early and slept in the room with her through the night. Heard nothing. Madame Maury's room was in a distant part of the house.'

Georges stroked his chin thoughtfully. 'So, Madame Maury has no alibi. She could easily have left the house about the time Maury was killed.'

The door to the cottage was still open where Maury in a drunken rage had broken in. The two officers searched the room thoroughly. Shards of tableware and parts of a chair lay strewn across the floor.

Georges wondered if Maury might have resisted before being shot. 'Was there a struggle here?'

'I don't think so,' Pioche replied. 'Maury himself caused this destruction, Saturday night, when his wife refused to let him in.'

The search proved fruitless. For the rest of the day, Georges and Pioche questioned Maury's fellow guardsmen, as well as people in the village who might have seen or heard anything unusual at the supposed time of Maury's death. Of special interest were Maury's gambling companions at the tavern near the barracks. They admitted despising the victim, but professed their innocence and gave each other alibis.

Joseph Mouton was the last to be questioned. He was on duty at the barracks cleaning muskets. His reaction to the news of Maury's death was a mixture of relief and anxiety.

'Where were you that night?' Georges asked. He had learned that Mouton had spent Saturday night on leave away from the barracks.

'Asleep in my bed.'

'Will you contradict your commandant? He says you were on leave.'

Mouton grew greatly distressed. 'I shouldn't try to deceive you. I simply can't tell you where I was.'

A point of honour, Georges realized, then guessed, 'Were you with Madame Maury that night?' He met the young man's eye. 'Don't lie to me. She doesn't have an alibi. I'll get the truth out of her.'

The young man hesitated, stammered, 'Yes, she came to me at the secret cottage. We had earlier agreed to meet there.

Maury terrified her. She was overwrought. We spent the night together.'

'Did you realize that she wasn't truly married to the lieutenant?'

'Yes, my father told me. I didn't have to kill him to marry her.'

'Right, but you believed that he killed your father. So you had another, even stronger reason: revenge.'

Meanwhile, early in the evening, Anne and Sylvie left Yvonne at Saint-Eustache and returned to the town house on Rue Traversine. Anne changed from her disguise and went home. For safekeeping, she had persuaded Yvonne to trust her with the copies, as well as her signed testimony. She put them on Paul's desk. The local police bureau couldn't be relied upon.

Anne had just put on a housedress and ordered supper when Paul arrived from Château Beaumont. They sat down to a meal of roast duck and red wine. He told her that the countess and her tenants, together with the Highway Patrol, had thwarted Gaillard's attempt to disrupt the grain trade and damage the estate's economy. The common struggle had also reconciled the discontented tenant Gigot with the countess and strengthened her situation.

Paul concluded, 'Our success should show other landlords how to put a stop to the duke's attempts to create panic in the countryside.'

'I also have good news.' Anne described her effort to discover the author of the messages falsely attributed to the baker Gagne. 'I've discovered copies. They are on your desk. Journeyman Duby dictated the originals to his partner Yvonne.'

Paul's eyes lit up. 'Under the former regime, her testimony would suffice to convict him of conspiracy to murder Monsieur Gagne. But in today's chaotic circumstances, we'll need stronger evidence to convince Mayor Bailly. He's reluctant to correct this miscarriage of justice since he risks provoking mob violence.'

Anne suggested, 'We could sneak into the basement of the police bureau and steal the originals. It shouldn't be difficult to find them. Monsieur Roland said Gagne's papers are in an unsealed box on the basement floor.'

Paul shook his head. 'I fear that stealing the papers from

the police bureau might throw doubt on their authenticity and prejudice the magistrates against our case.'

'What else can we do? If we wait much longer, the papers may be lost or stolen.'

'We must act quickly,' Paul granted. 'Tomorrow, I'll go to Mayor Bailly and the Marquis de Lafayette and argue for a new investigation into the baker Gagne's death. With the mayor's permission, we could retrieve the papers from the basement and give them to Comte Savarin. He could confirm their authenticity, as well as compare them to the copied papers and the handwriting on Gagne's application to the Bakers' Guild.'

'Can you reach him in time?'

'Yes, fortunately. This morning as I was leaving Château Beaumont, he arrived for an extended visit. I was pleased to see him. His groom and his valet are stout, former soldiers, and should add to Aunt Marie's security.'

Anne was surprised. 'I didn't realize that the count and the countess had become *such* good friends.'

'They've been seeing each other for months and were together at the town house for the symphony concert a week ago.'

'But this visit to her chateau looks almost permanent.' Anne didn't know the count's character well enough to fully approve this new development. But she didn't feel entitled to speak against it.

'True, a significant step in their friendship. I'm happy for her. But, back to the new investigation. When I speak to the mayor, I'll stress that Lieutenant Maury's initial investigation was a travesty. His lack of credibility should be obvious, especially to Lafayette whom he has deceived and disobeyed.'

'Who could carry out the new investigation?'

'Inspector Quidor. For another week, his authority will remain valid. Early in August, a new elective system will replace him and all the other inspectors who purchased the office. I don't know what will become of him. There isn't much time, so I must act quickly.'

A servant entered the room with a plum compote. When he had served it and left, Anne raised an idea that she had been thinking about since the day before. 'How could we persuade Madame Gille and her daughter to help us search Gaillard's office?'

'I see your point, Anne. It's more risky and dangerous for them than for us. At the very least, we should offer them a safe, improved alternative to the duke's service.'

'When you meet the mayor tomorrow, ask him to find work for the two women in the Louvre. It's the safest place that I can imagine, and the pay should be much better than the duke's pittance.'

'That's a good suggestion; I'll propose it to the mayor.'

A few minutes later, when they had nearly finished the supper, a servant appeared at the door. 'Monsieur Charpentier has arrived and asked if he may disturb you. He has important news.'

'Show him in,' said Paul.

His face flushed from exertion, Georges bounded into the room, caught his breath, and announced, 'Maury is murdered. We found his body today.'

He joined Anne and Saint-Martin at the table and described the discovery of the body and the subsequent investigation. 'We need to take a closer look at his gambling companions and the young man, Mouton. All of them have strong motives.'

'And,' Saint-Martin observed, 'they all have alibis. What do you make of the sword piercing Maury's heart?'

'It's a reference to Bertier's assassination and Maury's grotesque gesture in the City Hall, condemned by Maury's fellow officers and by Mouton.'

'But why would they call attention to themselves?'

Anne was listening carefully. Now she reminded the men, 'Gaillard and Laclos were heard complaining that Maury wanted too much money. Gaillard may have decided to be rid of him.'

'Quite possibly,' Georges admitted. 'We'll look into that.'

Twenty-Four

A Perilous Enterprise

Paris, Tuesday, 28 July

In the morning Colonel Saint-Martin met Mayor Bailly in his apartment in the Louvre. As they sat at the table in his study, he told Saint-Martin that the plan to move into DeCrosne's old office in the Hôtel de Police was going forwards. To Saint-Martin's mind, this move was a welcome symbol of continuity in the city's police administration. It was also an encouraging sign that the city's administration might be overcoming the chaos of the past two weeks. Bailly's demeanour hardly changed, but he appeared to feel more self-assured as the city's chief magistrate.

Encouraged, Saint-Martin summarized developments in the Harivel and the Gagne cases. 'They seem connected,' Saint-Martin opined. 'Lieutenant Maury is a central figure in both, part of a scheme to create a climate of fear in the city.' Saint-Martin paused, then added, 'But we can't question him. His body was found in Chaillot last night.'

Bailly raised an eyebrow in surprise. The news of Maury's death had not yet reached him. Saint-Martin filled in the details of the body's discovery. 'We have questioned several persons of interest but have not yet identified any serious suspects.'

'I confess, Colonel, that I'll not shed a tear for the man. Maury's role in Bertier's assassination was shocking. I shall never forget him holding up the victim's heart on the tip of his sword and trying to present it to us. What a ghastly, repulsive gesture!'

For an instant the horrific scene flashed before Saint-Martin's eye. A burst of anger nearly blinded him. 'Had I been there, sir, I would have killed Maury on the spot, regardless of the consequences. He was a treacherous brute. I deeply regret that I didn't follow Bertier's coach into the city. At Pont Notre-Dame, I could have prevented it from turning towards the City Hall and the mob gathered there.'

If the colonel's unusual display of temper surprised or shocked Bailly, he hardly showed it. He was quiet for a moment, then simply asked, 'What will you do next, Colonel?'

'Maury's death creates an opportunity to rectify a gross injustice against Monsieur Louis Gagne, the baker hung by a mob outside his shop on Rue Sainte-Anne. Maury merely pretended to investigate the baker's death, wrongly charged him with hoarding and profiteering, and declared that the mob's action was legitimate popular justice. The magistrates in the local police bureau accepted his version of the event.'

'Your conjecture is plausible, but is it based on evidence?'

'Yes, indeed, sir. The Abbé de l'Épée asked my wife to look after the interests of Gagne's deaf widow. While investigating the circumstances of Gagne's death, my wife has drawn signed testimony from several witnesses that exonerates the baker of any wrongdoing and proves that he was murdered.' Saint-Martin handed the mayor copies of Anne's interviews with Cécile Tremblay, with Gagne's son and his maid, and with Yvonne, the journeyman's partner. 'All this testimony,' Saint-Martin concluded, 'together with Maury's utter lack of credibility, should justify reopening the case.'

The mayor appeared to listen with cautious interest. 'And what do you propose that we should do?'

'You should instruct the local magistrates to retract their previous verdict in the Gagne case and choose a new investigator to replace Maury.'

'Can you suggest someone for the position?'

'Yes, Inspector Quidor, the most able and experienced investigator in the former regime. He initially offered to take on the job, but Maury rebuffed him.'

'If we were to put Quidor in charge, Colonel, we might provoke a strong reaction from the mob that killed the baker.'

'Correct, sir. And a similar response from powerful persons who incited the mob in the first place. Therefore, we need the support of the Marquis de Lafayette and his National Guard.'

A servant appeared at the door to the study. 'Sir,' he announced to Bailly, 'this broadside has just appeared in the Palais-Royal. I thought you would want to see it.' He handed a sheet to Bailly, who scanned it, frowned, and passed it on to Saint-Martin.

> Citizens of Paris, the minions of despotism have murdered Lieutenant Maury of the National Guard and hero of the Bastille. His body was found late yesterday in Chaillot. All good Parisians will recall this brave patriot. On July 23, as the people's strong right arm of justice, he struck down the erstwhile intendant of Paris. Enemies of the people, rest assured that we know who you are. Maury's death will be avenged with your blood.

'The reaction was quick in coming,' Saint-Martin observed. 'I recognize Gaillard's hand. Many desperate men and women will believe him. It's more urgent than ever to beard the lion in his den and stop his depredations.'

Bailly appeared incredulous. 'Do you really intend to attack Gaillard in the duke's palace?'

'In a manner of speaking, we do. We've found two women with access to Gaillard's rooms in the duke's palace who could be persuaded to help us search them and expose his criminal acts. That should undermine his influence with the people. The women are of course reluctant to risk their life and livelihood. Could you find work for them here in the Louvre where they would feel safe? One of them is deaf. My wife could introduce them to you.'

'Carry the war to the enemy, is that it, Colonel?' Bailly paused thoughtfully. 'I'll write an invitation to Madame Cartier and the two women to meet me here late this afternoon. Now we'll visit the Marquis de Lafayette.'

In the anteroom to Lafayette's office the air was warm and fetid, the noise deafening. Dozens of men and women jostled each other, demanding to see the commandant of the National Guard. Many of them had been waiting for hours and were grumbling that he should organize his time better.

Unperturbed, the marquis's secretary seated Mayor Bailly and Colonel Saint-Martin in a secluded part of the room, where they could at least carry on a conversation. An adjacent open window offered them an occasional draught of fresh air.

After surveying the scene, Bailly remarked, 'The marquis himself is to blame for this extraordinary press of business. He has many irons in the fire and tending to all of them is more than he can manage.'

Saint-Martin was irritated. 'If I may say so, the marquis is a poor judge of his own abilities. He aims to lead the French nation into a new era of liberty. That's impossible, even for leaders more gifted than he. His power depends far too much on his present popularity. The people are fickle and will turn against him when his reforms cause pain – as they must.'

The mayor demurred. 'He's our best hope for progress and more realistic than you seem to think. His National Guard will replace the former, inadequate police of the city and preserve the peace. That's a good first step towards a regime of liberty.'

'Unfortunately,' countered the colonel, 'the National Guard has assumed in the marquis's mind the character of a personal army. At sixty thousand men, it's far too large and unwieldy for him to manage efficiently.'

The marquis didn't keep the mayor and the colonel waiting long. After a few minutes, Lafayette himself opened the door and invited them in.

'What can I do for you, gentlemen?'

Bailly replied, 'We need a reliable detachment of National Guards to protect the witnesses, the magistrates, and the records and other evidence in the case of the baker Louis Gagne.'

Saint-Martin added, 'They must patrol Rue Sainte-Anne and guard the local police bureau.'

The marquis's brow furrowed. 'May I ask why? Has something gone badly wrong?'

Bailly deflected the question to Saint-Martin.

'Yes,' he replied. 'We can prove that a conspiracy including the late Lieutenant Maury wrongfully killed the baker Gagne.'

Lafayette interrupted. 'The *late* lieutenant, you say?'

'My men found his body last night. He was missing for almost two days.' Saint-Martin described the circumstances surrounding Maury's death. 'The lieutenant was apparently being paid by Laclos and Gaillard but had recently earned their displeasure. He had other enemies as well. All have alibis thus far.'

The marquis crossed his arms on his chest, his jaw tightened. 'As you both know, Maury deceived me by delivering Bertier to the Place de Grève instead of to the Abbaye prison. His obscene gesture with the heart later that night in the City Hall was appalling. What mischief did he commit in the Gagne case?'

Bailly replied, 'As the chief investigator, he gave the court a false report that incriminated the baker. For this and other reasons, we need to reopen the case and appoint a new, trustworthy investigator.'

Saint-Martin added, 'We suggest Inspector Quidor. For years he has worked in the area of the crime and is familiar with this case.'

'I trust your judgement.' Lafayette sighed. 'You've mentioned Laclos and Gaillard. In other words, the duke's faction is mixed up in this case. That must be why you want the National Guard's protection.'

Bailly and Saint-Martin nodded.

The marquis was silent for a moment, tapping his fingers on the table. 'I'll order the local National Guard to cooperate with your investigation. I'll also give you a patrol of guards on Rue Sainte-Anne and a few extra guards at the local police bureau. But I can't guarantee that these measures would ward off the determined assault of a well-organized mob.'

And that mob, thought Saint-Martin, was precisely what he expected Laclos and Gaillard to deploy – together with a pair of assassins.

As they left Lafayette's office, Bailly told Saint-Martin to recruit Quidor. Bailly himself would now visit the local police bureau and instruct the prosecutor and the magistrates to reopen the case.

'That will be a difficult task,' said Saint-Martin as they parted. 'God be with you!'

'Yes, thank you. The local court will be most unhappy. No one likes to admit making a serious mistake, such as wrongly condemning a man and pauperizing his family. But with patience and good reasoning, I'll bring my colleagues to the right path.'

Spoken like a true, enlightened scholar, Saint-Martin thought. The prosecutor and the magistrates will be keenly apprehensive. The pamphleteers at the Palais-Royal have persuaded the public of Gagne's guilt and of the justice of his punishment. Changing the verdict will confuse, even upset them. Worse yet, the mob who hung Gagne will be enraged and eager to react.

Saint-Martin found Quidor at the Hôtel de Police. His desk was as cluttered as ever, so he was still busy. But his eyes had lost their sparkle, his voice seemed tired, his manner was less brusque than usual. He slouched listlessly in his chair.

As perceptive as ever, Quidor anticipated the question that Saint-Martin was about to ask. 'You are correct, Colonel. I find less pleasure now in my work, and it shows. I'm tired. The mayor has asked me and my fellow inspectors to stay on, but perhaps I'll retire instead to a quiet village in the country and play dominoes for the rest of my life. Compared to our former lieutenant generals, like Sartine, Lenoir, and DeCrosne, my newly elected masters in the police bureaus, not to speak of the mayor himself, are feckless, clueless amateurs. The art of criminal investigation is utterly beyond their ken. They seek the approval of the crowd or political gain, rather than the truth.' He paused, gave Saint-Martin a crooked smile. 'But you haven't come to hear me complain. What can I do for you?'

'We can't afford to lose you, sir. Be patient. You can train your "masters". Some of them, like the magistrate Monsieur Roland, are willing to learn, but need protection, encouragement and instruction.' Saint-Martin paused, met Quidor's eye. 'I've come to ask you to take on a difficult task: the investigation of the baker Gagne's death.'

The inspector sat up. 'That case is finished, a travesty of justice, to be sure, but it's packed up. The mayor hasn't the wit or the courage to change the verdict. The duke has spoken: "Rid me of that pesky baker," he said. Laclos and Gaillard said, "Yes, sire." And it was done.'

Saint-Martin raised a calming hand. 'Granted, sir, that much of what you've just said is true. But it may surprise you to learn that the case will be reopened. My wife, Anne, has gathered sufficient evidence to undermine the verdict.' He went on to describe her interrogation of Cécile Tremblay, as well as the baker's widow, son and maid and Duby's partner.

'She has taken signed, written depositions from them all. She will give you the originals and keep copies.'

'Amazing!' Quidor gave the colonel a teasing smile. 'She's become a skilful investigator, thanks to Charpentier and me.'

Saint-Martin acknowledged the compliment with a slight bow. 'She'll be pleased when I tell her. She's grateful to her instructors.' He smiled, then caught Quidor's eye. 'This morning I presented the baker's case to Bailly and Lafayette and they agree that the verdict was wrong. I recommended you to carry out a fresh investigation and they accepted.'

Quidor's face brightened. 'Then I accept as well. When this case is resolved, I'll consider my options. Life in the country might bore me to death. Bailly has offered us inspectors jobs in the new regime. A change might be good for me. I've been an inspector of police for eleven years.'

'I hope that you will serve Paris for many more,' said Saint-Martin. He paused, smiled wryly. 'Lieutenant Maury will not stand in your way this time. He was found murdered last night.'

'I know, I read the broadside at my coffee hour in the Palais-Royal. I wonder if the duke's men got rid of him. He was out of control.'

'There are other suspects as well.' Saint-Martin told him briefly about Mouton and Maury's fellow officers. 'How else can I help you in the investigation?'

'You could allow your wife to assist me. The key witnesses in this case are either deaf or female or both. She knows them all.'

'I'll ask her. She doesn't need my permission. I trust her good judgement.'

That same morning, Georges returned to Passy and met with Brigadier Pioche. Together they went to the office of the surgeon who had examined Harivel's wound. He had now finished examining Maury's. 'Gentlemen,' he said, leading them into his surgery, 'the victim died of a gunshot wound to the heart. The murder weapon was a pistol, but it fired a larger ball than the one that killed Lieutenant Harivel. As you have surmised, the sword was inserted in the bullet wound sometime after the man had died.'

'Why?' Pioche asked. 'Can you think of a reason?'

The surgeon shrugged. 'The killer could see that the victim was dead. The sword was a whim, a sign of contempt. Who knows?'

Georges thanked the surgeon, and the two officers returned to Pioche's office in Passy with the weapon. Georges laid it on the writing table and gazed at it while he mused aloud. 'With this sword, the perpetrator of Maury's death would lead us to believe that fellow officers of the royal army killed him. In butchering Bertier, he had violated their code of honour and cast a pall of shame upon all royal officers. The offence called for a duel.'

'That could have happened in Maury's case,' Pioche agreed. 'The murder weapon might have been a duelling pistol. I can imagine his companions at the gambling table drawing lots for the honour of killing him. Maury was drunk. It would not have been a fair fight, more like sticking a pig. But that wouldn't matter if the proper formalities were followed.'

'In truth,' Georges argued, 'the killer could be a common soldier like Joseph Mouton, a man with complex motives for murder. He probably believes that Maury killed Harivel, his father, because of the interest he showed in his wife. Mouton also witnessed Maury's crime on the Place de Grève, and it profoundly disturbed him. Finally, Mouton is in love with Maury's wife – that's easy to see. He must have been angered by Maury's abuse of her. With Maury out of the way, she and Mouton could marry.'

Pioche raised a hand. 'Let's not forget Gaillard. He could have used this device in order to cover up the assassination of a man who had become a serious liability.'

Georges added, 'Gaillard might not have pulled the trigger. He would have ordered Simon or Nicolas to do it.'

Twenty-Five
Research

Paris, Tuesday, 28 July

While her husband met with the mayor and the commandant, Anne walked to the countess's town house and found Sylvie and Michou in the studio preparing for work. Michou was at her easel studying the portrait of the young woman in the gold locket. A nearly finished, enlarged oil copy of the portrait rested on the easel. As Anne approached, Michou looked up and signed, 'Adelaide was a frail, gentle soul. What is she, twenty years later? She's become like a lost sister to me. I must find her and restore the locket. Perhaps her brother, Monsieur Gaillard, will point the way to her.'

'I'll certainly keep her in mind,' Anne promised.

Sylvie was at the writing table, examining her sketchbook.

Anne tiptoed up to her and whispered, 'Am I disturbing your train of thought?' She glanced at the open book. Blocks of text were interspersed with sketches.

'Not at all,' Sylvie replied, smiling. She showed a few pages to Anne and explained that the sketchbook recorded several recent visits to the duke's art gallery. Under the pretext of studying his collection of paintings and sculptures, she engaged palace servants in casual conversations, typically beginning with views on art or the weather or events of the day, and slipping into serious palace gossip. André helped with introductions and his own observations.

The focus of the inquiry was Gaillard. 'A man of remarkable regularity,' Sylvie began. 'I learned his daily routine and his personal habits. He doesn't gamble, eats and drinks only in moderation, but he smokes a pipe. He's careless in his dress, slovenly in his hygiene, gross in his manners.

'He rises at dawn, when a servant brings him a tray of coffee and bread. He writes until noon, walks in the garden until two in the afternoon. He dines in a restaurant until four, when he goes back to his office. He finishes work at nine. Between nine and midnight he frequents cafés and brothels.'

Anne reflected for a moment, then asked Sylvie, 'Would his apartment be empty between nine and midnight?'

'No, his dog is kept in the office. During the daytime hours, his clerk sits at a table in the anteroom. An elderly servant takes his place at night. Both are served tea from the kitchen. I don't know how vigilant they are. Nor do I know whether he locks his door at night.'

A wave of doubt swept over Anne. How could she search Gaillard's office without alarming the dog, the clerk or the servant?

'Sylvie, I need to be reminded of the plan of his apartment.'

'Come back for dinner at two. André will join us. As you know, he's familiar with the office and should be able to answer your questions.'

Following the conversation with Michou and Sylvie, Anne went to her room on the top floor to be alone. She needed to think. For several minutes, she paced back and forth, mentally preparing for the search of Gaillard's office. She decided to accompany Madame Gille to the palace, next evening, disguised as her deaf daughter. Madame Gille could get them past the elderly servant in the anteroom and quiet the dog. While she cleaned the office, Anne would search through Gaillard's papers. Georges would find a way to join them.

Anne recognized the risk of the plan failing. They might get caught. But the most serious obstacle was the natural, reasonable reluctance of Madame Gille and her daughter to take part. They might lose their job at the palace. Laclos and his allies might retaliate. Anne would have to offer mother and daughter strong inducements, and only Mayor Bailly could provide them.

Anne found Madame Gille at home. The woman didn't seem surprised to see her. 'I want you to know that yesterday I called on the Abbé de l'Épée and inquired about you. He trusts you implicitly and urged me to help you. I also learned that the Comtesse de Beaumont is your patron.'

Anne was hopeful but still unsure how far Madame Gille was prepared to act. Nonetheless, she outlined her plan to search Gaillard's office.

Gille's face paled. 'Won't Gaillard find out that we've gone through his things and suspect me?'

'Our search will be secret. Actually, you will clean the room as usual. Georges and I will search through Gaillard's papers to discover his crimes, learn who he intends to murder or rob. We'll put everything back as it was. He'll never know we've been there.'

Gille's expression remained doubtful.

'I understand the risk you'll be taking. You won't want to continue working in the palace, even if you could. So my husband has asked Mayor Bailly to give you and your daughter safer, better jobs in the Louvre. We'll meet him there in his apartment late this afternoon. If we succeed in ending Gaillard's campaign of terror, you'll receive a reward.'

Gille appeared tempted, but her doubts lingered. 'You do look like my daughter but can you really act like her?'

'As an actress I've learned how to become another person for a couple of hours. Before moving to France three years ago, I performed for a decade in London theatres and music halls. True, I've met your daughter for only a couple of hours. But I can imitate her. Watch.' Anne walked to Gille's little kitchen and pretended to wash dishes.

'I'm impressed,' said Gille. 'You drag your left foot slightly when you walk; you tilt your head and slouch as you do the dishes – just like Adrienne.'

'I can also act as if I'm deaf. I've observed my friend Michou and other deaf persons and practised behaving like them.'

Gille agreed to meet the mayor and seemed resigned to the search. 'I'll have to consult my daughter. She's likely to favour your plan – she's not directly involved, would earn more money, and would be closer to her husband in the Louvre's royal printing shop. I'm the one most at risk.'

At two Anne returned to the town house and brought Georges along. He had done as much as he could in Passy for the time being. Brigadier Pioche would continue the Harivel and Maury investigations. Georges shifted his attention to the Palais-Royal. He would pursue the idea that Harivel's bullet was meant for Colonel Saint-Martin and came from a pistol hidden in Gaillard's office.

During the dinner, Anne asked André, 'Where would Gaillard keep records, documents, correspondence?'

'The large cabinet in his office probably holds his ordinary files. It's usually locked, but I've seen him open it and pull out papers. There's also a drawer in his writing table – I presume that it's locked. He might hide his diary there. I've seen it on the table. And, finally, there's a suspicious book-case in the wall behind his chair at the writing table. To judge from marks that I noticed on the floor, the bookcase is mounted on small casters and can be swung out from the wall. Behind the bookcase is probably a small room. I can only guess at what he might keep there, perhaps pornography, stolen goods, materials for extortion.'

'Thank you, young man,' said Georges. 'You've given us a sense of where to look. We'll search the office tomorrow night, God willing.' He turned to Anne. 'Are you ready?'

'Almost. From here I'll go with Madame Gille and her daughter to arrange with the mayor for their safety. Then we'll practise the search.'

Late in the afternoon of Tuesday, July 28, Anne went to Bailly's Louvre apartment with Madame Gille and her daughter. Bailly had sent Anne a message.

> This is an invitation to you and the Mesdames Gille and Bertrand to meet me here this afternoon. It should get you past the guard downstairs. To protect the mother and daughter we must keep their visit as secret as possible. I can assure them a safe place in the Louvre.

The mayor greeted them with perfect courtesy, smiling more than usual to put the mother and daughter at ease. Tea and sweet biscuits were served, and the servants withdrew. Bailly had the women tell their stories; Anne translated for Madame Bernard.

'Tell me,' he asked Anne, 'why it's so important to search Monsieur Gaillard's office?'

'It's really a matter of life or death, sir. Among other crimes, Gaillard is plotting to assassinate my husband. His first attempt failed in Chaillot, so he'll try again. When we search his office tomorrow night, we hope to discover his plans and take measures to foil them. We think Paris will then be a much safer city.'

The mayor frowned. 'Won't the search be too risky and dangerous for three ladies?'

'We've planned this for days, together with Monsieur Charpentier, who knows the palace intimately and will join us in the office.'

'Does Colonel Saint-Martin fully understand your role, Madame Cartier?'

Anne smiled indulgently. 'Yes, monsieur, and he has helped plan the search. It is risky, to be sure, but necessary.'

'Risky, especially for Madame Gille,' said Bailly, 'so I must make it worthwhile for her.'

She sat up straight and looked anxiously expectant.

'To compensate them for their efforts, I've found work for them in the Louvre at a rate twice what the duke would pay. For Madame Bernard, I've already found a position cleaning in the royal printing office near her husband. For Madame Gille, there's a room in the Louvre and a job cleaning this apartment and, if you wish, perhaps one or two others. Finally, if you ladies are successful, you will receive a reward. When the search is completed and you are ready, my steward will show you around and answer your questions.'

Bailly gazed at the women benevolently for a moment, then asked, 'Are these arrangements satisfactory?'

The daughter, who had hung on his lips, nodded vigorously. Her mother reacted much more slowly. 'This is the right thing to do, sir. Your arrangements are the best that we could ever expect. I accept.'

Anne thanked the mayor, who bowed to each of the women, then left the room. She turned to the mother and daughter. 'We'll move to the town house on Rue Traversine and begin to prepare immediately and continue tomorrow. There's much to do.' She fixed her gaze on Madame Bertrand, whose eyes were brimming with hope, and the expectation of a marvellous turn in her fortune. She would be sorely tempted to share the news. 'Madame,' Anne signed earnestly, 'you must not tell anyone, not even your husband, about the search or the benefits you would receive if the search is successful. It must be absolutely secret. Gaillard has ears all over Paris.'

Madame Bertrand appeared chastened, seemed to take Anne's words to heart, and signed, 'I promise.'

Anne put aside her lingering doubts and smiled. 'Now we must get to know each other. I want to act like you as much as humanly possible.'

Twenty-Six
A New Investigation

Paris, Wednesday, 29 July

Early on this cloudy, misty morning, Inspector Quidor was expected at the provost's residence to plot strategy. He had sent a messenger ahead. Almost a week after the hanging of Monsieur Gagne, the new investigation into his case would begin without fanfare. Fear of starvation and violence still gripped the city's population. Ruthless, self-serving demagogues like Gaillard could still raise powerful false alarms.

Anne and Paul were waiting in his office, discussing current reforms in the royal administration. 'Our meeting with Quidor reminds me,' Paul said, 'that the National Assembly in Versailles will soon abolish venality of office.'

'What's that?' Anne asked. She had little interest in the details of politics.

'It's a property right in an official position,' Paul explained. 'If you have enough money, the King will sell you an office like inspector or magistrate. Once it's yours, you can sell it to a friend or pass it on to your son. Back in 1779, Quidor paid perhaps as much as ten thousand *livres* for the position of inspector. The assembly thinks that such positions should simply go to the most qualified persons, who would receive stipends in return for satisfactory service.' Paul smiled wryly. 'But who could we trust to pick the right persons? I don't know who sold the office to Quidor. But he's as able an inspector as anyone could hope to find.'

'I agree wholeheartedly,' said Anne. He had appreciated her interest in detection and shared some of his vast experience with her. His ten thousand *livre* investment was now in jeopardy.

Quidor entered the office in his usual brusque way, as if nothing had changed. He waved letters from Mayor Bailly and Commandant Lafayette. 'These are supposed to ensure that the local police bureau cooperates with us. I'm cautiously hopeful.'

After a brief discussion, Paul said to Quidor, 'While Madame Cartier collects the maid and the boy, you and I shall visit the police bureau, deliver the messages from Bailly and Lafayette, remove the spy across the street from the institute, pick up the box of papers that supposedly incriminated Gagne, and send them off to Comte Savarin at Château Beaumont for examination.'

'Afterwards,' said Quidor, 'Madame Cartier and I shall interview the maid and the boy at the institute, then I'll ask Madame Tremblay to confirm her testimony to Madame Cartier.'

Paul turned to Anne. 'In the afternoon, while I persuade Monsieur Roland to return to the court, you, Georges, Madame Gille and her daughter will rehearse for tonight's search of Gaillard's office. Georges is already making preparations at the Palais-Royal, beginning with Gaillard's favourite brothel, and will join you in the afternoon.'

'In the meantime,' continued the inspector, 'I'll visit the Bakers' Guild and study recent thefts of flour and millers' marks on flour sacks. I'll also arrange for a temporary baker. Then tomorrow we'll be ready to interrogate and probably arrest the journeyman Duby at the bakery.'

Paul caught his wife's eye. 'Sounds like a full day's work, Anne. Are you ready for it?'

Anne had earlier indicated that she would rather not be noticed, but would help Quidor where she could. As much as possible, she wanted to avoid notoriety and malicious gossip.

Three years ago, a scurrilous broadside that circulated in the Palais-Royal called her a violent English whore for having exposed a corrupt police inspector.

Paul's enemies, especially Gaillard, would relish any new opportunity to fabricate false tales about her and make him look foolish in the public eye. Still, no reasonable person expected her to hide out of sight in a corner. Any kind of prominence invited slander.

'For the sake of appearances,' she said to Paul, 'I want Sylvie de Chanteclerc to help me bring the maid and the boy to the institute, where the inspector and I can question them. Sylvie can accompany me on similar errands as well. She is fast becoming skilled at drawing information from people.'

Quidor smiled, slapped his thighs, and rose to his feet. 'This is a promising start. If all goes well, Parisians will once again feel safe in their streets.'

At the local police bureau, a pair of armed National Guardsmen had already taken up positions at the entrance to the building. A patrol of guardsmen had begun on Rue Sainte-Anne, which would allow Cécile Tremblay and her mother to return home.

Saint-Martin and Quidor met the prosecutor and the two remaining magistrates and showed them the letters from Mayor Bailly and the Marquis de Lafayette. The local officials complained that the city leaders, especially Bailly and Lafayette, were encroaching upon the authority of the elected police bureaux. Nonetheless, an order was sent to remove the spy across the street from the institute.

Saint-Martin explained that the level of violence in the city was exceptionally high and required a strong, unified response. He reassured the officials of his full respect. They in turn promised him their grudging cooperation.

The box of bakery papers was brought up from the base-ment, examined and sealed in the presence of the magistrates, then dispatched to Château Beaumont to Comte Savarin for analysis. He had already received samples of Gagne's writing from the archives of the Bakers' Guild, as well as the papers that Yvonne had entrusted to Anne. Saint-Martin promised the magistrates a full report on the papers in a few days.

Anne picked up Sylvie at the town house on Rue Traversine, and the two women set out to find the murdered baker's deaf son. A few days ago, he had been hiding in a bakery near the Boulevard but was going to have to move. As they neared the site, Anne sensed that a man was following them.

She signed her concern to Sylvie. They stopped at a fruit stand. With a sideways glance Anne picked out a likely suspect. He had also stopped at a book stall and appeared to be browsing. The women repeated the manoeuvre a couple of times with the same reaction from the man. They recognized him from the garden of the Palais-Royal, the nondescript informer who worked for both Quidor and the duke.

He's probably now in Gaillard's pay, Anne thought. Was he scouting for Simon and Nicolas? Had they laid a trap ahead? She felt a surge of anxiety, and strained her eyes studying suspicious persons loitering by the food stalls that she and Sylvie would soon have to pass.

Suddenly, as the spy pretended to gaze into a shop window, two men jumped out of a coach, seized him, and drove off. As the coach passed Anne and Sylvie, one of the men inside gave a discreet signal and smiled. They were Quidor's agents. Anne surveyed the street scene and picked out two more agents following them at a safe distance. She and Sylvie breathed sighs of relief.

The women encountered no further danger. The boy was hard to find; he had moved frequently from one baker to the next. They had refused to shelter or employ him, fearing that he would attract mob violence to themselves or their shops and families.

Anne and Sylvie found the boy at last in the central markets, unloading produce from a cart. Thin, dirty and discouraged, he had tried vainly for almost a week to find a safe refuge. Anne assured him that the way back to the institute was safe; Quidor's agents would protect them. The new investigation would hopefully redeem his father, the murdered baker, and restore his family.

The boy appeared sceptical. 'My father's killers are still hunting for me. But I can't live like this much longer.' He waved an arm over the markets in a gesture of disgust. 'I'll go with you to the institute.'

The maid was also afraid to return but Anne persuaded her to join them. At midmorning, Anne and Sylvie finally delivered the maid and the son to Madame Gagne at the institute. It was a bittersweet reunion. They were together again, but still without a home and a source of income.

With Anne interpreting, Quidor confirmed the statements that they originally gave to her.

When the young people had left the room, Anne asked Quidor if there was sufficient evidence to exculpate Madame Gagne and to fix guilt on Gaillard and his men, or on Duby.

'We'll soon have enough,' he replied. 'I'll speak to Madame

Tremblay next. I expect her testimony to corroborate the boy's. Both were eyewitnesses to the hanging and will identify Simon and Nicolas as the killers.'

'That should convince the court,' Anne observed.

'Correct. They supply important pieces of the puzzle. Tomorrow, Georges and I should find more of them when we question the journeyman Duby and search his bakery.'

At noon, Colonel Saint-Martin arrived at Pierre Roland's apartment. The magistrate had had three days to recover from his beating, as well as to gain enough distance from the event to judge his situation more objectively.

At the door his wife tried to send Saint-Martin away, but Roland was up and about. From within the apartment, he asked, 'Who is there?'

'Colonel Saint-Martin,' she replied.

'Show him in. I want to speak to him.'

Reluctantly, she gave way, but with a caution. 'Remember the threat to me and the children.'

She led the colonel through an open door into Roland's study. He sat at his writing table, looking pale and drawn. He promised his wife to be mindful of the dangers to the family. When she withdrew, he greeted his visitor courteously. From where Saint-Martin sat, he looked over Place du Carousel to the Tuileries Palace's monumental east façade – an inspiring view for a promising young magistrate. Behind him, the walls were lined with shelves of legal books. A volume lay open on the table; pen and paper at the ready. Even in his battered state, the magistrate seemed eager for work.

The colonel asked Roland about his health.

He lightly touched the back of his head. 'Some spots are still sore, but otherwise I feel fit. I would actually like to return to the police bureau. But I'm concerned about Gaillard's threat to my wife and children. I say Gaillard, because I'm sure he wants to prevent any serious investigation into his affairs.'

'He will try but fail.' Saint-Martin explained the measures included in the new investigation. 'The mayor and the commandant of the National Guard are committed to restoring order and the rule of law. By becoming part of that effort, you could gain stature in the city, and among its leaders.'

Roland sat up, raised his chin. The colonel's appeal to the magistrate's ambition had struck a spark.

'Danger continues,' Saint-Martin granted. 'Still, there are risks in any worthwhile effort. The alternative is to hide in a corner and do nothing. Such a life is not worth living.'

Roland nodded thoughtfully. 'That's true.'

The colonel had a suggestion. 'Would you feel more inclined to cooperate if your wife and children were to spend the next few weeks at a safe place in the countryside not far from here? My aunt, the Comtesse de Beaumont, might be willing to offer refuge to them. I would ask her.' He described to Roland the successful defence of Château Beaumont against Gaillard's men. 'I'm sure we can defeat them in the city as well.'

Roland appeared to favour the idea of putting his family out of harm's way and then joining the fight against lawlessness. 'I'll speak to my wife and give you our response this evening.'

Twenty-Seven
The Search

Paris, Wednesday, 29 July

E arly Wednesday morning, Georges dressed himself as a businessman from Rouen, his usual disguise. While Colonel Saint-Martin and Inspector Quidor launched the new investigation into the Gagne assassination, Georges was preparing for tonight's search of Gaillard's office.

He thought of his task in military terms. As a young man, he was a soldier in the royal army. As the colonel's adjutant, he still served in a military organization, the Royal Highway Patrol. So he thought of the search as a mission to scout the headquarters of the enemy camp.

He began his task in the Palais-Royal's Valois arcade. At Gaillard's favourite brothel, he contacted one of Quidor's spies among the servants. For ten *livres*, a significant sum, the servant reported that the madame was expecting Gaillard that evening at nine, the usual hour. The servant also agreed to show Gaillard's movements during the evening, especially his departure, with lantern signals from the brothel's windows.

Late in the morning, Georges met André Dutoit and Sylvie at the town house. They gave a detailed and encouraging report about activity in the palace.

'Many residents and servants are away on vacation,' said André. 'Surveillance at the entrances and in the hallways is slack. Properly dressed visitors and guests move freely through the palace halls and rooms, except those reserved to the duke and his family.'

'What about Gaillard?' Georges asked.

'He's holding to his routine of work and leisure. He'll be in the brothel tonight.'

'Would you take my spy's lantern signals from the brothel and relay them to the office windows while we're searching inside?'

André agreed. And Sylvie offered to tell Georges when Gaillard left the palace on his way to the brothel.

That same morning, Madame Gille paid casual visits to friends and acquaintances among the palace servants. Her daughter came along to present the clothes Anne would wear that evening. No one noticed her face, mostly hidden by her bonnet. She was unusually shy among hearing people, a characteristic that Anne would have to imitate.

Early in the afternoon, Gille and her daughter arrived at the town house. Gille learned that her impressions of the palace agreed with Georges'. Her anxiety diminished. She felt more at ease with the scheme.

During the afternoon, Georges directed Madame Gille and her daughter to walk through their evening routine, again and again. Anne observed and imitated them until the routine became second nature. Georges coached them throughout the afternoon and discussed possible surprises. He helped Anne act as a deaf person – standing behind her, snapping his fingers, speaking to her, shouting at her until she wouldn't react. On occasion at home, she had blocked her ears so that she couldn't hear, then put herself into various situations. Paul joined in the exercises, calling to her from another room. This training gave her insight into her students' behaviour and empathy with their problems.

In the evening, they had a light supper together and waited in the town house until Sylvie came to report that Gaillard had left for the brothel.

At nine thirty, assured that the coast was clear, Anne and Madame Gille approached the servants' entrance on the garden side of the palace. Anne wore the deaf Madame Bertrand's dress, apron and bonnet and felt comfortable in the role – like being back on stage.

Entering the palace proved to be easy. The guards at the entrance were accustomed to speaking to Madame Gille and ignoring her deaf daughter. Madame Gille greeted them as usual and walked into the palace with Anne on her arm.

The two women collected brooms, mops, dust cloths and baskets from a storeroom, climbed the stairs to Gaillard's floor, and stepped into a short hallway serving the four apartments for which Madame Gille was responsible. Their occupants, other than Gaillard, had already left the city for the summer vacation. She would air and clean them just before they returned.

In the anteroom to Gaillard's office, the elderly watchman mumbled a greeting, rose from his game of solitaire with scarcely a glance at the women, took the key from his belt, and let them into Gaillard's office. Leaving the door half-open, he went back to the table, picked up his cards, and resumed his game.

Gaillard's dog, a large black mongrel, was resting on a rug in front of the fireplace. When the women entered, he raised his head, got up, and sniffed Madame Gille. 'Gaillard calls him Nero. We're old friends.' She petted him and introduced Anne, who scratched him behind the ears. Pleased with the visitors, he returned to his rug, lay down, and closed his eyes.

Anne surveyed the room to confirm André's report. Nothing appeared to have changed. The women began to dust the furniture and to collect rubbish. After a few minutes, while Madame Gille continued the cleaning, Anne stepped around Nero and searched the fireplace where Gaillard probably burned confidential throw-aways. She stirred the ashes and found several small, half-burned pieces of paper and tucked them into her bag. Off to one side was a piece almost intact, singed only on the edges. It was a note from Gaillard to the steward of the palace kitchen, asking him to buy fine white bread from Monsieur Duby's bakery.

Two windows overlooked a dark courtyard. In the distance were the illuminated arcades, in the centre of the garden the hulking shape of the Circus. Anne unlatched the windows, pushed them open, and drew a deep breath. The air outside was cool, humid, and still; it had rained off and on during the evening. She left the windows open to air the room. The stench from tobacco was nearly overpowering. Outside the windows was a narrow balcony. In an emergency, one could enter or leave through the windows. One end of a coiled rope was tied to the balustrade for a rapid descent to the balcony of the gallery on the floor below.

Anne pulled a dust cloth from her apron pocket and swiped the surface of Gaillard's table. Among the loose piles of paper, one sheet caught her eye, so she began to move it towards her for a closer look.

'Let that be!' The watchman's cracked voice carried across the room. Anne fought with her natural instinct to stop and turn around. For a few seconds she continued to draw the sheet towards her, then moved it back, as if dusting the surface under it.

Her heart beat faster. Heavy-footed and lame, the man shuffled across the room, muttering loudly.

Madame Gille spoke up. 'She's deaf, Monsieur. She forgot the rules. I'll warn her again not to move anything.'

That seemed to satisfy the watchman. He returned to the anteroom and his table.

Their chores finished, the women gathered their cleaning equipment, deliberately leaving behind a dust cloth. The watchman, in the middle of a great yawn, ignored them as they left.

At a safe distance down the hall, Madame Gille whispered to Anne, 'The maid with the tea should be coming up from the kitchen at any minute. We'll intercept her at the head of the stairs.'

She arrived as predicted, a stout woman, puffing and red-faced.

'I'll take the tray from you, dear,' said Madame Gille with a kind smile. 'We're going back to Monsieur Gaillard's office anyway.'

The weary maid gladly yielded her burden, stopped for a moment to catch her breath, and lumbered slowly back down the stairs.

Anne tested the tea. 'It's heavily sugared. He'll never notice this sleeping potion, a tincture of laudanum.' She pulled a small bag from her pocket and emptied it into the teapot. 'He'll soon sleep like a baby.'

They returned to Gaillard's office. Madame Gille placed the tray on the watchman's table and explained that they had left a cloth in the office. He waved her in with an impatient gesture. Meanwhile, Anne poured tea into his cup. He took a drink, smacked his lips with approval, and drank more. By the time Madame Gille returned with the cloth, his cup was half empty. He was lifting it again to his lips as they left him.

'He'll be asleep in a few minutes,' Anne said. 'About the time that Georges should arrive.'

Meanwhile, as Georges approached the servants' entrance to the palace, he tugged nervously on his coat lapels, unsure how carefully the guards would examine him, someone they wouldn't recognize. He didn't have proper identification, only the forged papers of a deceased palace servant he had known.

Georges had dressed, however, in a suit of the duke's livery, stolen years ago from the palace. He had worn it while spying for Lieutenant General Sartine, who was concerned that the then Duc d'Orléans had organized a conspiracy to undermine the government. The conspiracy proved to be little more than a small group of blathering malcontents. Georges moved on to other tasks, but he had gained an intimate knowledge of the palace, and he kept the livery. Given the natural rivalry between the junior and senior branches of the royal family, he might later be called upon for another palace investigation.

At the entrance he acted as if he were returning from a short stroll in the garden. 'Looks like we'll have more rain tonight,' he said. With an easy gesture, he offered a small bag of mixed candied fruit to the guards. 'Take one each,' he said. They glanced at each other, then each took a piece and waved Georges through.

He chose the servants' circular staircase as the safest way to Gaillard's office on the second floor. He was about to take the first step, when he heard loud voices and heavy feet treading down. On an impulse, he backed into a shadowed corner beneath the steps. Absorbed in conversation, grim-faced, Simon and Nicolas walked past him. Simon stopped by a lighted sconce, held a small pistol up to the candle, checked the flint, then put the pistol into his pocket. Georges felt sure that they could hear his heart pounding. But they continued on to the entrance and out the door towards the palace garden.

On any other occasion Georges might have followed them. They were most likely on their way to raise a riot or to assassinate someone. But Georges reasoned that he wasn't prepared to stop them. Instead he should help Anne and Madame Gille search Gaillard's office. He started up the stairway.

In the anteroom the watchman sat upright at the table, snoring lightly, sound asleep. Georges tapped a prearranged signal on the door. It opened a crack. Madame Gille peered anxiously at him, then relaxed and let him in. Nero woke, eyed Georges doubtfully, met him halfway across the room and sniffed. Georges scratched him with expert fingers, received a lick in return. Nero returned to his place and was soon asleep again.

Meanwhile, Anne was fingering through a stack of papers on the writing table. 'I've found Gaillard's receipt for money he paid to the director of the asylum on Rue Charenton. Gaillard pays a monthly sum for his sister Adelaide's keep. This information is for Michou. We must help her figure out how to use it.'

When Georges approached, she patted the stack. 'Agents are writing to Gaillard about their efforts to disturb the grain transport in the countryside.' She held up a sheet of paper.

'This one describes the failed attempt to destroy the grain at Château Beaumont. In the margin Gaillard has written, "Search for easier targets." He lists a few. I've copied them.'

Georges joined her at the table.

'Shall we take the more incriminating papers with us?' she asked.

'We'll leave them exactly as we've found them. Take notes on the most important. Give them to the colonel. He'll know what to do with them. But we don't want Gaillard to suspect that we've been here. We'll take with us only our notes and what we can store in our heads.'

While Madame Gille did the actual cleaning, and Anne continued to work on the stack on the table, Georges opened the table drawer with his tools. 'What do we have here?' He lifted out a box, unclasped the top, and retrieved a pistol. He measured the bore, examined the barrel, showed it to Anne. 'It's been recently cleaned. This could be the weapon that cut short Lieutenant Maury's life.' He replaced the pistol in its box and returned it to the drawer.

'And here's his date book.' Georges held up a small, leather-bound book and began to scan it. The handwriting was minuscule and cramped. In the beginning, the entries were mostly dates without comment. In the back were pages in code. They had to be left to another visit.

Among the dates that caught his eye was July 14 – the entry was merely 'Bastille'. On July 22, it was 'Foullon & Bertier', and on July 23, 'Gagne, Saint-Martin'. A thin line was drawn through the first three names. After the colonel's, Gaillard had placed a question mark. So, Georges wondered, did this entry indicate that Saint-Martin, rather than Harivel, had been the target that night in Chaillot and something had gone wrong?

On the 25th Georges found a line through Lieutenant Maury's name, followed by a question mark, and on the 26th Anne and himself, without lines but followed by question marks. For tonight, the 28th, the colonel's name appeared again. Georges was puzzled. He showed the entry to Anne.

'What can that mean?' she asked, a worried expression on her face. 'I think he's safe at home tonight, working in the office. If he were called out for any reason, a pair of armed troopers would accompany him.'

Georges recalled Simon checking the flint of his pistol at the foot of the stairs. 'The assassins will probably lurk near the provost's residence hoping for an opportunity to attack. They don't know about the troopers guarding the colonel or his plan to work tonight in the office.'

'I'm still worried, Georges. I want to finish quickly and go home. We can come back here another time.'

'Give me another minute,' said Georges. He quickly surveyed the sitting room, then opened the secret cabinet behind the writing table. As expected, it held Gaillard's collection of pornography, as well as files on a variety of prominent persons, potential or actual targets for extortion. Among them was the Marquis de Lafayette, involved in a curious way with a woman other than his wife.

Looking out a window, Madame Gille was also becoming nervous. Suddenly she exclaimed, 'Gaillard has left the brothel. André is giving us a signal.'

Georges closed the cabinet. 'Is everything as it was?' he asked the two women. They nodded. 'Then let's go.'

After locking the door behind them, Madame Gille fastened the key to the sleeping watchman's belt. They hurried down the stairway, returned the cleaning equipment, and walked past the guards. Their eyelids heavy with boredom and fatigue, they hardly looked up.

A few paces down the path into the palace garden, a slope-shouldered figure shuffled into view. For an instant the faint light of his lantern shone on his face.

'Gaillard!' Georges whispered in Anne's ear.

His lips twisted in a bitter curl, his eyes sunken, the man seemed absorbed in his own thought and took no notice of them as they passed.

'That was close!' Georges murmured. They breathed a collective sigh of relief.

Back at the provost's residence, Anne and Georges sat facing Paul at his desk. They had escorted Madame Gille safely home. The two assassins were nowhere in sight. They must have realized that their target wouldn't come out tonight. Paul leaned forward, attentive, while Anne and Georges described their search of Gaillard's office.

'Here are the estates that he ordered his men to attack.' Anne handed him the list.

He glanced at it. 'My troopers will be ready for them.'

Georges described Gaillard's diary. 'Your name is on the assassins' list. We think they gave up tonight but will look for an opportunity tomorrow.'

'Thanks, Georges, for the warning. I'd like to surprise them.'

Twenty-Eight
A Rogue Exposed

Paris, Thursday, 30 July

Late the next morning, Inspector Quidor met Georges Charpentier in La Vache Agile, the café across from the Gagne bakery. Both men were in civilian clothes to blend as much as possible into their surroundings. Their deception was in vain. When they attempted to question the barman and patrons about the bakery, they received blank expressions and mumbled evasions. They looked like strangers, if not police officers.

'I believe,' ventured Georges, 'that the people here are fearful of getting involved in possible violence. I don't sense that they are hostile or angry.'

'That may be true,' Quidor agreed. 'Still, before we try to talk to Duby, we had better take an accurate reading of the pulse of the neighbourhood, and especially of his customers. If they *are* hostile, they could prevent us from effectively questioning him.'

'That's right,' Georges admitted. 'We don't want yet another riot here.' Earlier, as a precaution, Quidor had also dressed his agents in civilian clothes and stationed them nearby.

A man joined them at the table. Georges introduced him as a retired master baker, elderly but fit. He would temporarily supervise the baking in the likelihood that Duby had to be replaced. The bakery must not be shut down. Too many anxious, hungry people depended on it.

For a few more minutes, Quidor and Georges watched a steady stream of men and women going in and coming out of the bakery, buying bread for the midday meal. From their vantage point in the café, the officers couldn't judge the customers' attitude towards Monsieur Duby.

Finally, Georges suggested, 'I'll fetch Madame Cartier's friend, Sylvie de Chanteclerc. She lives nearby and knows people in this area. They'll talk to her. We'll get out of the way.'

Sylvie was at home alone. Michou had gone with Anne to Charenton. Georges explained the problem, and Sylvie agreed to help. 'Over the past few days,' she said, 'Michou and I have observed the neighbourhood, in particular the bakery, for Madame Tremblay's sake. Simon and Nicolas used to appear on the street at least once a day and make people tense. But we haven't noticed them today, frightened perhaps since the National Guardsmen began to patrol Rue Sainte-Anne. I'll talk to some of Duby's customers.'

From a table near the café's door, Sylvie and Georges watched the flow of customers in and out of the bakery. Finally, Sylvie nodded towards a middle-aged woman leaving the shop with a fresh four-pound loaf under her left arm.

'I know her,' Sylvie said. 'She has a mind of her own and likes to share it with others.' The woman crossed the street, entered the café, and searched for a table. All were occupied by men. Sylvie beckoned that she was welcome to sit with them. She smiled, joined them, and signalled the barman for a jug of wine. Georges excused himself and sat with Quidor at a distant table.

Sylvie bought wine for herself and addressed the woman. 'I see you've come from the bakery. Could you tell me about it? I understand that the management has changed. I'm wondering if it's as good as it used to be.'

The woman studied Sylvie's smiling, innocent countenance. She seemed pleased to be questioned. 'My dear,' she began, glancing over her shoulder towards the bakery, 'they used to bake the best bread in the Louvre district. Honest weight, fair price, high quality. But a week ago, a band of villains hung the baker, chased his family away, and put his journeyman in charge.' She drained her glass and filled it again.

Sylvie leaned forwards, tilted her head expectantly, encouraging the woman.

She bent towards Sylvie and whispered, 'Since then, the business has gone downhill. You can't trust the bread's weight – if this loaf is really four pounds, I'm the Queen of France.

I think the baker is selling fine bread to friends, out the back door, so to speak, at a handsome profit.'

'How does he get away with it?'

'People are afraid to denounce him. Those two villains, Simon and Nicolas, swagger up and down Rue Sainte-Anne, and walk into the bakery as if they own it.'

'But you haven't seen them today, have you?'

'Come to think of it, no, I haven't. I suppose the guards are keeping them away.'

'I'm sure you're right,' granted Sylvie with a meaningful nod of her head. 'Maybe now someone will look into baker Gagne's death and the eviction of his family.'

The woman nodded cautiously. 'I'm of your mind, Mademoiselle. The journeyman Duby may have blood on his hands. It's time to find out.' She finished her wine, rose from the table, tucked the loaf under her arm and waved goodbye.

Sylvie signalled Georges and Quidor to return. 'I can tell you, Messieurs, that she's an honest woman and has given me the true sense of the neighbourhood. The baker Duby has no friends here.'

With renewed confidence Georges and Inspector Quidor crossed the street towards the bakery. Sylvie's report concerning the neighbourhood's resentment towards Duby had been reassuring. But they were still cautious enough to refrain from bursting into the shop. They waited perhaps a half-hour until the stream of customers had slackened to a trickle.

It was now dinnertime, at least for those households that could afford a proper dinner. A pair of young, pale-faced apprentices left the shop in the direction of the bakers' inn a few minutes' walk down the street. Baking was finished for the day. Time for recreation. The preparations for tomorrow's bread wouldn't begin until evening.

'Now is as good a time as we'll ever find,' said Georges. Quidor nodded. They had made the acquaintance of the National Guardsmen patrolling Rue Sainte-Anne. Former French Guards, they appeared to be trustworthy and were armed with pistols and sabres. Quidor asked two of them to remain nearby in case they were needed in the bakery. His request didn't seem to surprise them. Quidor also signalled his agents standing by to have a coach at the ready. If all went well, they were to haul Duby to prison without delay.

'Let's go,' Quidor said to Georges.

As they entered the shop, the young girl behind the counter was slicing a four-pound loaf in half for a female customer. The girl put a piece on the scales. 'Two pounds,' she declared. 'That'll be one *livre*.' The customer grimaced at the price but paid it and left with the bread.

The shop girl glanced at the two men approaching her. Almost immediately, her eyes filled with uncertainty, and a little fear. They were not ordinary customers, nor mere passers-by, but strangers on a mission. 'How can I help you, gentlemen?' Her voice wavered.

Quidor replied politely, 'We wish to speak with Monsieur Duby. Tell him that we are Messieurs Quidor and Charpentier of the police.'

'Monsieur Duby is resting and said that he must not be disturbed.' The young woman's eyes were now wide with fright; her lips trembled.

'We realize that a baker's work is long and tiring. We'll let him rest for a while. In the meantime we want you to show us through the bakery and to answer a few questions.'

For a moment the young woman stood frozen, her mind in the grip of Duby asleep upstairs. Then she began to weep. Georges went to the door to the street, beckoned one of the agents inside, latched the door, and put up a sign that said *fermé*. 'Guard the door,' he told the agent, then pointed at the young woman. 'Don't let her out.'

Quidor ordered her to show them where the fine flour was kept. A look of consternation mixed with her tears. Georges added, 'We know it's here. We've seen receipts.'

She dabbed the tears away and led them to a storeroom behind the bakeroom. Concealed by a canvas were three sacks full of flour, two sacks half empty, and a single folded sack.

'Look at the miller's marks, Georges. This morning at the Bakers' Guild I learned that six sacks of fine flour with these marks were recently stolen from a mill on the River Seine a few miles north-west of the city.' He nodded towards the young woman. 'She might have a record of the transaction between the thieves and Duby.'

Georges asked her, 'Where do you keep the secret account books?'

She pretended not to understand his question. He led her by the arm to the front room and pointed to a locked drawer under the counter. 'Here?' he asked.

She gave him a reluctant nod. 'I can't open it. Monsieur Duby has the key.'

Georges spoke softly. 'I don't want to wake him up – yet.' The lock appeared to be simple. He took out his tools and opened the drawer. He scanned the secret accounts, beckoned the inspector. 'Monsieur Quidor, would you believe that this stolen flour is baked into luxurious white bread for Monsieur Gaillard and other duke's gentlemen – at the duke's expense?'

Quidor inspected the accounts. 'I can't say that I'm surprised, Georges.' Then he turned to the quivering shop girl. In a low voice he said simply, 'Now it's time for us to speak to Monsieur Duby. Go wake him up.'

Head bowed, eyes cast down, she climbed a circular stairway to the floor above.

The two officers waited attentively at the foot of the stairs. Suddenly a loud voice burst out in anger. 'You stupid cow! I told you I'm resting. Tell them to go to hell.'

'I'll go first,' Georges said, and started softly up the stairs. Quidor followed. They emerged into a sitting room. The shop girl was cowering in a corner. Duby had not heard the advancing officers and was about to climb back into the sleeping alcove. He was wearing only underpants.

When Georges addressed him, he swung around in a fury. For a moment, he glared stupefied at the officers. They were dressed in civilian clothes. Then he uttered an oath and dashed towards a pistol on the mantelpiece. A pile of clothes snared his feet and he crashed to the floor. The officers quickly shackled him to a sturdy chair. Georges waved the shop girl downstairs.

'Now,' Quidor began, 'we shall have a civil conversation.'

'You'll regret this,' Duby hissed. 'I'll have you hanging from a lamppost before the day is over.'

'Before you do that,' Quidor said mildly, 'I think you should know that we've examined your secret account book, hidden under the counter. It proves that you're selling fine white bread illegally to the duke's kitchen. What's more, you are making a scandalous profit, rather like what the baker Gagne was accused of doing. If we were to tell the people, whom do you think they would hang from the lamppost?'

'Furthermore,' Georges added, 'we can prove from miller's marks on the flour sacks downstairs that the fine flour was stolen from a mill and hidden in your storeroom.'

Quidor continued, 'We've also collected the receipts of Gagne's purported illegal flour purchases and sent them out for handwriting analysis. In a few days, we expect to hear that Gagne never wrote them. Instead, you dictated them to a scribe.'

Georges added again, 'We've heard your customers complain of your bread's false weight. We must examine your scales and interrogate your shop girl downstairs.'

'Finally, Monsieur Duby,' said Quidor, 'I've neglected to mention that the Gagne case has been reopened. The authorities have determined that Lieutenant Maury's investigation was flawed. Monsieur Charpentier and I are carrying out the new investigation.'

Through this barrage of charges and insinuations, Duby's appearance changed dramatically. His defiant expression gave way to anxiety and craven fear. At the end he was perspiring.

'You're trying to trick me,' he said in a faltering voice.

Georges pulled the secret account book from his bag and held it up. 'How's this for a start? We already have enough evidence to send you to Bicêtre for many years.'

'Or perhaps to the gallows,' Quidor added. 'That depends on whether you cooperate.'

Duby paled at the mention of the gallows. 'What do you want from me?'

'We know that you aren't the chief villain in this piece. You must tell us who recruited you.'

Duby fell silent, desperately calculating his options. None of them looked good. 'If I name them, they'll kill me.'

'Not if we can apprehend them first,' Georges said.

'If I implicate them, they'll call me a liar and deny everything I say. I'll have compromised myself for nothing.'

'We don't depend on your word alone. You are one of several witnesses. Their testimony against the villains will strengthen yours. When we bring this case before the magistrates, they'll easily see who lies and who tells the truth.'

Duby was silent again. A small man, he seemed to shrink into himself. 'If I reveal my part in this affair, what will the magistrates do to me?'

'If we tell them that you didn't kill Gagne, and that you are cooperating with our investigation, they will feel much more kindly towards you than if you lied and balked.'

'Alright,' he sighed. 'I'll tell you how it was.' He went on to explain that Simon and Nicolas first approached him the day after the Bastille fell. For selfish reasons, or so they claimed, the baker Gagne was opposing the duke's plan to open up opportunities in baking for the most clever and enterprising among the journeymen, men like Duby himself. 'I told Simon and Nicolas that I was interested in the duke's plan. They arranged for me to meet Monsieur Gaillard the next day.'

'This is what we shall do,' Gaillard had said. 'We'll remove Gagne and his family, and you will take over the bakery. If you demonstrate that you are capable, you will become the owner.'

'But I have no money for wood and flour and other supplies,' I told him.

'Don't worry,' he said. 'I'll see that you receive extra sacks of fine flour and arrange for you to sell the bread at a premium.'

'At later meetings with Simon and Nicolas, I was told that I had to forge receipts for the flour, which I had begun to suspect would be stolen from a mill.'

'Why didn't you stop at that point?'

'I protested. But they said I couldn't drop out of the scheme. I knew too much.'

'Too much?' Georges asked. 'Did you know that they were going to kill Gagne?'

'They never told me that. I thought they would just remove him from the bakery. I was surprised and shocked when they killed him. Afterwards, when I complained, they said never mind. In the eyes of the law, I was as much involved as they were.'

Quidor drew Georges aside. 'What do you think of his story?'

Georges reflected. 'Most of it has the ring of truth, though he was probably more aware of Gagne's fate than he admits.'

'I think we should put him in the Châtelet to prevent him from backsliding.'

'And for his own protection.'

'Yes, if he remains here, he's marked for death.'

Quidor's agents carried Duby downstairs still shackled, put him in the coach, and set off for the prison. A small crowd of the curious, mostly from the neighbourhood, had gathered in the street. Sylvie emerged from the café and spread the word that the police had discovered baker Duby selling bread under weight and keeping false accounts. He was going to prison for further questioning.

Just as concern began to grow that no more bread would be baked in the neighbourhood, the temporary retired master baker arrived to replace Duby. The newcomer had already met the two young apprentices returning to the shop, and he announced that he was reopening the bakery. The guild would soon licence a permanent baker.

The crowd slowly dispersed, many retreating into the La Vache Agile for further discussion. Georges turned to Quidor. 'What shall we do with Duby's shop girl?'

'We need her as a witness against him. But who will replace her at the bakery?'

Georges consulted Sylvie.

She said, 'Bring Madame Gagne, her son, and the maid back to work in the bakery. Local opinion favours them. For the time being, confine the young shop girl to a convent while you question her. Otherwise she'll disappear, most likely into the river.'

At the provost's residence Anne and Paul sat down with Georges to a supper of green bean salad with an oil and vinegar dressing. Quidor was looking after the shop girl. The mood at the table was optimistic. Georges informed them of progress in the Gagne murder case. With the arrest of Duby, the chief hurdle was overcome. It was now up to the magistrates to do the right thing and clear Gagne's name.

Anne said, 'I'm especially pleased that I could help restore Louis Gagne's family to their home and livelihood. That's what the abbé had hoped for.'

'Congratulations,' Paul said, then turned to Georges. 'I noticed that Inspector Quidor contributed to your success.'

'Yes, I'm pleased to report that he no longer seems discouraged or talks about retirement. He and I were a perfect team.

We had Duby on his way to prison before he knew what had happened to him.'

A question troubled Anne's mind. 'I hope this wasn't just a temporary burst of energy. Do you think he can continue?' She valued the inspector as a mentor, respected his tenacious pursuit of evidence.

Paul replied thoughtfully, 'Recent events in Paris have turned much of Quidor's world upside down. The professional, experienced officers, like DeCrosne, whom he knew and respected, are gone. Bailly and the other new men have not yet earned his trust.'

'I see,' Anne said. 'Quidor would prefer to carry on as before. It remains to be seen whether he'll find his way in the new order of things.'

After the soup came Paul's report on the magistrate Pierre Roland. 'He'll return to the police bureau and help us prevent Gaillard and the duke's men from upsetting our resolution of the Gagne case.'

Anne remarked to Paul, 'I hope Roland's wife and children will be welcome guests at Château Beaumont. With Comte Savarin and his retinue there as well, your aunt will have her hands full.' Then she added, 'I believe she will enjoy the challenge and manage it to everyone's satisfaction.'

When the bread, a soft cheese, and fruit were served, Paul remarked, 'Much unfinished business remains.' He spoke of the unsolved murders of Lieutenant Harivel and Lieutenant Maury. 'What do you think, Georges?'

'The chief suspects in the killing of Harivel are Lieutenant Maury and the villains Simon and Nicolas. In Maury's death the most likely suspect is the young National Guardsman, Joseph Mouton.'

Paul shook his head. 'I'm inclined to believe that Simon and Nicolas also killed Maury on Gaillard's order.'

Anne didn't feel as involved in these investigations as she had done in the baker's case. But she listened with particular interest to news of the Harivel case. What concerned her most was that the target had in fact been her husband.

Twenty-Nine
Charenton

Paris, Friday, 31 July

At noon, Anne met Michou in her studio. She was seated at her easel contemplating her finished copy of Adelaide's portrait. 'I'm wondering,' Michou signed as Anne pulled up a chair beside her, 'how did this beautiful young woman go from Monsieur Hall's studio to an asylum for the mentally ill in the course of twenty years?'

Anne shrugged. 'I don't know who could answer your question, other than Gaillard. We can't discuss the matter with him. We might find someone at the asylum to help us.' Anne shared Michou's fascination with Adelaide's tragic story. The simple desire to return the gold locket had evolved into a need to discover the woman in the portrait. What could the locket mean to her? Could she be trusted with such a valuable item? The answer was to go to the asylum and meet her.

Before leaving the studio, they discussed whether to bring the locket and decided not to. The piece was too valuable. Instead, Michou wrapped her copy of the portrait and put it in her bag. She had framed it, thinking of it as a possible gift – depending on the circumstances.

During the coach ride, Anne signed to Michou a brief description of the asylum on an estate at the south edge of the Bois de Vincennes. A religious community, the Brothers of Charity, had established it more than a hundred years ago as a home for the elderly. Over the years it housed instead the insane of both sexes. According to Paul, a recent inspection criticized conditions there. The inmates were chained to the walls, confined in wicker cages, shocked in cold baths. No attempt was made to cure their illness. The director,

Paul said, ignored Doctor Philippe Pinel's recent successes in mental care.

'Does the director allow visitors?' Michou asked. 'He should be ashamed to show his poor work, especially since the inspection.'

'He's cruel and greedy as well as ignorant. Conditions remain unchanged. In fact, the critical report has intrigued the idle rich. They now come to the asylum to stare at the inmates, ridicule them, mimic their antics. The director charges a fee for admission. I can imagine that the money goes into his pocket.'

'Poor Adelaide,' Michou signed, her expression very glum.

The director sat behind his brown mahogany writing table in a large, well-furnished office. Head tilted to one side, he studied his two visitors until he seemed pleased with their appearance. Anne and Michou had worn their best muslin gowns, tied at the waist with blue ribbons. Anne introduced herself and Michou in proper French and explained that they wished to visit a patient named Adelaide Gaillard.

'What's the reason for this visit?' the director asked, a hint of wariness in his voice.

Anne had anticipated the question. 'My companion, Micheline du Saint-Esprit, has painted a portrait of her as a young woman. It might please her to see it.'

'Would you show it to me?'

Michou understood him, took the painting from her bag, unwrapped it, and handed it to him.

He pursed his lips in surprise. 'Did you paint this yourself?'

She nodded calmly, accustomed to the question.

'You couldn't have known her then; you're not old enough. How did you do it?'

'I painted it from a small portrait that I found. Madame Cartier helped me trace the portrait to your patient.' Anne translated for her.

'How did you do that?'

'Monsieur Pierre Hall, the artist of the original portrait, was helpful. The Abbé de l'Épée knew the family.'

The director appeared satisfied that these two women had money and good connections, and wouldn't cause him any trouble.

Anne spoke up. 'We would be happy to make a financial contribution to the work of the asylum.'

That was what the director was waiting to hear. 'That would be generous of you. I'll arrange for a nurse to show you to Mademoiselle Gaillard's room.'

The nurse was an older woman, past sixty, Anne thought. Stout, heavy-footed, the nurse called herself Ruth and said she made a living this way. The director explained that Adelaide had lived with an uncle. When he died three years ago, her brother Monsieur Gaillard brought her to the asylum and paid the nurse to care for her.

On the way to Adelaide's room, Anne asked the nurse, 'What's wrong with the patient?'

'She talks to her father who has been dead twenty years. She thinks I'm her mother who died at her birth. Many years ago, I used to be an actress. So I play my part and don't argue with her. We get along.'

'Does she recognize her brother?'

The woman hesitated to respond, then spoke guardedly. 'He visits once a month, brings her treats. She looks forward to him coming. I doubt that she knows who he really is.'

The woman led the visitors from the main building to a cottage beside a garden. Her route avoided the unseemly sights that the inspectors had complained about. The cottage was simple but pleasant enough.

The nurse left the visitors at the door, while she went in to prepare her patient. In a few minutes she emerged and beckoned them in. The room was dimly lighted. It took Anne a few seconds to notice a woman seated in the shadows near a half-shuttered window. The nurse made the introductions and seated the visitors. She opened the window and let in more light.

Adelaide was knitting what would become a scarf, Anne thought. She responded to the introductions with a quick bow and a brief smile. Her face was gaunt, her body little more than skin and bones. She looked much older than her forty-odd years.

'May I offer you something to drink?' she said to the visitors, then turned to the nurse. 'Mother, bring us cool cider.'

The nurse winked at Anne and left the room. A minute

later, she returned with glasses of water. Adelaide glanced at the glasses but seemed not to notice their contents. A conversation ensued about her recent vacation in Normandy with her father and mother, obviously but one of many fictitious stories she could tell.

'I even milked a cow,' she said in a childlike voice. 'And Father was so amused.'

'Did your brother go with you?' Anne asked, trying to probe that relationship.

'I don't have a brother,' she replied, and went on about the birds and flowers she had seen.

'Who is the gentleman who visits you every month?'

Adelaide played coy. 'Oh, I really shouldn't say. Just a hopeless suitor. I try to discourage him, but he comes anyway. I do enjoy his sweetmeats.'

She glanced at Michou, seemed irritated, and asked Anne, 'Why does your friend stare at me?'

'Michou means no offence. She's trying to read your lips. She's deaf, you see.' Anne paused, pointed to Michou's bag. 'She's a painter and has something to show you.'

Michou brought out her copy of the portrait and held it before Adelaide in the window's light.

The woman gasped in disbelief. 'Why, that's me. That's exactly how I look. How wonderful!' She turned to the nurse. 'Mother, bring me the mirror.'

The nurse hesitated, looked uncomfortable, and began to demur.

'Mother! I said bring me the mirror.' Adelaide rose from her chair, a wild expression on her face, and confronted the nurse. 'Do as I say!'

The nurse threw a desperate side glance at Anne and left the room. She returned with a large hand-held mirror. Adelaide impatiently beckoned her. She came closer and raised the mirror.

Adelaide let out an ear-piercing scream. 'That's not me!' She swung her fist at the mirror. The nurse pulled it away just in time and scurried from the room. Adelaide stared piteously at Michou's painting. 'That's me,' she wailed again and again, then began to cry.

To calm her, Michou lowered the portrait and was about to wrap it up.

'Let me keep it,' Adelaide said. 'At least for a while.' Her tears subsided. 'I hate the woman I see in the mirror. She's so ugly.'

Michou took her hands, gazed into her eyes and smiled sweetly.

Adelaide responded with a tentative smile. 'I would like you to be my sister. I really don't have one. But we'll pretend.'

Michou nodded.

Anne wondered just how deluded Adelaide was.

Thirty
Hostage

Paris, Saturday, 1 August

'Michou has vanished!' Sylvie exclaimed. She had rushed into the garden where Paul and Anne were having breakfast. The young woman collapsed in a chair, weeping. Anne knelt beside her, put an arm around her shoulders, comforted her. But it was a minute before Sylvie could explain in halting words what had happened.

Michou had risen at dawn and walked to the river's bank to sketch, one of her favourite pastimes. She had gone there alone many times without an incident. This time, however, she didn't return.

Sylvie waited an hour, then went to the river, looking for her at all her usual places. With a shock Sylvie recognized her sketchbook lying at the foot of the embankment. A few fishermen and other boat people recalled having glimpsed her on the Quai du Louvre. But the early morning mist often hid her. She might have climbed down to the water's edge, stumbled, and fallen into the river.

'Could someone have thrown her in?' Paul wondered aloud.

'Who would do that?' Sylvie asked. 'She had no enemies.'

'But we, her friends, have enemies,' replied Paul. 'They might hurt her in order to afflict us.'

'Did Michou act normal last night and this morning?' Anne asked, hesitating even to suggest suicide.

Sylvie nodded. 'Her usual self. But it's sometimes hard to know how she's feeling. She keeps her troubles hidden. Deafness is a huge hardship. Her frustrations build up and she feels depressed. Maybe that's what happened this morning. Still, I can't even imagine that she would drown herself.'

Anne walked Sylvie back to the town house on Rue Traversine. 'Rest a while. I'll wait here for you. Then we'll speak to some of our friends at the Palais-Royal and at Abbé de l'Épée's institute. The police probably shouldn't be called into the search for her – not yet.'

At midmorning, Saint-Martin was sitting at his writing table, too distracted by Michou's disappearance to concentrate on his work. The porter appeared at the open door. Saint-Martin beckoned him in.

'Sir, a boy left a message with me at the front gate, said it was for the provost. I tried to hold the boy, but he wrestled free and ran off.' The porter handed over a plain folded paper, addressed to the provost. The porter bowed and started to leave.

'Stay,' said Saint-Martin. 'I may need to question you.' Already he sensed the nature of the message. His hands trembled as he unfolded the paper and began to read it.

You must stop investigating the deaths of the greedy baker Gagne and the treasonous aristocrats Foullon and Bertier, condemned and punished by the people. If you continue to oppose the people's will, your little spy, the deaf artist Micheline du Saint-Esprit, known as Michou, will die within twenty-four hours. And if you persist, your wife will be next. The People's Avenger.

Paul stared at the paper as he laid it on his table. He drew a deep breath, then asked the porter to describe the messenger.

'A street urchin, about ten years old. Sly and quick beyond his years. Spoke with a lisp. Light-skinned. Had a small, rose-coloured birthmark on the right side of his jaw. Walks on the balls of his feet.'

Saint-Martin was not surprised by such a detailed description. The porter, after all, was a middle-aged police spy, who had served Inspector Quidor for several years. Quidor had loaned him to Saint-Martin two weeks ago, when he determined to improve the security of his residence. Trustworthy as well as observant, the porter was much appreciated and well paid.

'I sense that you've seen him before.'

'Yes, sir. He lives in a brothel in the Palais-Royal and runs errands for the madame.'

Saint-Martin tilted his head, as if amazed at the porter's knowledge of the city's low life.

He waved his hands in a dismissive gesture. 'Three years ago, sir, the police inspector, my former master, ordered me to observe a band of little boys, believed to be thieves working for the madame. This boy was one of them, her favourite. She protected him; the others went to prison.'

'You've been very helpful. I want you for a special mission. Ask one of the other servants to take your place at the gate, then come back here.'

Saint-Martin sent for Georges, showed him the message, and relayed the porter's information. 'Investigate the brothel with the porter. Observe the boy. He may lead you to Michou. Be very circumspect. Her life is at stake.'

Anne received a message from her husband just before she and Sylvie left the town house on Rue Traversine.

'Michou's a hostage.' She handed the message to Sylvie. 'But there's still hope. Someone may have seen her being abducted or hidden away.'

Sylvie read the message, shook her head. 'It's hopeless to comb Paris in search of her. Let's speak to André. If anything bad has happened to Michou, the cause of it lies in the duke's palace. Someone in André's network might help us.'

'I can't add to what you already know about Michou's disappearance,' André said as he sat with the two women in their secret meeting place, the puppet theatre in the Camp of the Tatars. 'A few minutes ago, I had tea with the cook. She had heard only that a young woman had been abducted on the Quai du Louvre.' André paused, signifying that a revelation was coming. 'However, I can tell you that Monsieur Gaillard suddenly left the palace early this morning. He sent word to the cook that he was going on vacation to the countryside and might be gone for a few weeks.'

'What could that have to do with Michou?' asked Anne.

'Perhaps nothing. But I met him on his way out. He seemed unusually agitated, not at all as if his mind were set on a stroll in sylvan glens or any other country pleasure. There was a gleam in his eye that suggested he was looking forward to leading a riot or doing damage to an enemy. I followed him to the garden gate, where a coach was waiting. He told the coachman to take him to Passy.'

'There must be hundreds of dwellings in the village,' Anne surmised. 'Where would he stay?'

'I asked the cook. She didn't know for sure, but she had heard that Gaillard's friend, the madame of his favourite brothel, owns a property just outside Passy where she spends the summer vacation. You might find him there.'

Anne thanked André. 'You've given us a promising idea to pursue. I'll take it to my husband.' As she rose to leave, she turned to Sylvie. 'We now have at least a glimmer of hope that we might find Michou as well as Gaillard.'

Disguised in simple brown woollen suits and wigs, Georges and the porter stood at a safe distance from the entrance to the brothel, one of many in the Palais-Royal's Valois arcade. It occupied the first floor above ground level. Gaillard's favourite brothel, it was possibly a place to conceal Michou. But it seemed too busy. There was constant traffic of tradesmen, customers and women in and out of the building.

'What do you know about the madame?' Georges asked the porter.

He replied, 'Most of what I know comes from Inspector Quidor's files. She is rich, clever, unscrupulous, a strict mistress of the women in her house. In her youth, she was a striking beauty. The old duke was fond of her. The present duke is indifferent, though she's still attractive. If Gaillard so wished, he could close down her house and put her in jail. But she surely pays him for protection and grants him free access to the house and its women.'

'And grants him other favours,' added Georges. 'Like perhaps holding Michou hostage somewhere. If not in that building, then where else? How shall we find out?'

'Quidor thought that she owned property outside the city, perhaps near the village of Passy.'

For an hour, they watched the entrance. Then the boy appeared, glanced left and right, and set off across the garden. 'This might be a wild chase to nowhere,' said Georges, 'but I think we should follow him.'

At Rue Saint-Honoré he turned west, stole a handful of cherries and an orange from a fruit stall. Again, he looked around, then climbed up on to a slowly moving, empty cart, joked with the driver. Hitching rides in a similar manner, he made his way to Passy.

Walking through the village, he stole a small loaf of bread from a baker's basket and tucked it into his shirt. A half-mile beyond the village, he turned right up a carriage lane of prosperous farms producing fruits and vegetables for the city markets. Occasional walled gardens lay to the right and left of the lane, behind the country homes of wealthy city dwellers. At the last house on the road, the boy stopped and looked around, then opened a gate, walked up to the house, looked around again, and knocked.

After a moment's delay, the door opened a crack, then wider. A tall man ushered the boy in, and the door closed.

Throughout this journey, the porter took the lead, following the boy from a distance, deftly anticipating when he might turn around or glance over his shoulder. Georges held back, keeping the porter in sight. Now he caught up to the porter hiding in a grove opposite the gate.

'This must be the madame's country house,' the porter remarked. 'And the boy may have delivered a message.'

Georges agreed. 'Michou might be inside. But, if we stormed the building, her captors would kill her before we could rescue her. They might also outnumber us.'

They hadn't waited long when a young woman wearing a kitchen maid's apron came walking up the lane with a basket of groceries on her arm. Georges turned to the porter. He shrugged. The same tall man let her into the house.

It was now near noon. Georges felt they were at an impasse. How could they search the house without endangering Michou? For lack of a better idea, Georges told the porter to watch the madame's house while he spoke to the farmer next door.

In the middle of a large field, the farmer was overseeing two servants harvesting a row of carrots. 'For the city market, tomorrow,' he said when Georges inquired. A patient donkey stood nearby, hitched to a cart half-filled with produce. The farmer bent down and picked a few carrots himself and tossed them into the cart. He scarcely looked at the visitor.

'So, you rise early,' Georges remarked.

'With the sun,' the farmer replied, pulling a large, thick carrot from the ground. He brushed off the dirt, inspected the vegetable with a critical eye. He nodded with satisfaction and threw it on to the cart.

Georges quickly calculated the time a cart would take to go from the Quai du Louvre to this country road. 'Early this morning, as you took your cart down the lane towards the river, did you meet anyone coming in this direction?'

The farmer brushed dirt off his hands, stretched, and met Georges' eye. 'Why would you want to know?'

Georges assessed the man's frank, open countenance. He would want a straightforward reply. 'I'm interested in the tall man next door.' Georges pointed with a slight toss of his head towards the madame's house.

'Oh?' The farmer was intrigued. 'What about him?'

'He may have kidnapped a petite young woman of my acquaintance and brought her here early this morning.'

The farmer nodded. 'If we stand here too long together, we might be noticed and arouse suspicion. Wait for me at the back door of my house where they can't see us. I'll be there in a few minutes.'

Georges did as he was told; and the farmer soon joined him and let him into a tool shed. 'We can talk here,' he said, and pulled up a couple of stools. 'You're from the Highway Patrol, aren't you?'

'How did you know? Am I so obvious?'

'Your disguise is fine. I happen to recognize an officer when I see one, especially if he's pursuing a rogue like the man next door. I also know the officers at the Passy post only a mile away. Brigadier Pioche was here a few days ago, also asking about that house. Trying to find Harivel's killer, I suppose. Asked me to keep an eye on the people coming and going.'

'That's right. The chief suspects may be there.'

'I'm not surprised,' the farmer remarked. 'Four weeks ago, several suspicious men settled there. Among them are the tall man with a cropped ear and his companion, short and fat. They receive visitors of the same ilk.' He paused. 'But to get back to your question – yes, I met the tall man coming up the lane early this morning, carrying a large flour sack on his shoulder. From its shape I knew it wasn't flour. Now I suspect that it was a small woman. Probably unconscious, because she didn't stir. The tall man frowned when he saw me. But I bid him good morning just the same.'

'Can you tell me what goes on in that house?'

'You probably know that it belongs to a rich madame at the Palais-Royal. We get along fine. She uses it mainly in the summer, sometimes for parties with gentlemen. When it's empty for a while, as in winter, she pays me to look after it. The rooms are nicely furnished, a temptation to thieves. I'm supposed to keep them away. I've not been in the building since the beginning of this month when those men moved in.'

'Where would they keep my acquaintance? She's deaf, by the way.'

For a few moments, the farmer pursed his lips, stroked his chin. 'In the basement there's a wine cellar and a storeroom, both rooms with thick walls and no windows. Either would make a good prison cell. There's also a room in the attic.' He paused, a question teasing his mind. 'What are they going to do with her, do you know?'

'She's a hostage. They're using her to force the police to end an investigation. They'll kill her during the night unless we stop them.'

The farmer blinked, shook his head. 'That's a pity! What can I do?'

'Send one of your servants to fetch Brigadier Pioche at the Passy Highway Patrol post and send the other to the provost's residence on Rue Saint-Honoré.' Georges took out pencil and paper and wrote two brief notes. Give these to the servants to deliver. Tell them to be quick. It's urgent.'

Thirty-One

Rescue

Paris/Passy, Saturday, 1 August

Late in the afternoon, Anne arrived with Sylvie at the farm. They had trudged up a path to the back of the property rather than come by the carriage road. The rogues in the madame's house might notice any increase in traffic.

Georges had written that Michou might need their support, once they had freed her. Anne realized that Georges anticipated a violent struggle. Michou might be hurt in any number of ways. The kidnapping itself must have been a shattering experience. Her 'liberation' might compound the injury.

Brigadier Pioche and Paul had come by the same path with six troopers. Counting Georges and himself, Paul had a force of nine professional armed men. The farmer and the porter, also armed now, would serve as scouts. Anne and Sylvie joined the men around the kitchen table to discuss strategy.

The farmer described the madame's house in detail. 'The servants' door is in the rear and opens directly into a large kitchen. Next to it is a dining room, then a sitting room or parlour and an anteroom to the main entrance. There are also two sleeping rooms on the ground floor. Upstairs are the servants' quarters, and in the basement are the wine cellar and a storeroom.'

'Is there a way to enter unannounced?' Paul asked.

'Last winter, I made a copy of the key to the servants' entrance.' He held it up for all to see.

'I'll use it,' said Georges and put the key in his pocket.

Then Pioche spoke about the servants. On his visit a few days ago, he had questioned them. The cook and the kitchen maid claimed to know nothing. Simple women, easily frightened, they would offer no resistance but no help either. The groundsman was a rude peasant, surly and strong. 'Beware of him,' Pioche warned. 'We suspect that he leads a band of rogues that steals grain in the countryside and sells it in the city.'

The farmer agreed. 'He usually carries a long knife, has a hot temper, and is feared in the neighbourhood.'

During the afternoon, the boy had returned to the city, and Simon and another man had arrived, both probably armed. Thus far, however, the villains appeared unaware of the attack being mounted against them.

Paul asked the farmer, 'Could you describe the stranger who arrived with Simon?'

'An older man, lean, slope-shouldered, shuffled up the road.'

'Gaillard!' exclaimed Anne and Sylvie together. 'Why would he come tonight?'

Silence fell over the room. 'Perhaps he wants to oversee Michou's fate,' replied Georges softly.

Paul nodded. 'We can't afford to make a mistake.' With his usual caution and attention to detail, he laid out his plan to surprise the villains and to keep violence to a minimum. Accompanied by Pioche and a trooper, he would approach the front entrance and knock. Georges and two troopers would enter through the servants' door. The remaining three troopers would take up positions around the building to prevent any escape. The farmer and the porter would guard the carriage road and stop any unwanted visitors.

'Any questions?' Paul asked.

Anne waved a hand. 'Are you really sure that Michou is in the building?'

He smiled. 'Not really, but I hope so. Otherwise we will have stirred up a hornet's nest in vain.'

There was no response to Saint-Martin's knocking on the door. An instant later, at Pioche's loud whistle, Georges unlocked the servants' door and rushed into the kitchen, his troopers close behind, all with pistols drawn. Seated at a large heavy table, the occupants of the house were lingering over the last vestiges of dinner.

'We're from the Highway Patrol, and we're going to search this house. For now, everyone stay where you are.' He nodded to one of the troopers, who dashed to the front door and opened it for Saint-Martin, Pioche and the remaining trooper. Simon and Nicolas exchanged glances. Georges cocked his pistol and glared at them. 'Hands on the table,' he ordered.

They slowly complied. 'What do you think you're doing here?' demanded Gaillard. 'This is an outrage. You will pay dearly.'

'Thank you for the note you sent me this morning,' said Paul with thick irony. 'It helped us to trace you. We're searching for the deaf woman Michou. Your men kidnapped her this morning on the Quai du Louvre and brought her here. Since you threatened to kill her, we've had to do without the polite forms of gaining entry to a house.'

In the meantime, the troopers had searched the house and found no sign of Michou. 'Search the basement,' Saint-Martin commanded.

The troopers went downstairs and checked the wine cellar and the storeroom. Still no Michou.

'Shackle the men,' said Saint-Martin to the troopers. 'And make them lie down on the sitting-room floor.' To Georges he murmured, 'Question the cook and the maid. They must know.'

The cook was an older woman, the maid hardly nineteen. Both probably came from madame's brothel and were firmly under her thumb. Georges sat at the table facing them. 'We know the woman was brought here. Where is she?'

'We don't know,' they stammered in unison.

Georges pounded on the table. 'Do you think I'm stupid? Of course you know.' He glared at them. 'If you don't tell me, I'll put you in La Salpêtrière with all the other demented, crazy and criminal women of Paris and throw away the key.'

'Those men will kill us if we tell,' croaked the cook, glancing in the direction of the sitting room.

'They might want to, but they won't have the opportunity. They're going to the naval prison at Brest, where they'll break rocks and scrape barnacles for the rest of their lives. So you may as well tell me.'

The young woman moaned, swayed in her seat, and fell over in a faint on the table. A trooper rushed up and tried to revive her. The cook glanced desperately about the room, then, shielding one hand with the other, she pointed downwards and gave Georges a knowing look.

He nodded. With a wink to the woman he exclaimed with feigned anger, loudly enough to be heard in the sitting room. 'So you won't tell me. That doesn't matter. I have a hunch.' He summoned two troopers. 'Move this table.'

He studied the tile floor. One tile was loose. Beneath it he found a lever and pulled open a trap door. With a lighted lantern, he climbed down a steep stairway into a black abyss. A moment later, he reappeared. 'Call Madame Cartier and Sylvie. I've found Michou.'

Anne and Sylvie were waiting anxiously in the farmer's house. At least they heard no gunshots. That was encouraging. Part of their anxiety was due to the uncertainty about Michou's location. Was she in the madame's house? If not, where was she?

Finally, a trooper burst into the room. 'They've found your friend. Come.'

Michou was lying on a bed in a ground-floor room, semiconscious, covered with blankets. Paul and Georges were at her side.

'How is she?' Anne asked.

'She has not signed to us yet. There's a big bruise on the back of her head. We think Nicolas knocked her out, put her into the large flour sack and brought her to Passy by cart, then carried her here on his shoulder.'

Georges added, 'I found her in a windowless basement room hidden below the kitchen table. She was bound and gagged, unconscious, lying on the damp floor in her shift. Simon was supposed to throw her into the river tonight. We found his instructions from Monsieur Gaillard, together with a broadside denouncing Michou as a treacherous spy.'

Anne and Sylvie approached on opposite sides of the bed. 'Michou!' Anne caressed her cheek. She moaned, stirred, opened her eyes.

Sylvie signed, 'You're safe now.' She patted her hand.

Michou whimpered. A tear rolled down her cheek. Anne wiped it dry. Michou smiled and closed her eyes again.

Paul drew near to Anne. 'I think we should take her to our residence.'

Anne agreed. 'She'd be safer there than anywhere else in Paris. How shall we move her?'

'The troopers will fetch two coaches parked at the foot of the carriage lane. One is for Michou, Sylvie, you and me. And the other is for our prisoners. Georges will deliver them to the Châtelet when he completes an examination of this building. Pioche is interrogating the cook and the maid. The two women can stay here under guard for the time being.'

It was dark. The coaches had just arrived. Troopers were about to pack the rogues into one of them. Saint-Martin drew Georges aside. 'Before you leave, tell me what you've learned.'

'Simon and Nicolas refused to reply to my questions,' Georges replied. 'They may change their tune after a few days in prison. Gaillard claims he had no idea that Michou was in the house. His men were guilty only of an excess of zeal on the people's behalf when they abducted her. They thought she was one of the King's spies.'

'And the groundsman?' Saint-Martin asked. 'Would he talk?'

'Yes,' Georges replied. 'He's far from an honest man – he helped steal the flour that was sneaked into Gagne's bakery – but he doesn't want to sink with the others. He insists he had nothing to do with Michou's abduction, nor with Gaillard's murder of Lieutenant Maury.'

'What?' The colonel gave Georges a sceptical glance.

'That's right,' Georges continued. 'He was present in the kitchen when Gaillard shot Maury and helped throw Maury's body into the secret cellar under the table. I found pieces of fabric and a coat button on the floor at the bottom of the stairs. Probably came off Maury's coat when his body was hauled up the stairs. Simon and Nicolas moved the body to the Chaillot hill. I'll check with Pioche. He has the coat.'

'Why did Gaillard kill Maury?'

'They had quarrelled about money. Maury had already been paid for killing Bertier on Place de Grève and for falsely investigating the baker's hanging. Now he demanded an enormous sum for shooting Lieutenant Harivel. Gaillard refused to give him a sou. He claimed that no one should get paid for killing the wrong man. Maury lost his temper, called Gaillard a lowborn hack and extortionist, and threatened to expose him. Gaillard replied, who would believe a cuckold who shot his rival in the back on a dark night? Maury reached for his sword. Gaillard pulled out a hidden pistol from his coat and shot the lieutenant through the heart.'

Saint-Martin added, 'If brought to trial for murder, Gaillard would obviously plead self-defence.'

Georges nodded. 'At the time the groundsman told Gaillard he would back him up. But now it's in his interest to distance himself from Gaillard and let him take full blame for his crimes. The groundsman also claims that he condemned Gaillard's plan to abduct and kill Michou.'

'I hope to hear him testify against Gaillard. If allowed to go free, Gaillard would be a constant threat to Michou, Sylvie and Anne – not to mention the other evils he might commit.'

'A propos of Harivel – it *was* me rather than him who was meant to be killed that night?'

'Yes, sir. Gaillard instructed Maury to kill you. But instead he deliberately shot Harivèl, who he accused of seducing his wife. There was no mistake. Maury knew that Harivel was on his way to the barracks. A spy followed him from Passy to Bailly's door, saw him about to mount your horse. He hastened to Maury, waiting in the alley.'

Anne beckoned to her husband from the coach. 'Remember Michou! We must leave.'

He smiled and waved back. 'Just a moment more.' He turned to Georges and remarked, 'By a curious twist of fortune, I owe my life to Harivel.'

Thirty-Two
Finale

Paris, 2–25 August

Early the next morning, Saint-Martin hastened to the Louvre for an emergency meeting. By messenger, he had given Bailly and Lafayette a brief account of the previous night's dramatic events in Passy and had persuaded them to meet in the mayor's apartment, even though it was a Sunday. They feared that the duke's faction might violently protest Gaillard's arrest.

The three men gathered around the writing table in Bailly's study. The door was shut. The mayor leaned forward, unruffled, his arms resting on the table, his hands clasped.

'Please give us the full story, Colonel.'

Saint-Martin presented a detailed report of events from Michou's disappearance to Gaillard's arrest at the country house.

At the end, Lafayette exclaimed, 'How brazen the duke's men have become. That has to stop.'

'What do you want from us, Colonel?' asked Bailly evenly. His calm, attentive expression had scarcely changed during Saint-Martin's narration.

'I want the authority to search Gaillard's apartment in the duke's palace before his papers are removed or destroyed. He's charged with a capital crime, the murder of Lieutenant Maury, among other major offences. In the past, in cases of murder or treason, the King's agent, the Lieutenant General of Police, could authorize an invasion of the duke's private domain. Now, under the new dispensation, that power should belong to the mayor to whom the lieutenant general's office has passed.'

'I agree with you, Colonel,' said Lafayette. 'And I would go a step further. In our new democratic society there should be no private fiefdoms, such as the duke's at the Palais-Royal. The police investigator must be free to go wherever the evidence leads.' The marquis raised a warning finger. 'But, in today's dangerous circumstances, we have to proceed with great caution. The duke's faction has significant resources and, if threatened, will use them ruthlessly.'

Of all men, *you* should know, thought the colonel, recalling the obscene image of Maury offering Bertier's heart to the marquis at the City Hall. Nonetheless, he gave the marquis a deferential smile. 'All the more reason to act immediately, sir. We must present the public with convincing evidence of Gaillard's guilt before the duke's men can rally. We should also brand Gaillard and his accomplices as rogues, acting without the duke's knowledge or permission. We could point out that this is not the first time Gaillard has violated the duke's trust. Two years ago, he fenced artworks in London that were stolen from the duke's collection. At the present time, he's profiteering in the sale of fine bread to the duke's kitchen.'

'I see,' said Bailly. 'The duke could therefore, without severe loss of face, discharge Gaillard from his service, allow National Guardsmen to remove his paper and other evidence from the palace, and hold them in the local police bureau for examination.'

Lafayette frowned. 'Or so we might hope, sir. The duke often appears ignorant of his own best interest or acts contrary to it.'

Bailly countered, 'We can't allow Gaillard to affront the law. The case against him should be as strong as we can possibly make it.' He turned to Saint-Martin. 'Thanks to your adjutant and your wife, Colonel, you do have an idea of what you might find in his apartment.'

'Yes, I do. This must remain between us, messieurs. With the mayor's knowledge, my adjutant led a secret search of the apartment a few days ago and discovered a detailed diary and a trove of incriminating files in a hidden cabinet.'

The mayor and the marquis appeared reassured.

'We'll hope for the best today,' Bailly said, then addressed Lafayette. 'I'll provide the colonel with written orders for the search.'

'I'll countersign them,' said the marquis, then asked Saint-Martin, 'Do you need a detachment of National Guardsmen?'

'Yes, they would be a useful reserve but should remain out of sight unless needed. An open show of force might provoke a violent reaction in the public. I'll go to the palace with my adjutant, Monsieur Charpentier, and two unarmed guardsmen.'

The men parted, Saint-Martin less sanguine than he might appear. Much could go wrong.

At midmorning, he and his men entered the palace by the servants' entrance. The duke's guards, lolling in their chairs, jumped to their feet, aware that these men had come on serious business. The colonel presented his papers and declared he would search Monsieur Gaillard's apartment. The guards exchanged glances, their mouths agape.

Saint-Martin allowed them no more than a few seconds' delay, then said, 'We know the way. Inform Monsieur Choderlos de Laclos, the duke's secretary, of our arrival.' He gave a signal to his men and strode to the servants' stairway. He had learned that the duke was away from the palace for the day. Just as well; there would be less bother. Laclos could act on the duke's behalf.

The colonel had delayed the news of Gaillard's arrest as much as possible, asking everyone connected to the case to remain silent. But such a secret couldn't be kept long. André Dutoit reported hearing it in the palace an hour ago. Therefore Saint-Martin wasn't surprised to find the door to the apartment open and three men inside. They must have arrived only a few minutes earlier. The dog Nero was already gone. But the room was otherwise undisturbed.

Saint-Martin recognized tall, thin Laclos in his rumpled black coat. 'Sir, I must ask you to leave. Mayor Bailly and Commandant Lafayette have authorized this search as part of an ongoing murder investigation.' He handed his papers to Laclos.

The secretary hesitated for a moment, while he probably thought of calling on the palace guard to eject the intruders. He took the papers, closely examined them. Then he studied Saint-Martin, Georges and the two National Guard officers. Finally he capitulated.

'Your papers appear to be in order, Colonel.' He handed

them back and signalled his companions to leave the office. At the door he turned to Saint-Martin. 'May I speak to you privately?'

After instructing Georges to search the office, Saint-Martin joined Laclos in the anteroom.

The secretary sniffed, adopted an officious tone. 'I spoke to Gaillard at the Châtelet a half-hour ago. He claims to be innocent of all charges.'

Saint-Martin could barely contain his scorn. 'What else did you expect him to say? Here are the facts. I set out to investigate the murder of Harivel du Rocher, one of my officers. The trail of evidence led to Gaillard. Along the way, I found him involved in several other crimes. A credible eye-witness, for example, has testified that he saw Gaillard shoot Lieutenant Maury.'

Laclos' sickly yellow complexion turned grey. 'Really?' he murmured with disbelief.

'Incredible but true. They quarrelled over a failed plan to kill me.' Saint-Martin gave Laclos a brief summary of Harivel's death in Chaillot and the subsequent investigation. 'Among Gaillard's lesser crimes,' the colonel concluded, 'is the sale of luxury white bread to your palace kitchen at fancy prices, bread baked from stolen fine flour. Can you imagine, sir, such brazen profiteering in this time of the people's great want? They'll be outraged when they hear of it.'

Laclos flinched, surely realizing that the scandal might touch the duke, sully his reputation for beneficence. 'I must speak to the kitchen steward. He'll certainly hear from the duke.'

As Laclos was leaving, he cast a glance at the door to Gaillard's office, whence came muffled sounds. 'You may come across files unrelated to your investigation, Colonel. For much of his journalistic career, Gaillard was a collector of piquant information about prominent personalities. Possibly our own duke was one of them. I expect you to treat such files with discretion.'

'Don't worry,' said Saint-Martin. 'I'll return them to the persons whom they concern. Gaillard was an extortionist and deserves to be put out of business.'

With a slight bow Laclos left the room, apparently reconciled to the search. Saint-Martin breathed easier and returned to Gaillard's office. The secret cabinet stood open. Georges was browsing in a file and looked up. 'This contains a record of his sister's mental history, instructions for her care at Charenton, and financial statements of the legacy her uncle left her.'

Saint-Martin said, 'Send the file to Madame Cartier. She'll want to study it. Gaillard may have cheated his sister.'

'I'll see to it,' Georges said, then added, 'I've also set aside the personal files to be returned to Lafayette, the duke, and several noblewomen in the Queen's circle of friends.' Georges winked. 'We're leaving the pornography for the duke to add to his collection.'

Several sealed boxes stood in the middle of the room. Georges explained, 'They're ready for transport to the local police bureau and from there to the Châtelet and Gaillard's trial. They contain his instructions to Simon and Nicolas concerning the attack on the Gagne bakery, their attack on magistrate Roland, an attempted attack on Madame Cécile Tremblay, and their abduction of Michou. We found plans also for Lieutenant Maury's attempt to assassinate you, and Gaillard's plans for the assassination of Foullon and Bertier.'

Saint-Martin gazed at the boxes. 'They record a great deal of evil. May they help justice prevail, finally.'

At midmorning Anne found Michou standing in the shade of a tree, fully dressed, staring up at a pair of sparrows. She greeted Anne with a wan smile. The sun was already hot. They sat down at a table under the tree.

Last night, during the ride from Passy to the provost's residence, she hadn't reacted to her liberation. Even allowing for the blow to her head, she should have at least expressed relief, not to mention gratitude.

Anne and Sylvie had put her to bed in a safe, comfortable room in the rear of the house, next door to a servant family who would look after her. A doctor had found her to be physically sound. He said that the shock would wear off and the bruises heal in a few days, and he had given her a sleeping potion. Still, Anne wondered if her abduction might have seriously damaged her mental health.

After a few still minutes together, Anne signed, 'Do you want to tell me about yesterday?'

Michou shrugged and began signing. 'I was sitting on a barrel on the Quai, sketching an old river boat. Suddenly, someone hit me from behind. Because of my deafness, I couldn't hear his steps on the paving stones. In the mist there were no shadows to warn me. I never saw him. When I awoke, I was gagged and bound and lying on a cold damp floor in the dark, I knew not where. The hours seemed like eternity: no light, no movement or touches. Complete isolation. Every minute I feared that they would come to violate and kill me.'

Her signing was listless, her large green eyes dull and life-less. It was as if she were thinking about another person distant from herself.

'What would you like to do, Michou?' Anne asked. 'You should stay here for a few days to recover before returning to your studio. If you'd like, we could bring you paint and brushes and canvas or just a sketchbook and pencil. You could paint or draw our garden scene.'

Michou shook her head. 'You are kind, but I feel like just sitting here and watching the birds. Nothing interests me now. My painting and sketching seem useless. Who really wants anything that I do? I'm just a poor little deaf woman who survives by the kindness of a few people who feel sorry for her. I can't defend myself or manage my own affairs. Sylvie looks after my money.'

Anne thought Michou would burst into tears under the burden of her woes. But she continued, dry-eyed, 'I really don't like myself. Look at me now, ugly and full of self-pity.'

'You've had a dreadful experience, Michou. It's going to haunt you for a while. Would you feel better at Château Beaumont? It's a safe, beautiful place. We could go there today and stay for a week or two until your spirits improve.'

'My spirits aren't going to improve. For the past few years I've been fooling myself: learning to read and write, walking about the Palais-Royal like a lady, setting up a studio and selling portraits. Though I'm stone deaf, I had begun to think of myself as almost a normal person.' She shook her head. 'What a fool!'

Anne waved a dismissive hand at Michou's pessimism. But her friend ignored the gesture and went on, 'I forgot how unfair and dangerous the world is and how vulnerable and frail I am. Even in this peaceful garden I feel afraid. Still I can't hide here forever. How dreadful it will be for me to live outside these walls.'

'The present dangers won't last,' Anne assured her. 'Mayor Bailly and the Marquis de Lafayette will soon restore order, perhaps even better than before.'

Michou shook her head. 'For the first time the common people have really tasted power and enjoyed it. Clever rascals, more ruthless than Gaillard, will step forward and tell them how to use it. Badly.'

For all Anne knew, Michou could be right. But it was pointless to argue. Anne sensed that Michou was labouring under the influence of earlier painful episodes in her life. She had probably been abused as a young girl after leaving the convent where she was raised. Then, three years ago, she had witnessed the brutal murder of Antoine Dubois' mistress and experienced an intimidating police interrogation. She had retreated into herself for months.

Michou lapsed into silence. Anne sighed inwardly, gave Michou a parting embrace, and left, hoping that nature would heal her friend.

Michou's physical recovery was quick. In a few days, she looked like her old self. On 5 August, she moved back to her studio on Rue Traversine. But her heart and mind appeared to heal slowly, if at all. Though she continued to sketch, she lost interest in painting and withdrew from Marc Latour's studio. His *Coriolanus* remained unfinished with the Salon just four weeks away.

Anne continued to visit her. They played dominoes or walked in the back garden. After the second week Anne sensed that Michou was beginning to feel bored and restless. On 19 August – Anne's thirty-first birthday – she and Paul invited Michou to join them for dinner at the Grande Taverne de Londres, a popular restaurant in the Palais-Royal. Its chef, Antoine Beauvilliers, had cooked for the King's brother, the Comte de Provence, and was now setting a lofty culinary standard for Parisian restaurants. Neither Anne nor Paul frequented high-toned restaurants or pretended to be connoisseurs. They both preferred a simple cuisine. But they hoped this dinner would stimulate new life in Michou.

Out of shyness, their friend hesitated to accept the invitation, but not for long. Her innate good sense prevailed. Sylvie and Anne helped dress and groom her. She entered the restaurant in a low-cut yellow silk gown that flattered her petite figure. Her large green eyes glittered with pleasure. As they were shown to their table, she carried herself with self-confidence and grace. Men and women noticed her.

After a few glasses of wine and light conversation, Anne signed casually, 'I visited Marc's studio today. He's growing desperate. So much to do and so little time. Could you help him, Michou? Your portrait of the *Coriolanus* child remains unfinished. Marc can't seem to get it right.'

Michou smiled wanly. 'I see through you, Anne, trying to lift my spirits. Still, I have worried about Marc. His career depends so much on success in the Salon. Maybe I can clean his brushes. I'll visit him tomorrow morning.'

The following afternoon, Anne stopped by Marc's studio, slipped in unobserved, and immediately felt a rush of joy. In her painter's smock, brush in hand, Michou was working intently at her piece of Marc's painting. The two young artists seemed joined in a perfect harmony.

Early one evening in the last week of August, while waiting for Paul in their garden, Anne opened her diary and looked back over the past six weeks. Her feelings were mixed. The country remained feverish and discontented. Its economy failed to improve. The financial situation worsened. In Paris, unemployment remained high. The debate on a new constitution was contentious. The members of the National Assembly didn't trust the King to govern democratically and refused to give him veto power. But they could not agree among themselves what form democracy should take in France.

She was, nonetheless, aware of signs of progress. The Royal Highway Patrol had restored peace and good order to the countryside. The National Assembly had declared the end of legal privilege: all citizens were now equal before the law. In Paris, the National Guard became more effective and reduced crime. Mayor Bailly had moved into Lieutenant General DeCrosne's office in the Hôtel de Police and had brought order to the city's administration.

On Rue Sainte-Anne the Gagne bakery thrived. In Passy, National Guardsman Joseph Mouton had become engaged to

Maury's 'wife'. With help from Brigadier Pioche and Colonel Saint-Martin, the young man joined the Royal Highway Patrol, hoping to follow in his father's footsteps. At the Salon, the public and the critics had received Marc Latour's *Coriolanus* favourably.

Anne heard footsteps and closed her diary. Paul entered the garden and sat down next to her. He had been at the Châtelet for the trial of Gaillard and his companions. 'I have a mixed report for you,' he said, then signalled a servant and ordered two glasses of cool white wine.

'Tell me the good news first,' Anne said.

Paul smiled. 'The Comte Savarin's handwriting analysis of the papers taken from baker Gagne's shop proved that they were fraudulent, maliciously composed to incriminate him.'

'So what did the magistrates decide?'

'They condemned Simon and Nicolas for the baker's murder and Michou's abduction and sentenced them to life in the Brest naval prison. Lieutenant Maury was convicted posthumously of killing Lieutenant Harivel. Gaillard was convicted of conspiracy in the death of Gagne, in the failed attempt to kill me, and in the abduction and failed attempt to kill Michou. He too was sentenced to life in the Brest prison. The magistrates concluded that he killed Maury in self-defence.'

'He should also have been convicted of illegal trafficking in bread,' Anne protested.

'That charge was dropped because it might stain the Duc d'Orléans' reputation.'

'Is that why no one is going to be hung, burned, decapitated or broken on the wheel on Place de Grève? That's how these crimes used to be punished. Maury's body could be burned for the killing of Harivel. Simon and Nicolas should be hung for the murder of Gagne.'

'I see your point, Anne, but I can only guess the magistrates' mind. They probably shied away from yet another grisly spectacle on Place de Grève, especially since it would involve men from the duke's faction. The people's reaction would be hard to predict. They might riot. It was much safer to send the malefactors to rot in Brest. They will soon be forgotten.'

The servant brought the wine, poured, and withdrew. As Anne quietly sipped from the glass, the question of Bertier's death edged into her mind. She was reluctant to raise it, aware that it continued to pain her husband.

Finally, Paul read her thoughts. 'I've failed Bertier and Foullon a second time,' he muttered, nearly choking with emotion. 'I gave a report to the prosecutor on their assassinations. He refused to bring it to the magistrates. They would have ignored it anyway. The people's verdict stands. And so the victims remain dishonoured. Bailly and Lafayette, the King, and now the magistrates have made a mockery of justice.'

Anne added, 'There's some comfort in the fact that Maury is dead and Gaillard, Simon and Nicolas will at least be severely punished for other crimes. After all, the Brest naval prison is called the antechamber of Hell for good reason.'

She reached out a hand to her husband. He caressed it. For a few minutes they sat quietly drinking their wine, listening to the birds, gazing at the roses, while their spirits recovered a measure of peace.

'What have you learned about Adelaide Gaillard?' Paul asked. 'I understand that she's mentally healthier than first thought but still not competent. Who is responsible for her, with her brother in prison?'

'The magistrates have appointed Monsieur Roland as her guardian. He has transferred her to Dr Pinel's clinic. Hopefully, we'll see improvement in her condition.'

'Can she afford the treatment? Pinel will expect to be paid.'

'Unfortunately, Gaillard had depleted her legacy. But Michou has come up with a solution.'

Paul looked puzzled.

'This afternoon, she and I went to the jewellers Böhmer and Bassenge and sold the gold locket. Michou deposited the money in Adelaide's trust fund. Roland says that her income should now cover her costs at the clinic. Michou also gave Adelaide the oil portrait in place of the one in the locket.'

Paul took a thoughtful draught of his wine. 'If she recovers, she may regret the loss of the locket. It was dear to her father.'

Anne shook her head. 'She may realize that her father would be pleased that the locket helped buy her good health.'

Anne and Paul relaxed for the moment, satisfied with their accomplishments at least in the short term. Then they heard the sound of thunder in the distance. Soon rain drops began to fall.

Paul rose from the table. 'We must move indoors.'

Anne picked up her glass and followed him into the garden room. Rain soon pelted the garden. Gusts of wind lashed the trees and bushes. Anne reflected aloud, 'I feel that there are storm clouds in this country's future.'

'That's true, Anne, but they shall not spoil the rest of this evening.'

They put aside their glasses, gazed fondly at each other, and embraced.

Author's Note

B efore the fall of the Bastille, July 14, 1789, Paris lacked self-government. It was ruled in the King's name by a royal minister, Baron de Breteuil, at the time of the Anne Cartier series. Reporting to him was the Lieutenant General of Police, Thiroux DeCrosne. To maintain public order he had a force of about 1500 watchmen and municipal guards to patrol the streets. In emergencies he could call upon the French Guards, a regiment of soldiers stationed in the city, as well as a regiment of Swiss mercenaries nearby. In the twenty-five districts of the city, commissioners and inspectors exercised local oversight and justice. Four of the inspectors, including Inspector Quidor, an historical person, were responsible for criminal investigation. The oversight of civil administration, royal property, taxation and finance belonged to a royal intendant, Bertier de Sauvigny.

During the month following the fall of the Bastille, the city's government was transformed. An elected council took the place of the royal minister and the royal intendant. An elected mayor, Sylvain Bailly, replaced the royal lieutenant general. The new National Guards, a municipal militia under the Marquis de Lafayette, absorbed the French Guards and the municipal watchmen and maintained order. The twenty-five city districts were reorganized into sixty. The commissioners and inspectors continued to function but in an uneasy, ambiguous relationship to newly elected district police bureaus. The Royal Highway Patrol continued to police the area around the city within roughly a sixty-mile radius.

The assassinations of Delaunay, Foullon, Bertier de Sauvigny and Harivel du Rocher are historical facts, lightly fictionalized in this story. Justice was denied them and their families. The killers of the first three victims were known but never charged. A fellow dragoon accused Bertier's assassin of cowardice and killed him in a duel. In Harivel's case, the killer was never identified, nor motive found.

For a readable account of Sylvain Bailly, first mayor of Paris, go to Gene A. Brucker, *Jean-Sylvain Bailly, Revolutionary Mayor of Paris* (Urbana, 1950). For the Marquis de Lafayette, consult Louis Gottschalk and Margaret Maddox, *Lafayette in the French Revolution through the October Days* (Chicago, 1969).

The Duc d'Orléans (1747–1793) lacks an English-language biography. I have relied upon Hubert LaMarle, *Philippe Égalité 'Grand Maître' de la Revolution* (Paris, 1989). As the Revolution grew more radical, the duke gave up his title and adopted the surname and the cause of equality. As a member of the first French Republic's National Convention, he voted for the execution of his cousin, Louis XVI. Philippe himself was guillotined in November 1793.

Steven L. Kaplan's works offer authoritative discussions of every aspect of bread in the lives of eighteenth-century French men and women. See especially *The Bakers of Paris and the Bread Question, 1700–1775* (Durham, 1996).

The baker Gagne's misfortune was suggested by the mob hanging of the baker François in October 1789, who was alleged to have hoarded fine flour and profiteered in the sale of luxury bread. He was actually providing the bread to the National Assembly.

Pierre Hall (1739–1793) is arguably the greatest miniaturist of the epoch. Born Peter Adolf Hall in Sweden, he moved to Paris in 1766. His portrait of a young woman – Adelaide in this story – is #157, p.126; colour, p.89, in Régine de Plinval de Guillebon, *Pierre Adolphe Hall* (Paris, 2000).

Literature on the French Revolution is abundant, but often partisan and conflicting. For reference, consult William Doyle, *The Oxford History of the French Revolution* (Oxford, 1990). Warren Roberts, *David and Prieur: Revolutionary Artists* (Albany, 2000) offers helpful discussion of images of the Bastille's fall and the subsequent political assassinations.